Collecting Rayne: Volume One
By Rayne Havok

In order of publication:

May offend

My Christmas Story

The Boy

Degenerate

Retaliation

Devour

XXX

app

The Embalmer

My Christmas Story

LYDIA IS SPENDING CHRISTMAS ALONE FOR THE FIRST TIME. AT LEAST HER HOUSE IS BEAUTIFULLY DECORATED.

ONE

The cuckoo clock on the wall tells me it's 11:15pm. Every time I look at it, I'm reminded of one of our European trips, this one took us to Germany, where it is practically mandatory to leave with one.

We'd chosen well, I think, the clock had spoken to both of us, with its intricate design and beautiful craftsmanship. We'd known right away this was perfect for us. It's small, having to fit in a bag to take on the airplane back to the states, but somehow commands the space on the wall where it hangs.

A constant reminder of my love for him. We had gone for our one-year wedding anniversary, it was a trip I could never forget. During that vacation, if I really thought about it, had been the moment I truly and fully fell in love with Henry. I had always loved him, this was simply the spot I could pinpoint it falling into place, knowing it would last forever. He had finally made his way into my heart and it grew to the point that only his love filled the space in there.

I sigh, the thoughts of him looking so happy and full of life and potential. I almost lose a tear from my eye but, I smile through it.

The tree is especially beautiful now, I'd put some finishing touches on it tonight. We'd put the tree up together right after Thanksgiving, one of our many traditions; always so excited for this time of year.

In fact, Christmas day is our wedding anniversary. Both of us knowing right away that it would be the only day that would encompass us and mean the most.

Our celebration together would have happened in about an hour from now, and here I sit, alone for the first time in all our years. The first time I've had to wait alone for the clock on the wall to sound midnight, making it officially our day and marking another year. This would have been twenty.

This time the tear does fall and then another. How am I supposed to do this without him? How am I supposed to fill this house with Christmas cheer without the person that had been my source of happiness for all these years?

I can't think about it anymore. The fact is, he isn't coming back; he won't be here for anymore anniversaries or Christmases. I will be doing it without him. I'm filled with a loneliness so deep it tears my chest apart and my throat seizes up.

I can wish and hope all I want, but the facts are the facts and no amount of wishing or hoping can bring somebody back to me.

My head falls back onto the head rest behind me and my eyes close. I have to be strong right now. This is a new journey in my life; I am alone and without my partner. And, in less than an hour, I will ring in our anniversary alone. First of many. This will be the hardest, my loss still so new. It should begin to get easier after this, as each year passes; so, they say.

The thought settles me. I will be ok— I have to be.

I walk over to the tree, his gift for me underneath. I have no idea what it is, even though I had been looking at credit card statements, trying to see. He must have used cash.

I hate surprises, contradicting my love for Christmas. But it was never about the gifts for me, it was about all the love everyone feels during this time of the year.

The box is large, I lift it; heavy.

The modern gift for twenty years is platinum. I was expecting a piece of jewelry, even though I've never been the type for anything other than my wedding ring. I thought, like me, he would have gotten me a replacement band. I went to the best jeweler and picked the nicest band I thought would fit him well and engraved "you own me" into it.

I've always felt that way, he truly had owned me. My life consisted only of pleasing him, making sure to show and tell him every chance I got. Now, I'm out of time.

This box tells me he hadn't thought about it even though we had stuck to that tradition, starting out loosely; selecting only the ones we liked. We had made it a tradition once we'd begun to truly love finding just the right thing to fit under those guidelines. I had been hinting at what could be a great idea for months leading up to the holiday.

I wipe at my arm absentmindedly when a drop falls onto it.

I pull at the beautiful bow tied around the large box. Had never been one for wrapping so this had been prepared by the gift- services wrappers. I never minded. It was sweet that he knew I love beautiful wrapping but was unable to attain that level himself.

I myself, always took my time to gently and lovingly wrap his gifts. He would tear into them like a child though, always too excited for theatrics. I never thought it uncouth, just loved seeing his joy.

Another drop.

I get through the paper, shiny and thick; good quality. The box gives nothing away, it's simply a brown cardboard. I pull at the tape and it gives way; unfolding the flaps I see instantly what it is. A mother fucking blender. I'm absolutely shattered. That bastard. It was a slap in the face if I've ever seen one.

I bet that *bitch* got something. I bet whore woman fucked him until he forked over whatever the fuck she wanted, sucked his cock like some come guzzling vampire. I know what he was like. Insatiable. Needing it often and everywhere. I was mistaken to think that I would be enough.

It took a lot to confront him with what I had found. The emails I should have seen long ago, the texts he'd not even hidden; I'd simply been stupid enough to trust him.

Being so in love myself, I was unable to see what was in front of me; the longer evenings at work, the need for more and more time away from me.

I just thought it was his need to be successful in his career; never having kids pushed him to excel at work. I had sacrificed my time with him for him to have his purpose.

I wanted him to be happy, and he was, but it had been her more recently, *Ashley*– from the name on the emails. The sweet things he'd been saying to her in them, all the love and kind words he wrote her. I read all the happiness he had for her and all the times he had told her he'd wished he was with her and stuck here... with me.

It shattered me to read those things. How could I have been so fucking stupid? How had I been unable to sense it? I had lived with this man for twenty fucking years. How had I lost him; I'd catered to his every whim, sexually and otherwise.

He was a demanding man; he knew what he wanted and I wanted it for him. I wanted to be the one to give it to him, no matter what. I wanted to please him in every way. All his kinky and wild fantasies, I needed to be the source of fulfillment in those. I did everything for him.

Reading those emails told me he'd been getting them met by her as well. I know that had he told me he wanted another woman I would have done anything to find just the right girl and invite her to share our bed, for him. I think he knew that. So, I have to assume he had meant to leave me this whole time– since the moment this started with her. Possibly just waiting for the right moment to devastate me.

Another drop, this time I look at the source.

"Oh, Henry, I wish you'd continued to be a good man." I finger a part of him now; the source of the dripping. The piece of him I'd ripped from his torso; slick and wet, hung neatly, woven around the branches in true garland fashion. Who knew intestines would look so beautiful wrapped around a Pine? And there was plenty to decorate with, much longer out of the body than I realized.

TWO

Earlier that night...

I wait patiently for Henry to make it home, allegedly at work—after what I've learned I can't even believe that any more.

I hear the front door close quietly, he calls out to me. "Lydia?"

"In here." I stay seated in my arm chair. I take a deep breath, trying to steady my beating heart.

He stops in the door way of our neatly decorated living room. "How was your day, love?"

Love? Was he fucking kidding me? "Fine, how was work?" I say sweetly.

"Oh, you know, same old shit, different day." He empties his pockets of wallet and change, coming toward me. I'm sure he expects his devoted wife to be more welcoming than I am.

"You, ok?" he asks, knowing me too well to let my mood go unnoticed.

"Fine." I say shortly, which only leads him to inquire again.

"You don't look fine; something must be the matter." He comes to sit with me on my seat, I don't scoot to give him room, so he is left to half hover on the cushion.

He reaches out to me, touching my face softly with the back of his hand.

It infuriates me that my body responds to his touch like it always had. That gives me the final push to tell him what I've uncovered.

"I know about Ashley." I say unceremoniously.

His face pales. I see the pulse in his throat quicken. He doesn't try and deny it. I'm grateful for that. What he does say doesn't ease any of my pain though. "I was wondering when this might happen."

It's my turn for shock. My hands begin to shake and I can't hold back the anger I feel; the heat of my body radiating. "What the fuck have you done, Henry?"

"I was going to tell you after the holidays."

"Tell me what? Why don't you share it with me now?"

He moves to his own seat, the matching pair to my own. "I never meant to hurt you; I don't want this to be over."

I can see in his eyes he is telling me what he thinks I want to hear. My fingernails dig into my palm. Rage brews inside me.

"I don't know what you know." He seems to wait for me to fill him in, and when I don't, he continues. "I met her at work, she was a temp a few months ago. It means nothing...meant nothing." He corrects himself.

"So then, it's over? You can end it with her?" I'm only trying to get a read on him, I know from the email sent last night that they had plans for New Years– a get-away. And with that being the time we go on a trip ourselves; he was going to make the break with me between now and then.

"Of course, sweetie. She won't come between us, we have so much together."

The lies from his mouth flow so eloquently that I'm sure he's learned along the way how to manipulate me. And he thinks he is doing it now.

"Really Henry?" I go overboard on the hopefulness in my voice and he doesn't notice; he thinks he's maintaining the upper hand.

I slink from my chair, landing on my knees, I crawl toward him. I see the arousal hit him. After all these years he knows what is coming, his hands itch to move for his zipper, but he knows he shouldn't assume that's what might be happening right now.

I crawl my hands up his legs and unzip him. His cock is already hard, throbbing as I take it in my hand. I hold his eyes with mine as I bring my mouth to the wet tip, working him the way I know drives him crazy. Deep and hard. I relax my throat and let it pass my tonsils.

He groans loudly, gripping the knot of hair on my head, he moves my head and his hips in unison, fucking hard against my mouth. I can feel him close to his finish and pull away from him. The question is in his eyes, but he doesn't ask it.

I stand and pull him up with me. I undress him quickly and then myself. He tries to touch me but I back away, playing coy. I widen my legs and touch my pussy, sliding my fingers through the slit; I rub my clit. His breathing quickens and his hand moves to his cock, pumping quickly.

My heart is pounding so hard as I walk to him and reach into his hair, the beautifully lush head of hair I'd run my fingers through countless times while he lays in bed waiting for sleep to catch up to him. I wrap my fingers around it and drag him roughly to his knees. I push his face into my pussy and his tongue instantly goes to work. I let him taste me even though I'm furious. I'm hardly ever demanding, so this is a treat for him. He loves the occasions I take control and force him to do these things– to an extent. He would never relinquish it completely.

I pull his head back and lean over to kiss him, his mouth taste like me. This time when I bring his head forward it's my knee it hits. Hard. Like the self- defense classes have taught me. I bet he regrets having talked me into going to them now as his nose explodes. The crack is loud in the quiet room.

I turn my wrist and force his face upward to me, the shocked look in his eyes sends me over the edge and I laugh, "You stupid fuck!" I smash his face again with the heel of my palm, shoving his nose upward. His body becomes slack as his lights go out, landing hard against the wood floor.

I'd always been so demure, so submissive to him. He must have taken that to mean weak this whole time. My small frame only adding to it, I suppose. The feeling that is in me now must be all of that pent up, because I feel euphoric. I never knew this lived in me.

I take advantage of this feeling and the fact that he is out cold and get a sheet from the linen closet. I roll him onto it and as I'm dragging him, he comes to.

Quickly, remembering his predicament, he moves fast, but not faster than me. I'm on him before he can roll to his knees and make his escape.

Situating his arms at his hips, I kneel on his hands and straddle his lap. He starts to say something but my fist landing against his jaw stops him. I hit him over and over. I've never punched anyone my whole life, but something deep inside me knows just how to deliver them, avoiding his teeth so to not bloody my knuckles on them.

I feel his jaw loosen, teeth giving way, as my strikes become more furious and forceful; sweat pouring from my hair, into my eyes, as the effort to keep the pace with my hatred pushes my body to the limits. The adrenaline taking over, which is why I don't see right away that he is out again.

I stop, breathless. His mouth slack and empty looking from the loss of teeth. I pull his lips back to survey the damage, removing the lost teeth as far back as his throat. I collect eight whole and two fragments. I place them in the candy dish we had set out for decoration on the coffee table. They give it a more appropriate feel for this Christmas.

I drag his limp body with the overhang of the sheet to the vintage radiator that sits under the window. I go in search of a few items to restrain him.

I unload an armful of items next to him. Zip tying his arms above his head to the radiator and tie a thick rope around his ankles, and the other end tightly to the exposed support beam in the middle of the room to keep his legs in place.

When he finally comes to, his bloodied and swollen eyes connect with mine. I'm sure a part of him is wondering, but the bigger and more deviant part of him doesn't care why I'm on top of him, or why his cock is inside of me.

He seems to have forgotten all about me lashing out on his face and that he is restrained. He pushes that aside somehow, bucking his hips up repeatedly to meet my pace. I bounce on him, the way he likes, the way that makes my tits bounce like a porn star; the way that makes him come the hardest.

"I bet she doesn't know how to fuck you like I can, how to make you feel so fucking good."

I slow my pace and squeeze my pussy tightly around him. He moans, completely lost in this.

"I bet she doesn't feel this good wrapped around your big cock." I rub myself, sitting hard on his thighs; shoving every inch inside of me. My fingers working fast.

He tries to watch, but is unable to get the angle to see so he looks at my face instead, his eyes holding mine as he watches me enjoy myself.

My breath comes faster as I climb closer to my finish. I let out a shaky moan as I finally come. Leaning over his heaving chest, I kiss his mouth, sucking his bottom lip; tasting the blood that has settled and dried there.

Pulling myself off his still overly- swollen cock, I kiss down his chest until I reach it with my lips. It's glistening with my come and I taste myself on him as I suck his dick into my mouth. It fills my throat as I swallow it down, fucking him with only my mouth until I taste the hint of come settle on my taste buds. I pull up on it, licking around the head, salivating at the taste of us together.

"Does she make you feel this good?"

"No. Never." He breathes. And I believe him. I know what makes this man; I know everything that makes him tick. He may have wanted something different, but if I wanted him to, I know I could have him back. I know, if I could forgive him, we could be so good together, still. But I can't. And won't.

I bite down teasingly on the head of his cock, purple from being without release. He cries out excitedly. I lick him and push it down my throat again, sucking hard all the way up the length– slowly, over and over; all the way up and then down again, milking him. Quickening the rhythm until I feel the tell- tale stiffening before the finish.

Just as I taste his semen on my tongue I drag the box cutter across the base of his cock, above his emptying balls. He doesn't feel it at first, too caught up in the release and

19

somehow it makes it more erotic for me, the come exploding in my mouth and the blood mingling as I work him through his finish.

I know the second he feels the cut, my saliva bringing it alive, and still one more pulse of come evacuates.

I replace my mouth with my hand and the look in his eyes, as I lick my lips to collect the fluid mixture around my mouth, tells me he is well aware of my intentions now. I show him, this time, the source of his pain, the box cutter I had stashed next to us for this purpose. Pulling up on his cock, making it taught, I dig the blade into his flesh and circle around until it comes off in my hand, finishing the job.

I hold his cock up to his face, pale from shock. His face contorts as I lick the head, the sound that comes from him is one of fear. Pure terror. Not even the loss of his cock is as horrible as seeing me blow it now, after it's been removed.

He sees the side of me that I've been able to keep hidden, the side he's been keeping at bay with his love. Now that that is gone, I let myself out of the cage.

My lips make a popping sound as I pull his cock from my mouth. "And now it's too late for poor *Ashley* to try harder to please you."

His bleeding gets out of hand, but I don't try and stop it. "Don't worry, it doesn't seem like you're going to have to live too much longer without it."

"What the fuck? You crazy bitch!" he shouts.

"Oh, honey, I wouldn't yell at the woman who literarily holds your cock in her hand. Doesn't seem smart." I boop him on the nose with it.

He looks shocked that this could be happening to him, it fuels a rage inside of me. I want to rip him apart, this man who had promised me a forever with him has ended it for some pussy, he himself, has said is not up to par with mine. This man who promised 'till death do us part'. I thought it would have been a more natural type of death, but he's brought this on himself and now it's one of my doing.

I watch his eyes fall heavy and become slow to open. "Do you have anything you want to say before we begin?" I ask.

"Before we *begin*? You're holding my dick in your hand! How have we *not* begun? That should be the end."

"Oh, honey, I don't think I could live without you having a cock. You know how much I love it."

He loses it then. "Are you going to *kill* me?"

"You killed yourself when you started this whole thing with her, when you stuck this," I hold his cock up again, "inside of her; you killed yourself." then toss it aside.

"So, nothing to say, then?" I slide the razor across his thigh. Blood dots and the gathers together then falls down either side of his leg, pooling on the sheet.

"Bitch." He says through gritted teeth. "You can't do this to me, you fucking cunt." His voice betrays him and cracks in fear.

"I think I am doing this. And your insults are lacking."

I push the triangle edge of the blade into his skin as deep as it will go and drag it a couple of inches, the blood is pouring out of this one. I climb up his body and slash repeatedly at his arms, I move quickly, cutting his flesh. X's mark from wrists to armpits.

He opens the floodgate of his lungs and cries sobs of fear and hatred for me.

I slap his face, trying to bring him back. "Shut the fuck up, Henry."

He does no such thing, if anything, he gets louder and more frantic.

"Shut. The. Fuck. Up. Henry." I shout over him.

When he still will not heed my words, I reach down to his feet and grab his cock, shoving it deep into his wide-open mouth, mid scream, closing my hand over it to keep it inside.

When attached, it was close to eight inches, it probably lost an inch in the removal process, and limp now—giving room for manipulation; he shares none of my throat-opening- dick- sucking skills himself. He is choking and the screams have become frantic heaves. His eyes are watering now, no longer from fear, they're flowing freely from gagging.

"Do you want to die like this, Henry? With your cock vying for a spot in your throat, or do you want to die with dignity? It's up to you."

I sit back onto my heels and wait for him to make his choice. He calms himself, as much as a man with his own cock shoved down his throat can, so, I take my hand from his mouth. The appendage folds out, sliding down his cheek and flops to the floor.

His chest heaves, trying to replenish the air. He regains some composure quickly.

"Shall we continue now?" I drag the razor from his adam's apple to the vee-juncture of my thighs, at his belly button. Blood fills the line and I slide my finger along the incision, not deep enough to do anything other than superficial damage. But he doesn't seem to know that, the pain is overwhelming.

I run my hands through the blood on his arms, painting him in it, then smear it across my breasts, squeezing my always- hard nipples. I wasn't prepared for this to be so erotic. My pussy tingles from the sight of him restrained and red, slices marring his always-perfect looking skin. "Fuck, Henry, you look so sexy right now. I'm going to use this image for years to come."

I cut at him again, over his chest, the slashing is quick and deep; gaping in many spots. His screams are back, hitting me right between my legs, but this time I revel in them. I grind myself against his belly, slick with blood, I slide freely; the pressure building quickly. "If I'd have known this would be so hot, I'd have left your cock attached until the end." I rock harder against him, pushing my fingers against my clit. My breath coming almost frantic as I reach for my finish.

Coming down from my orgasm, I realize that his screams have stopped and that I had been leveraging myself on his throat; like he often loved me to do. I check his pulse, it's still there; shallow, but there.

I look down at our bodies, mine— tingling in the orgasmic aftermath. Red and slick with wetness; slathered in the blood of the man I'd been more in love with than myself and now, I'm getting off on his bloodied body. I look beautiful, more alive than I ever have. His— barely holding on.

I hit his face to rouse him, smacking lightly at first, but when nothing happens and I start hitting him harder. Something takes over, I stop trying to wake him and the hate overwhelms me.

This face that looked at me in the morning and made love to me. This face that kissed me 'goodnight' every night and fucked me until I was exhausted enough for sleep. The face that I had memorized and loved, who loved me back so deeply there were never any secrets. Until there was one. *Her*. The reason I will be alone now, the reason for hatred when I look into his beautiful face, the reason I can't stop my arms from lashing out at him now. She did this— and he let her.

His face is split and actively bleeding, I realize quickly that I've got the blade in my hand and that I've been gouging his cheek and throat; the arterial spray alerting me, quite vividly, that this will be the end. Blood is pulsing quickly out of his body like a geyser, spraying me and the walls. I watch as it dies down to a stream, coming quickly still.

I don't miss him as he slips away, I don't have any remorse. He had brought this upon himself, his death is on *his* hands.

I do miss the man I thought he was, though; the idea of our forever. I hold on to the years that were good, the idea that he was mine for that time. He still is, in fact, this part of him will always be mine.

I climb off his body and go in search for what I need to finish the job, coming back with an arm full of tools. I kneel next to him, leaning over his chest to make the first cut– the Y incision performed in an autopsy I've seen countless times depicted on the crime shows we loved to watch.

He hasn't been refrigerated which is why, I assume, there is blood seeping from the wound I create at his shoulder blade. Either that or TV just gives the illusion it's less messy. The razor slices through easily, the thin layer of fat on top of his muscle he carried around his midsection needs another inch or so to get deep enough to see his insides.

It surprises me that there are varying shades of pink and flesh toned pieces, slimy and wet looking. I cut along the sinew that hold his flesh to his ribs, finally pulling it back; enabling me to expose everything.

I remove the already tumbling intestines and set them aside, clamping before cutting, knowing the smell of what's inside would be much worse than what I've already encountered. It leaves him almost hollow looking– they really take up a lot of space in there.

Reaching for the center of his rib cage, I take the knife I use in the kitchen for deboning. It takes a few sawing motions before I'm able to make progress, but, as soon as it's in there I'm able to slice through the bone. I take a triangle piece from it and set it aside, exposing what lies beneath.

His heart; I reach for it right away, cutting the pulmonary veins, thick as my finger and set it aside. Next the lungs liver and spleen, cutting the connective tissue that hold each organ in place.

Hollowed and empty, I feel a bit of vindication, knowing I've made him as empty as he's made me.

I cut at the skin around his neck and pull it over his face, cutting where I need to along the way to remove the skin and hair from his head. Essentially scalping him from front to back. His skull looks nothing like I thought it would. Nothing like him.

I send the cleaver through the neck bone a few times until it detaches. I hold up his skinned face to mine and look into his empty dead eyes.

Grabbling a stake- like piece of wood I'd found in the backyard— left over kindling for the fire pit. I find the softer part at the base of his neck and push them together hard enough to pierce. I hold it up by the shaft and walk him over to the tree, tying a long piece of twine around it and the stem of the tree a few inches from the top where it is thick enough to hold the weight. I replace the star at the top with his head, stepping back, I admire it. It's leaning a little, but I don't mind.

I unwind his intestines and rope them around the front of the tree, back and forth until they're gone— a garland of intestines. Beautiful. I put his heart in my stocking, giving it as a gift to myself. I quickly remove his balls and replace the mistletoe with them, I chuckle at the thought of kissing under them, something he'd always loved for me to do. That soft tissue of his taint always his favorite to have teased.

More of his teeth into the candy dish, and the other organs become part of the decorations.

I sit back into my arm chair, and fully naked, drenched in the spray of blood, covering me in the most erotic way, I catch sight of his amputated cock and I have nothing more to use it for but a tool to get off right now.

It's heavy in my hand and I crave the feel of it inside of me, so that is where I put it, hitting the spot I need it to, and though I can't fuck it— its flaccid, I push my pussy against the chair and hold it inside of me as I work my clit. Rocking my hips against the edge of the chair, wildly bucking as I fuck myself. My pussy convulses with the oncoming orgasm and, lost in the depraved nature of what I'm doing I come a second time, launching his cock a full foot in front of me, flopping to the floor.

Coming down from my orgasms doesn't stop me from laughing at what happened.

THREE

The cuckoo clock chimes twelve times, alerting me of our day– our Christmas anniversary that will be my first alone.

Kicking the blender box with my foot as I take my feet, I stand and admire the beautiful scene; how my husband has made the room feel even more like a home.

I climb up the stairs, into our– now my– bed. Still covered in his blood, not bothering to shower, knowing as soon as I wake, I'll have an awful mess to clean. I fall asleep quickly.

Epilogue

One year later...

I take the next box down from the top of the closet— the tree topper from last year. I saved it, after cleaning his skull, wrapping it and putting it away. I wanted him to spend the future Christmases with me as a reminder of us. "Hey, honey." I say to it after unfolding the flaps of cardboard.

I set it with the other boxes.

I test the lights, like I do before stringing them. I realize there are a few strands that will need replacing, not making it for this season. I put that on the list of things to get at the store.

Having finished going through the boxes, I grab my purse and the list off the table and I head out.

My cart is full of all things Christmas and I'm reaching high upon a shelf for the last few boxes of the multicolored lights I love, when I'm interrupted by a man.

"Would you like help?" he asks.

"Thank you." I step back to let him have room.

"I just love Christmas; it's my favorite." His eyes meet mine and ignites a fire inside me.

The smile that crosses my face is electric– like our connection. "Mine, too." I breathe.

I don't know if we'd make it twenty years– or a week for that matter. But I look at him and know just the spot I'll put him when it ends.

The End

The Boy

CHOP HAS THAT FAMILIAR CRAVING. THE ONE THAT MAKES HIM ITCH; DRIVES HIM CRAZY UNTIL HE GETS HIS RELEASE.

JOIN HIM TONIGHT AS HE INVITES HIMSELF INTO A FRIENDLY NEIGHBORHOOD HOME AND INDULGES HIMSELF IN ALL THAT IS NOT OFFERED.

CHAPTER

ONE

Chop

Hey, Chop, you leavin' man?" Gabe, the fucking idiot who loves to follow me around asks.

"Yea, got shit I gotta do."

I don't have anything in particular that I really have to get away for. But I can't be here another second. My skin is crawling; itching to leave.

The bar is usually my second home— the place I come to escape. The shady dump with dim lights and sticky floors has been my hunting ground and home away from home for a long time now. Tonight, I need something else.

I give my card to the bartender, Jenn— a hot little red head who's down to fuck most nights. Settling my tab, I head for the door.

Gabe stops me again.

Fucker.

"Cha need?" I say when he grabs for my elbow. All my self- control teetering toward punching him in the face.

"Just wondering if you heard from Jamie?"

Fucking Jamie.

The bitch that he's been after forever. She's had a thing for me and wouldn't leave me alone, no matter how shitty I treated her.

"Nah, man, I ain't seen 'er." I say it in a way that makes that the end of the conversation. I leave before I have to do something painful to him for holding me up.

It's late, the only people on the street are drunkards trying to find their ways home. I have steam to blow off and I've had too much to drink to get on my bike without alerting law enforcement to my predicament. So, I hoof it; not really heading home directly– got too much going on in my head for such a short walk to be enough.

It's dark, save for the outdated street lights with yellowing bulbs doing nothing to help you see inside the shadows of the darkened alleys, here more for the aesthetic look of them.

One of the ladies on the street catches my eye, she's alone and stumbling in her heels. The skirt she's wearing is hiked up and the bottom of her ass is hanging out. It's a nice round ass, I can see her black laced thong stuck inside the crack.

I follow behind her for a while, she doesn't seem fazed by me. She stumbles and falls to her knees; her arms catch her before she face-plants. I come to her aid, reaching out a hand for her to take.

Once she has made it back to her feet, she reacts to seeing me for the first time and the telltale look in her eyes says she wants me. She bites her lip and gives me her best impression of 'fuck me' eyes I've seen in a long time. I can smell the alcohol and desperation on her.

If I was in the mood for something consensual, I'd be all over this chick. Her long blond hair and blue eyes are usually what I like. Her hot little body and barely- there clothes would get any man in the mood. Not for me... not tonight.

"Hi." She smiles.

"You ok now?" I ask.

"I think so." She surveys her body with her hands, one of which has a small cut on the palm and she smears it across her chest without realizing it. I almost change my mind.

Almost.

"You better get home then."

"You want to follow me? Make sure I get home safe?"

I read the message between the lines. "You got this, girl." I smack her now fully- exposed ass harder than I intended, the sound of it echoing through the night, and start walking again.

I hear her huff, but I don't turn. I'm even more irritated now than I was when I left the bar. I hate nights like this, the nights I can't stop thinking about it–the thing that lives inside of me.

I walk faster, picking up speed; trying to outrun the swirling thoughts fighting for attention in my head. I can't fucking do this. I can't get rid of the itch, though. It grows until I have to listen– until I have to follow its orders. Don't get me wrong, I love that little demon that lurks inside of me, but it has been getting more demanding and leaving me with not much else to think about.

I'm sure I could have made that girl *not* want me after we got into it, I could scare her into a fight; maybe she'd even like to play like that. I think about going back to find her, but I don't. Something inside me knows it's not going to be enough.

Fuck.

I wander into a neighborhood; completely lost in a fantasy of everything I need– all the fucked-up things that I crave. Sometimes it helps to live in the past– to revel in the memories. I feel it strongly in my bones. The need.

Looking around for something to get my mind settled, a distraction from the urge. My eyes land on a window, the vertical blinds are open. My breath catches, exciting me more than calming me. I get that feeling deep inside me, the feeling I spend most of my time shoving down, knowing I can't encourage it. It hits me like a brick in the gut.

I can see straight through the house, a long room that starts with a living area and opens into a dining room. From here, I can see six adults, three women and three men, seemingly coupled up and three teenaged kids. They are a good-looking group of people, so happy and unassuming. Middle class house and the people in there seem to fit the stereotype of what would be found inside.

They're drinking wine, something trendy, I'm sure. The kids are grouped together on the large sectional sofa away from the adults on their phones. As close as kids these days come to social interaction.

Walking across the manicured lawn, I get closer to the glass, standing inches from it. No one is paying any attention to me and the darkness that comes from having no street lights is giving me perfect refuge.

I watch as conversation flows between the people around the table. Laughing and enjoying life. I catch sight of one of the women in particular, uptight and snobby looking. My favorite— if I had to choose. I would love to break her down and show her who the fuck is really in charge. Break her to the point of tears, begging for me to stop. Deep down, knowing I won't. Women like her always so on top of their social circles, vying for queen bee. I love to rip that illusion away from them.

My cock stirs.

This woman is perfect. I can tell she is leading the conversation, everyone angled toward her. She commands the room.

I reach my hand into the front of my pants and squeeze my aching cock. Giving a quick look around the street before finding her in the room again. I don't want to come right now. I love the need that comes from being right on the edge of not finishing, stopping just before I explode. Instant gratification has never been my 'thing', I love the chase of it. The need that I feel going after that high, not wanting it to be over too soon.

My mouth is dry, I can't hear anything over my heavy breathing, coming faster as I pump my cock. I pull my hand away just as I feel the end near. I swallow what saliva I have to wet my throat and reach for the back of my pants, patting the waistband where I keep my gun.

This has to happen. I need this right now.

I watch a few minutes longer to see if anyone else may appear from somewhere else in the house. Nothing happens so I head for the door.

I settle for the 'my truck broke down' approach as I ring the doorbell. I hear a woman call "coming" just before the door opens.

It's her—the one that enticed my cock. My eyes go right to her full tits, but I'm able to pull them up to where it's more acceptable before she notices.

"Don't mean to interrupt you, ma'am." I give my best attempt at 'friendly guy who needs help'. "My truck just crapped out on me. Cell phones dead." I hold mine up; using it as a prop in my lie.

"Oh, um." She seems confused as to what I would need from her in this instance, worrying her bottom lip. I almost snatch her out of her house right then. I stop myself before I do, my hands itching to touch her.

"Is there a phone I can use? Out here, of course." I add when a panic comes into her eyes.

"Um... yeah, I think I can do that." She closes the door tightly after going inside, coming back in a flash.

She steps out onto the porch and shuts the door behind her, putting her less than a foot from me. I can smell her perfume; something sweet and heady. She hands me the phone as a second thought.

Her eyes take me in. I am gruff looking, dark hair, green eyes and about 6'4". To this woman I may seem like a giant, probably no more than five feet herself. Petite and obviously into yoga or some other sort of body toning bullshit. Shoulder length, wildly curly blonde—with a hint of strawberry hair and the prettiest whiskey-colored eyes, looking up into mine, softening a little as she sees nothing in mine to worry about. I definitely don't look like the monster that hides inside of me.

She seems to release the rest of her tension after I take the phone and put it to my ear after adding numbers into the keypad.

I watch her watch me. I've sobered completely, the adrenaline pushing the alcohol from my veins, she looks away self- consciously whenever our eyes meet— which is frequently because I've not stopped and she keeps returning to mine time and again.

I mumble some bullshit into the phone about needing a lift and hit end on it before handing it back to her. Her hand missing it when her eyes refuse to look away from mine to pay attention to the device.

I can't help but tease her, when her hand finally stumbles its connection with the phone, I don't let go on my end. She pulls harder. I let go finally with a half- sided smirk on my face. Something registers in her eyes, close to confusion. She turns quickly toward the door. I grab her hand before it reaches the knob.

"What's your name?" I ask, my tone in any other instance would be considered flirting. She seems to know that, squinting at me to try and calculate how to respond.

"Amy?" she says it like a question. Pulling her hand out of mine harder than it needed to be done; her elbow hitting the door with a thud. She hisses in pain, which only adds to this shit I have going on with me. I love seeing her grab her elbow and baby it. It goes against everything a normal person feels when watching someone hurting, I actually enjoy it. It looks so fucking good on her. Her brow scrunching and the sharp hiss she makes could be confused with the sound she would make while fucking.

"You ok?"

She nods, shaking her arm to rid her funny bone of the pain. "I should get inside."

She turns to the door again.

"What are you doing tonight?" I ask just before the door flies open. The man who had brought on this distraction is tall, only a few inches or so shorter than me. His frame is thin and tapered, where mine is thick and muscular– hours spent at the gym burning off the intense energy I often feel.

I reach my arm toward him in a gesture meant to be accepted with a shake. "I'm Chop." I tell him.

He looks at Amy, trying to gauge her feelings about this and he must not see anything alarming in her eyes because he shakes my hand; harder than necessary—to show me he isn't soft.

"Dan," he says flatly.

"You get everything taken care of, babe?" he wraps his arm around her waist, marking his territory.

My cheek twitches as I fight the laugh that begs to be heard. I could knock this fucker out in one hit without using my full strength and he wants to enter a pissing contest with me. I almost hope he tries something tonight. I'm usually more of a fucker than a fighter, but anything that gets the blood pumping is good for me.

Ok.

I move quicker than either of them can stop me and the gun is leveled at his temple. Amy is who I want my eyes on– to see her reaction to this, but mine stay trained on Dan. His eyes are a cartoon version of shock.

Dumb fuck.

I do laugh now; his face is too comical to not. "Let's take this inside— wouldn't want the neighbors to think something strange is going on."

They do, walking in front of me. Amy stumbles over the threshold and I catch her sore elbow in my hand before she can spill over. My fingers envelope her whole bicep, which is muscular but thin. She yelps when I dig my fingernails into her flesh.

I think of a few ways I could use this woman. I'd fucking break her in half if I went at her the way I'd really like to, maybe I'll get a chance tonight. I could very well make sure to leave enough time for it.

I fling her arm away from me, propelling her forward. The room falls quiet as everyone realizes what is happening. A quick count tells me that everyone is here and accounted for. I tell them all not to move. No one seems to have thought that they might have anyway. Shocked, as a collective whole, is all I read in them.

It's a nice neighborhood, things like this aren't supposed to happen here, thusly, making people like them unable to function when it finally does. I thank the 'false sense of security' gods as I give them further instructions.

"Everyone to the table. Phones right here." I point to the floor in the middle of the two groups. Hands start reaching around for devices. The clattering of them hitting the floor happens quickly after.

I nudge this fuck- face forward with the barrel of the gun. I can see the defiance in his eyes, but he is not crazy enough to try anything. *Yet*.

Amy stays close by his side, probably feeling a sense of protection toward him— like she could do anything about it if I pulled the trigger. I think I'll test that loyalty tonight.

Everyone has made it to the chairs around the rectangle table, scooting close together to keep their backs from facing me; choosing to butt against the wall instead. I tell these two to get there now as well.

The fear is evident on everyone, although the questions they have go unasked.

I take a minute to collect my thoughts— how this is going to go down tonight. I look around the neatly decorated, but mostly feminine room.

"Ok, so, this is what we're going to do." My voice is loud and commanding in the space, startling them. "I want to play a little. Nothing too horrible will happen tonight if you all can just follow directions. Think you can do that?" It is not true most of the time, and definitely not on a night like tonight where the little demon wants to play, but if I told them the truth it would be anarchy.

Silence. "I think I asked a fucking question. Do you all think you could follow some simple instructions if your lives depended on it? Because you fuckers can't even answer a simple fucking question."

Losing my cool really loosened their vocal cords; this time I get a mixture of nods and verbal confirmations. "That's better. Now, whose house is this?"

Amy answers that it is hers.

"Who else lives here?"

"Just Travis and me."

I look toward the man who came to her aid outside. "You Travis?"

He just shakes his head, offering me no more information.

"Ok... then who the fuck is Travis?" My voice is showing my irritation by progressively getting louder.

"I am," one of the teenagers who was sitting on the couch earlier says. Blond kid with shaggy hair, tallish for his age and trim. I can see it now; he has her rare colored eyes.

"You her kid?"

"Yea," he says.

"Who are your parents?" I ask the other two kids.

They both point to the same set of people— the youngest looking couple of the group.

"So, you don't have kids here?" I ask the last couple.

They shake their heads. His fat chins jiggling back and forth with the rapid movement. He is much older looking than her, who looks at least ten years his junior, bleach blonde, big tits. She looks like a trophy wife, probably the reason that there are no children between the two of them.

"My name is Chop, and now that we've all been so nicely introduced, let's fucking do this."

The expressions on their faces encourage me, fear of the unknown written everywhere. I love this part– the part that lets them all in on their fates. "I'm going to ask you, Amy, to please come here– stand right here." I point to the spot right next to me.

She takes a deep breath before standing and making her way over. I pull her closer to me, wrapping my arm around her shoulders. She stiffens but doesn't pull away. The man she is with– her boyfriend I assume, seethes.

"So, Amy, which of these fine people would you be least likely to miss if something were to happen to them?"

"What? You said if we followed your instructions no one would get hurt." She's panicking, pulling against my restraining hold.

"Well, sometimes people have to show that they mean business. I'm merely trying to show you I'm serious. It could be a hypothetical question, maybe nothing will happen to this person. I mean, it seems unlikely, but it *could* be the case. Either way, I'll need that fucking answer from you or I'll have to choose and you won't like the choice *I* make, I'll be sure of it." I give her a cocky smirk.

She holds her pleading eyes to mine. She must see what needs to be seen in them to make her choice because she swallows hard and says, "Stephen."

I know who Stephen is right away. It is him who jumps from the table, toppling over his chair. "Amy!" he shouts at her, the accusation thick in his voice. He tries to scramble away, but there isn't enough room for his large body to move quickly.

The polo shirt tucked tightly into his khaki pants makes me hate him instantly. I level the gun to him, "Come over here, Stephen."

He looks ready to hyperventilate.

"Would you rather do it yourself, or should I?"

"Please, you don't have to do this." He is shaking with fear, his legs nearly buckle as he reaches the spot on the floor, I indicate for him to stop.

"I know, but I *want* to." I pull the trigger and half his face explodes, landing with an oof as his lungs empty of air when his body falls hard onto the floor.

Amy escapes my grasp, but only to slide down my body to the ground, her legs giving out.

The gasping and screaming that fills the air is from multiple sources— sounding together it is almost comedic. His wife doesn't do anything overboard, like I usually see, she simply looks at his dead body, tears rolling from her eyes. This furthers my idea that she is a trophy wife, a marriage of convenience and money, possibly.

I catch Travis in the corner of my eye, he is unaffected by the gruesome scene. The only one in the room who hadn't responded to the violence. I watch him until his eyes meet mine.

He doesn't look away. *Hmmm.*

CHAPTER

TWO

Travis

I watch as this big fucking dude put a bullet into Stephen's face. Something I wish I could have done a thousand times. His wife is always over here bitching about all the horrible things he does to her. (All the things that *I* want to do to her)

She tells my mom she hates fucking him because he is so mean about it. He essentially rapes her whenever he wants to. I stay close by when she visits to hear all the details, fantasizing it would be me one day to force her into doing whatever the fuck I want to do to her. I jack off to that thought more often than not. Even now, as she is crying over him, all I can think about is how her tits are heaving as she cries.

CHAPTER

THREE

Chop

I pull the fat fucks body out of the way, leaving behind a smear of him along the floor.

"Ok, now everyone knows I mean business. Amy, thank you for helping out on that one."

Her response is almost a hiss. "Fuck you." She scrambles back to her seat, dragging her knees through the mess.

The words hit me in the dick. "I wouldn't talk like that to me, I already have my eye on you. I like a lady with a nasty mouth."

This seems to alarm her, but she snaps her mouth shut.

"Ok, now that that is out of the bag. You," I point to the man who is with the lady that didn't just witness her husband's brains burst open. He is in good shape, on the shorter side but looks like he may be able to handle himself against a man of equal stature. "This is going to sound like a strange request. But you know after someone loses someone dear to them, they need a little companionship."

His wide eyes tell me he may know where I'm going with this.

"Don't you think Miss Trophy Wife over there looks so lonely after Mr. Fat Fuck lost his head?"

He shakes his head wildly.

His lady, and mother to two of the children looking on, looks horrified herself. "In case it's not clear, I'd like you to fuck her."

"I... I can't do that."

The boy, Travis, seems a little pissed now. I wonder where that's coming from.

"Travis."

He looks at me, lifting his eyebrows in response to his name being called.

"What's got you all pissy now? You want a chance with one of these girls?"

He looks away finally.

"Which one?" I ask.

His eyes meet mine for the briefest second before looking down again.

"You a virgin?"

His face turns red as confirmation.

"Which one you want? This one?" I walk over to the girl looking to be about his age and pull her up by her hair. She screams from the pain.

I watch closely and see his eyes subconsciously shoot to the trophy wife. I drop the girl back into her chair, being of no further use to me right now. I go to where his eyes were drawn. "You want this one?"

His tongue licks his lips before he looks up at me through his eyebrows.

I might actually like this kid. "Come 'er."
He stands quicker than is polite for what I'm about to ask of him. I hold back a laugh.

I tell trophy wife to get undressed and lie down on the couch. She does it without being asked twice, going into auto- pilot and looking a little shaken by the whole experience. The task is quick, she was wearing a sundress with no bra and a strip of fabric as panties.

I can see what the boy sees in her, her large fake tits are perfect and her tiny waist with wide hips make her look even better naked. I almost think about giving her a go myself, but the thought of tearing Amy apart later holds me back.

"Alright, boy, go on over there and give it to her." I shove him a little, although he doesn't really need the extra push. I do it more for his sake– to give it the illusion the he's not so ready for this. I don't know why I feel the need to protect his perversion, but I do.

"I can't," he says once he's standing in front of her. The bulge in his pants says quite the opposite.

"You gonna need help? You want the girl to get you ready?"

He shakes his head before I can go collect her.

"You want me to bring your mom over there for you? Make her get on her knees for you?"

He looks at me; the thing that flashes in his eyes is not one of disgust.

"We may have a thing for the same woman." I can't really blame the kid, all those hormones and a hot as fuck mom has got to be confusing.

He looks panicked, so, I let up on him.

"Alright then, get started. Take your clothes off. Better yet, why don't you undress him?" I tell miss trophy. "His dick isn't going to suck itself– open up wide for him."

When she doesn't move, I pull her up from her prone position by her hair and force her face into his crotch. "I told you to do something. You want to end up like the fat man?"

She shakes her head and moves her trembling hands to his zipper. I see the boy take a shaky breath and swallow hard.

"You ever had a blow job?" I ask him.

"No." His voice cracks.

Amy, his mom, shouts at me to stop, to leave him alone. I let her outburst go, this time– enjoying this shit too much to take my attention away from it.

Once his cock is out, harder than men my age gets anymore, I push her forward until she is forced to open her lips. I watch as she moves him in and out of her mouth. She's pretty good at it, too. She takes him deep.

"You want in that pussy, boy?"

His eyes close, so I let him enjoy himself.

I reach between her legs. "Spread."

She does, moving the two inches I need to fit my hand between her naked thighs.

I put my fingers inside of her smooth pussy– easily as she seems to be wet. The fucking slut could be getting off on this.

"You like him, huh?" I fuck her quickly with two fingers, her pussy clamping down on them, squeezing tightly.

"You're gonna want to get in this, boy." I slap the mound of her pussy. She whines, but doesn't let up on him, the slurping sounds remain in perfect rhythm.

He looks at me, asking for help, in a way. He knows that I know he is a sicko like me.

"Maybe you need some alone time with her? Take her to the room right here." I point to the bedroom I see down the hallway with the door open, just off the dining room. "Stand up, whore."

She does it with tears flooding her eyes. "Get in the room, lie back on the bed and wait for him."

The boy tries to follow her in, but I stop him. "You listen to me, you try anything I won't put a bullet in you, I'll make it much more fun for me."

He nods.

"Now, get in there and make her scream. I want everyone out here to hear her."

"Leave it open." I tell him when he tries to close the door. "I'll be watching. No fun if I can't see it."

He looks at me a long moment before pulling his shirt over his head and going in for the girl, who is waiting on the edge of the bed for him. I smile a knowing grin at him. That girl is about to get the fuck of her life time in there.

I keep an eye on the remaining people in the dining room, but my real attention is drawn to what is going on in the bedroom, the light blue paint and sunflower border is a direct contradiction to what's about to happen to that woman on the bed in a minute.

The boy is inside of her already, wasting no time pushing her onto her knees and entering her slick hole from behind, pumping quickly; holding tightly to her hips and pushing into her hard.

She is soundless, though, not that she could be heard over the banging of the headboard or the squeak of the bed frame. Her face is vacant, the boy's ferociousness possibly scaring her.

"That's it, boy," I say to encourage him.

He seems to know what to do and thrusts deeper still. I cover my hard on with my hand and give it a good squeeze. This boy really knows what he wants. He is going at her like a madman. "You watch porn? You got some good shit going on there."

His grin tells me he appreciates the compliment.

"If you can't fuck her 'til she screams you better find a way to make her scream— we have an audience to impress."

He takes no time to understand what I mean, ripping her head up off the bed by her hair, making her yelp.

"Hit her," I grunt.

He puts his fist into her back, right at her kidney.

She screams.

"Nice." I say, massaging my cock. It's like watching porn, only better. I can practically smell the musky sex smell from here.

He does it again, then wraps both his fists into her hair and uses it like a rein to keep her in place as he forces himself inside her. I have a great side view of what he's doing to her. His eagerness is amazing.

She is squealing like a stuck pig now.

The others in the dining room are looking a little worried for her welfare, which only makes me enjoy this even more, he is savage.

And just when I think it can't get any better— or worse, depending on what side you're on— the kid fucking turns her face up toward him, looking her in the eyes then punches her right in the jaw. The crunch is louder than both the pounding and her screams that follow.

I can't believe it. I laugh before I can stop myself. "Fuck, boy, nice going. You got everyone in here worried for her. You got anything else in there for 'em?" The blood around her mouth is beautiful. If I wasn't on guard duty I'd go over and fuck it right now.

"What are you making him do to her?" I hear from Amy. Poor mom didn't know he'd be capable of something like this. I kind of feel sorry for her, shattering her illusion of her perfect little all- American blond-haired boy.

I ignore her question, completely absorbed in what's happening with the woman and her wildly bouncing tits.

He seems to think about my question for a minute. Then, before I know what he's doing, he spits on her ass, and quicker than I've ever seen, he shoves his hard dick into that hole.

She looks ready to pass out from the abrupt and painful maneuver, losing her strength, her knees slide out from under her, leaving her sprawled out on the bedspread.

He barely misses a thrust, but he only lasts a few more before he grunts his own finish deep inside her torn ass.

CHAPTER

FOUR

Travis

I can barely keep it together; I shove her forward until she is bent over the bed. "Get your knees up there, Kelly." She does and I get the perfect view of her meaty pussy. Chop was right, she is wet. Maybe she is so used to being used by Stephen that her body responds to it now.

I slide my fingers through her slit and spread her open, ramming into her as hard as I can to fill her up. My first time in a pussy– so much better than I have ever imagined. And trust me, I have imagined– this in particular.

The closest I've come to fucking was watching an old babysitter get fucked by her boyfriend. I must be doing a good job, though, Chop has his hand on his crotch, much like I had mine while I jacked off watching that little slut get fucked. Or spread open while being eaten by her boyfriend countless times.

CHAPTER

FIVE

Chop

She is openly crying now. Something that doesn't go unnoticed in the room full of people— his mother looking the most horrified of the bunch.

"Come on now, boy, get cleaned up." I grab his pants from the floor in front of the couch and toss them at him.

He pulls his pants over his hips after wiping his bloody cock off with the cream-colored comforter. As he passes me in the doorway I tell him, "Nice job, Travis." Clapping him on the sweaty shoulder the way a proud father might.

He hides his smile before joining the rest in the room.

His mother is looking at her son like he is a stranger, the things that went on in the room are not known to her, but there is no mistaking that it was horrible. She stays sitting instead of comforting him like a mother might want to do after her son had been forced to do those things in there. A part of her knowing he was possibly glad to accept the challenge.

The girl in the room is struggling to stand, her bloodied shaking legs unable to hold her weight. I do not let her get too far, spraying her brains on the wall behind her. The thwack of the gun startling everyone.

"She's better off dead after what happened in there, she'd never be the same after that." I laugh. She would definitely have some therapy bills, for sure.

There are sideways glances toward the boy, the questions of what actually happened in there written across their faces. They may be as scared of him as they are of me— maybe more so— I've only killed people.

Amy, his mother, seems to be taking it the hardest, probably devastated her son was capable of whatever made that bitch scream like that. Fuck, I'm a little shocked myself. Mom has got to be taking it hard.

Kinda like the dead girl— she took it pretty hard, too. I laugh at my own joke, confusing everyone not privy to my inner thoughts.

"Now that we've taken care of them, let's see here... you," I point to the mother of the two children. "What's your name?"

"Nancy."

"Ok, Nancy, it looks like you're up."

She pales and the excitement fills my insides.

"This is your husband?"

She nods slowly, hysterics building inside of her.

"You love him?"

"Very much." Her chin quivers, trying to hold back her tears.

"These his kids?"

Another nod, then the damn breaks and she loses it.

"Would you rather him die or one of the children?"

She takes a shaky breath between sobs. "Please, don't do this. You can just leave now and everything will be fine. Nothing..."

I cut her off, "That's not going to happen. Just answer the fucking question or I'll make you regret not."

She takes a long look through her tears, into her husband's eyes and just before she loses it again, he speaks up.

"It's ok, love, I know you have to protect the kids. I love you so much. I could never blame you for this choice he's forcing you to make."

She is crying again, sobbing. "I can't let you hurt my children," she says by way of an answer.

"Ok, great, then I'm going to need a few things." I turn away from her snotty, wet face.

"Boy, go find something– like a rope? Anything like that around here?"

He nods, "We have some in the garage. You want me to get 'em?"

I hear the eagerness to be helpful in his voice.

"You need me to threaten you with violence if you try anything stupid?" I don't really feel like I'd have to; this boy is the perfect assistant.

"Nah." And he leaves before I even can.

While he's gone, I tell Nancy to place one of the dining chairs in the center of the room, underneath the exposed wooden ceiling beam. I take the rope from the boy, as he hands it over, and truss it up and around the beam, catching the end of it as it wraps snuggly around.

"Get over here, Dad," I say. "Up on the chair. Your wife made a decision that your life is less important than your children's, so, let's see if we can get her to follow through with that, shall we?"

"Nancy, come here." I tie the rope into a noose and place it around his neck.

He stares into my eyes, raging with hatred for me.

"Nancy, I'd like you to move the chair out from under him when I say. If you don't, I will kill one of your children." I drag her teenage son, by his throat, over to the scene and hold the gun steady to his head.

He is shaking under my hand.

"Do it now, Nancy."

She puts her hands on the chair back, but doesn't move it. "I'm so sorry, baby. I love you so much." She looks at me, begging. "Please don't make me do this, I could never live with this." She crumbles to her knees.

Before I can give her further instructions, her husband kicks the back of the chair, toppling it over and drops the few inches of slack before catching himself around the neck by the rope.

I roar and pull the trigger at his son's head. "I fucking told *her* to do that."

As his eyes see what he has done to his child with that decision, his legs kick frantically to find the chair and right himself, his fingers claw at his neck to get free of the rope.

"You did this, fucker." I kick the kid hard, with no response from him as the bullet killed him instantly.

A full minute later the man's hands slip from his neck, his shaking body stops— no more life left in him to fight. I watched as the light in his eyes dulled. Keeping mine on his, so they'd be the last thing in this world that stupid fucker saw.

Nancy is crawling herself to her son, screams pouring from her lungs. I thought she was hysterical before– that was nothing compared to what the fuck is going on now. She is blubbering incoherent words to the dead men on the floor.

His sister pulls mom away, trying to calm her. They are holding tightly to each other, both knowing the other's pain.

"Come 'ere, girl. Your turn."

Nancy's red and tear-streaked face pales, she hasn't had any time to properly mourn the rest of her family and she knows she's about to watch something horrific happen to her daughter, but she's too weak to do anything about it.

"Nooooooo," she whines.

I don't think I've enjoyed torturing a person quite like I'm enjoying this– her screams are like Viagra. She really knows how to make my efforts feel worth it.

The girl isn't standing up fast enough so I snatch her up. She stumbles twice before she can stay up on her feet– her mother grabbing hold of her ankles to keep her away from me. When she has control of her feet, she tries her best to act tough, setting her shoulders back and glaring at me.

"You know what happens in a strip club? All those hot young girls grinding against poles."

I love the look this her eyes. I can see a little of her reserve falter but she nods.

"Great, why don't you go show him a good time?" I point to Amy's man, Dan.

He stiffens, not knowing yet which of the two of them my target is.

"Get undressed," I tell him. "We got to make sure she's doing a good job."

"You're just going to shoot me anyway. So, fucking do it now and save everyone from this."

"That's not the way this works. I *want* to see it. Shooting you is the nicest way I could kill you. Do you want to hear about all the ways I could make you feel pain *before* killing you? All the things I've done in the past— that I dream about when I go to sleep, or the things I'm just aching to try. Do you like the thought of being my guinee pig? Do you want to see me *not* being nice?"

He begins to unbutton his polo shirt— really drawing out the time it takes him to get it done. "You got something wrong with your fingers that's making you move so fucking slowly? I'm not a very patient man, I'd hurry if I were you."

He picks up his pace, not quite as fast as he would normally go about it, but I let that slide.

He hesitates again when it comes to his underwear, stopping with his thumbs in his waistband, looking at me for permission to quit.

"I could lop your dick off if I don't see it in the next three seconds."

He sits back into the chair when he is sufficiently naked.

"Ok, girl, go show him a good time. Strip for him— for us. Make it sexy."

"I don't know how to do that." She says frantically.

"Move slow and take your clothes off— it's not too hard."

She starts to sway her hips side to side, walking closer to him.

He seems nervous and won't look at her.

"You're going to keep your eyes on her. All of you watch her— don't be rude."

Everyone's eyes go blankly to her. Travis eagerly watching now that her thin sweater has come off. *Good boy.*

"You liking this, Travis?"

His eyes are glued to her and without looking at me, he nods.

I smile. Watching his mom, Amy, look at him from the corner of her eyes, horrified.

"Everyone else having fun?" I don't get an answer, but then, I really don't expect one. This girl is *very* close to barely legal.

"Alright, girl, let's see those tits."

Amy, looking all the more horrified to learn her son was not the only monster in her midst.

"Amy, what do you think about your boy- toy fucking this hot little piece of ass?"

She snarls at me, making me chuckle. I can't wait for her turn.

"Why don't we get a look at your little ass now, girl? Take it all off."

Silent tears are running down her cheeks, she's no longer dancing. She does what she is told, pulling her skin-tight jeans down her legs, kicking out of both them and the panties I saw earlier for the briefest moment.

Hot pink.

Fuck.

"Grind your little pussy against him, let's see if he can hold back with that."

"Fucker!" he yells at me. Dan's semi- hard cock is growing now. He can't hide his excitement any longer.

"You sick pig." Amy hisses at him.

"Amy... I'm sorry. I don't want this, I promise. You know me, I'm not like this man. I don't know what it is— stress or something maybe? Oh, god, please," he begs to no one in particular.

"Why don't we just skip the grinding part, honey, his cock has made itself known."

"Quite the grower." I say as an aside to Dan.

"Why don't you just slip him inside of you on your way down to his lap?" I say to the girl.

She cries finally, looking at the massive cock she is up against. "I can't put that inside of me."

"Why don't you help her out? Get down there and make sure she's wet so it's not so scary for her."

He looks at me questioningly.

"With your mouth, idiot. Give her a little to get excited about."

He gets on his knees in front of her. "I'm so sorry, Lizzy," he says before spreading her open and positioning his upturned head between her thighs.

Her sobs are louder now.

"Put some fingers inside her. You're a big guy… do you want to tear her open?"

His grunt is muffled by her pussy; not pulling away to answer. It wasn't the grunt of a man who is not enjoying himself, it doesn't go unnoticed by the people in the room, particularly Lizzy who panics, pushing against his head.

He does what I say and pushes his fingers inside of her.

She yelps.

"You want to fuck her now?"

He doesn't answer, but sits back onto the floor. His mouth is glistening with saliva.

"Get her on it," I say.

He lays back, pulling her arms along with him, helping her situate herself into a straddle around his thighs. Grabbing the base of his cock, holding it in place as she settles against it.

I push her shoulders down until she is fully impaled

She squeals as his full length fills the inside of her.

"Lizzy, I'm gonna need you to make him happy. Why don't you do a little bouncing on his big dick?"

She does what her body will let her do while convulsing in hysterics, which is not as exciting as I need this to be.

"Help her out, she's new at this. Buck your fucking hips, mother fucker, the sooner you come the sooner it's over."

The slapping of her jiggling ass against his solid thighs is barely audible over her screams, his jack hammer approach to fucking her would do that to anyone.

He is grunting from the effort to keep this pace and just as I see signs of his finish, I put a bullet in her head. She collapses onto his chest.

Instead of stopping, like a gentleman might, he gets more frantic, her convulsing body flopping about. He thrusts faster into her, gripping her hard around her waist to keep in her place, drawing out a moan for the duration of his pulsing cock emptying inside of her dead body.

"You fucker!" her mother yells, but not at me. She is on her feet and screaming at him. "You sick fucking pervert. Fucking her was one thing, being forced to do that, but you really had to fuck my little girl while she was dying? You sick piece of shit!" she has gotten so loud she's screeching.

She leaves the room, I let her only out of curiosity.

She comes back with a large knife from the kitchen and before the man can defend himself— still coming down from what I can only imagine was an awesome nut— and trapped by the full weight of Lizzy's dead body, she puts the knife into his eye socket.

He's not moving. I'm not sure if that worked to kill him, there's a lot of blood on the floor and the knife is buried to the hilt, so I have to assume he is. He died in what I can only imagine was the happiest state he's ever been.

I leave them attached by their crotches and move on, ripping the woman away from her victim.

"Well, now that it's just the four of us, and we're all a little worked up. Why don't we have a little fun together?"

I wait for everyone to become curious enough at my words to look at me.

"Travis, you want a go at her?" I point to the woman covered in the blood of her family members I've killed tonight– and the man she's taken it upon herself to do without help.

"Yea," he says, not hiding behind anymore masks of being a normal boy.

"Alright, but you fuck her you gotta kill her."

"You got it." He pulls the knife from the man's head, using two hands as it becomes clear it had been lodged into his skull.

He walks over to the table, setting the knife down as he undoes his pants and lets them fall to the floor. He drags Nancy to the spot her daughter's body was brutally raped and then killed– kicking Dan's arm aside, and hikes her skirt up over her ass, ripping her thong at the seam, effectively removing them. Already hard, he pushes her face onto the table and enters her from behind.

The woman is all cried- out, however, his mother is in complete hysterics, becoming massively undone as he drags the knife across Nancy's throat and then fucks her dying body. Pulling her head back by the roots of her hair– it opens the gash in her neck and she gurgles around the sprays of arterial blood leaving her neck and spurting across the room.

She dies before he finishes and when he does, he is laughing, fully lost in the sick nature of what he has just done.

CHAPTER

SIX

Travis

The thought of that, all the blood, much like the brutal underground porn I love to watch, excites me.

"You got it." I pull the knife from Dan's eye socket, which takes effort; that bitch stabbed him pretty good.

I drag Nancy to the table, letting my throbbing dick out of my pants. I lift her skirt over her ass and tear her underwear away. Her pussy is not wet like Kelly's– not as meaty either. I'm sure I'll still like it in here, but it may take a little something extra to really enjoy it. And as soon as the thought is in my head, I know nothing else will work to get me off.

I fuck her hard until I'm sure how to go about it and then I drag the knife across her throat. And yeah, that fucking did it. Her pussy is in the middle of the most-extreme fight as her body writhes in the throes of her death.

I fuck her harder once she's dead, her body fitting me like a glove. Sweat pours from my forehead as I exert the last bit of energy to feed her pussy my come. Breathing hard, I collapse on her while I recover.

CHAPTER

SEVEN

Chop

"Jesus, boy," I say, keeping a tight hold on his mother as she squirms against me.

"What? You didn't tell me what order I had to do it in." The boy has a fucking *smirk* on his face.

Oh, my fuck. This kid.

I wonder then, what it would be like. I've fucked my fair share of 'dead fish' women who just lie there while I fuck them. That was nothing like the excitement I got from watching Travis slice open her throat and fuck her.

"How was it?" I ask.

He walks over to me, dick still wet, and takes the gun I have pointed at his mother and puts a bullet right between her eyes. "Why don't you give it a try?"

Holy fuck.

I catch her body before it hits the floor and I do try it. I fuck her for longer than I've fucked anyone, coming inside of her pussy– and a moment later, when I'm hard again at the thought of her ass, I have a go at that, too.

Nothing had ever been that good. Although, I love the fight of a clawing and scratching woman I'm fucking– this is something different. All my effort could go into the fucking– not having the struggle deplete my energy. I pounded relentlessly into her body. Growling like a fucking animal with all the power.

Travis watching has him interested in his girl again, and he gets another round in with her.

We fuck them until absolutely and utterly spent– the both of us.

After getting dressed, while I'm still wondering what to do with this boy, he answers my unasked question. "Where to now, Chop?"

Seems I've got a hunting buddy now and the boy is full of great ideas, but I have a few that could change his life, too.

I plan on taking him to meet Jamie, the girl Gabe was asking about tonight. The play- thing I've been enjoying in my basement for the last week. "I got just the girl for us."

He looks excited, even after all we've done here tonight; he could probably give Jamie a few good rounds when we get home. Maybe we could have a go at her together? One on either end like a pig on a spit.

"Grab some shit, boy, I got just the place.

The End

DEGENERATE

AFTER RECEIVING NEWS OF HIS FATHER'S
UNTIMELY DEATH TYLER RYDEK SETS OUT ON A
JOURNEY BACK TO HIS CHILDHOOD HOME. HE
LEARNS QUICKLY THAT HE WASN'T THE ONLY
ONE KEEPING SECRETS IN THAT HOUSE.

Chapter One

"Hello, am I speaking with Tyler Rydek?"

The unknown number that I answered thinking it was Cammie calling from a friend's phone asks. I should not be in charge of my devices after a night of binge drinking. I can barely think right now.

"Yea," I say, rolling over onto my side to look at the alarm clock. Seven fucking thirty. Who the fuck calls someone at 7:30am?

I stumble into the bathroom, bumping into the wall as I pass, unsteady on my still drunken feet, not fully listening to the man's voice. He's going on about something I can't hear over the stream of alcohol pushing its way out of my mornings semi- hardened cock.

"What's this about?" I ask after climbing back into bed, pulling the covers over my naked body up to my chin. I must have left a window open last night. The chill in here is too much. I think about going to close it but I can't climb back out of the covers to do so right now.

"Mr. Rydek, I'm your father's attorney. I'm sorry to be the one to tell you this... but he has passed. The hospital called last night; he had been mugged—stabbed multiple times by the assailant. Seems he didn't recover. There was too much damage to his organs. They thought he would be alright after surgery, but he passed while he was sleeping."

I can't wrap my head around this. My father was 45 years old, still young and full of life. "Did they catch the guy?" I ask.

"No, no witnesses were at the scene when he was found. A woman came across him lying there in the alley. She told police he was the only one there when she arrived."

"Wow." I don't know what else to say. It hasn't hit me yet, the words he's saying should be enough to hit me, to bring the tears. He was my best friend, a great father, the man I idolized growing up. My hero. But they don't come, I don't cry, instead I ask him why he is the one calling me.

"He gave me strict instructions upon making his Will that I be the one to call if he were to meet his fate. I'm simply following his request."

"Oh, so what now?" I ask, not sure I even want to know. My eyes are getting heavy with sleep.

"I'll ask that you come to my office, he has some things he'd like me to give you personally. Then we can go over his last Will and Testament."

"Where's my mother?" I haven't talked to her in years, she is the reason I had to get out of that fucking town.

She's a lot to handle. And that is the fucking understatement of a lifetime.

"Mr. Rydek, I have no idea of your mother's whereabouts. I'm your father's attorney. I had no dealings with her."

"Ok. So, when should we do this?"

"I'd like it to be as soon as possible, he's told me there are time sensitive things for you."

"Well, I can't be there sooner than tomorrow night. It's a long drive for me; I'm no longer in town."

"That should be fine; I'll have everything ready for your arrival."

"I need an address." I look around the room, I don't even think I own a pen to take it down, but it's a small town, I should have been able to retain enough to find it.

"Absolutely, I'm at the old textile loft on First Street. Are you familiar with the building?"

Oh, fuck, that old loft was the hang out for all the stoners; of course, I know the place. "Yea, I know where you're at. I'll be there tomorrow night. Thanks for the call."

"I'll see you then, sir. I'm so sorry for your loss; your father was truly a great man— a friend of mine for years."

"Thanks, I'm sorry you lost him, too, then." I push end on my cell before he can say anything else, pulling the comforter over my face to warm my nose I pass out in seconds.

CHAPTER TWO

The morning– or afternoon rather, comes quicker than I am ready for it. The sun coming from the large bay window is beating down on my face.

I pick up my phone and check for a missed call from Cammie. Nothing. She is so good at avoiding me. I roll my eyes at her antics, I don't know why I even want a fucking girlfriend, they are definitely more trouble than they're worth. The occasional blowjob or fuck is not worth the hassle of all the emotional bullshit I have had to tolerate from them– her in particular. Say or do the wrong thing and this girl will fight with you for a week and ignore you for a second one.

It's becoming too much for me. Still, she does have the best ass and tits I've ever seen– when she actually lets me have access to them, that is. The girl is also very much a prude, little miss catholic school girl– and the kind that doesn't go wild and fuck anyone and everything. She's the boring kind that wants you to marry her and shit. That's not for me, but I tell her whatever she wants to hear to let me inside. She gave me her virginity. After some major manipulation on my part to get her to do it, I'm not giving up on that tight hole before I'm done with it.

I climb my hung- over ass out of bed, remembering the call from earlier, I think of all the things I need to do to be ready to head out soon. It's going to be a long night of driving, nearly a thousand miles. I could not have gotten far enough away when I left.

I relieve myself then head into the kitchen for coffee, passing the front door that is standing wide open— the source of the cold last night. Not the first time I've neglected to close it. The damn thing swings wide open if you don't slam it.

I do now, the thunderous sound shaking the walls.

The smell of coffee brewing is finally doing something to rouse my mind— waking me. My mouth is salivating for the dark drink. I take a too- big swallow of it after it's done. Burning my mouth but not caring, I go for a second one, topping my cup off before heading back to my room to get packed and ready for the trip.

I pull on a pair of jeans after loading a few other pairs into my bag, throwing some tees on top of the stack and then call Cammie's phone. Voicemail. I leave her a message explaining why I'll be gone for the next few days and that I need to talk to her and then slip the phone into my back pocket. I pull on a t-shirt and my favorite hoodie and take the bag to my car.

I look around the house before leaving, making a quick checklist of things I may have overlooked. I can't think of anything more I'll need while I'm there so I fill a travel mug with the remainder of the coffee and lock up the house.

CHAPTER THREE

I've always hated this drive. After leaving my parent's house and coming here for college, I've made the trek a few times. Before I didn't, choosing one day not to go back.

When college was over, I got a job, got a house, got a life and didn't want this fucking town to be a part of it anymore. So, it wasn't.

I've been on the road for almost three hours, making my way through my favorite playlist when I see a girl on the side of the road—telltale hitch-hiker thumbs up. I don't give it much thought; I just pull over to the side of the road when I reach her. She is blonde and tall, short skirt and a top that shows off her tits. Her face is nice, but not beautiful—I notice when she sticks her head in the window that I opened for her.

"I'm going about a hundred miles west, think you could help me out?" she sounds sweet, but the eyes she's giving me tells me she may be a little naughty.

"I can do that." I tell her, hitting the button to unlock the door for her.

"Thank you." She throws her bag into the back seat. "What's your name?" she asks after settling in the seat next to me.

"Tyler." I say, looking a little too long at her thighs, exposed after her skirt gets hiked up from sitting.

She notices, opening them slightly more— possibly subconsciously. I've always had a way with the ladies. My all- American boy good looks have made it easy for me to get what and whom I want. I run my hand through my shaggy blond hair and look her in the eye, my eyebrow goes up in a way that tells her I know that she wants me. The way she bites her bottom lip lets me know I was right.

"I'm April."

Before pulling away I ask her, "So, April, you got gas money?" I don't really want it; I want her to offer something else in return.

"I don't have any money."

Good. "What else could you repay this kind favor with?" My cock is growing in my pants just thinking about the possibilities.

"Umm, what do you want?" she asks, squirming a little in her seat, showing me she knows what it might be.

I reach my hand over to her face, sliding my thumb in between her lips and she fucking lets me.

Slut.

"How about you put this to work?"

Her tongue tastes my thumb, sending a shock to my dick. "I could do that," she says shyly. The shy shit must be all an act because she's far too eager to get her hands on my zipper.

The feel of her warm mouth on my excited cock makes me hiss. Her ass is high in the air, knees on her seat as she leans over the console in the center. I can see her cheeks peeking out of the skirt. I pull it up more, exposing her completely. Her little black thong tucked nicely in between. I give one side a smack and she moans, humming around my cock. The girl is good at it, she is taking me deep— I can feel the back of her throat against the head.

I tuck my hand under her— between her legs. She spreads to accommodate it. I feel how wet she is instantly— her panties are soaked. I bypass them quickly and slip my fingers into the slit of her meaty pussy.

She moans again, growing hungrier for me. My finger finds her hole and I push inside of her without a care. Her juicy cunt is all too excited for me. The wet sounds coming from her hole as I pump my hand quickly mingle nicely with the sounds of her throat fucking me.

I wrap my fingers into her hair and hold her tightly in place, bucking my hips to reach past her tonsils. She gags but doesn't try and pull away. Her pussy accepts another of my fingers and she rocks against them.

I get lost in the feel of her throat, my thoughts go to Cammie– she would never let me do anything like this. Sure, she's ok with the occasional blowjob but I'd never get her to deep throat me. She is more a put your mouth around the head until I tell her it's good enough and to stop so we can "make love" and then spreading her shy legs in missionary position until I come– which often times takes too long, as she likes it slow and sweet.

This girl here can really take a cock. I might have to take advantage of this again before I let her out.

My hips buck faster, pushing deeply into her, her breathing is labored and the noises coming from her throat encourage me. The sound of her gagging as she takes my cock thrills me and I'm so fucking close to coming. "Are you going to let me come in your mouth?"

She nods, barely able to move.

"You want to taste me, don't you?"

Another nod.

"You gonna swallow it?"

She moans in reply.

"You're a hungry little slut, aren't you?"

"Mmhmm."

I pull my fingers out of her and the bitch fucking whines like a dog in heat. "Make yourself come for me. I want you coming with me so hurry the fuck up."

Her hand works her clit fast, I watch as her arm moves quickly, rubbing herself aggressively.

I tilt her head so I can see more of her face to watch how my cock looks inside her mouth. Her eyes are wet from choking and her mascara has made her look like a raccoon. She has her jaw wide but her lips wrapped tight. I move her head slowly up my shaft; her lips pop as I leave her mouth. Then I push my swelling cock back in, her throat accommodating me now that it has been accustomed to the girth.

She tries to keep her eyes on mine but I fuck her faster– crashing her face into me. It makes her come only seconds later, her mouth losing focus on me a little but it gives me my opportunity to really fuck it– with her mind on her own orgasm I pound her mouth harder than is polite, ravaging her throat.

I'm grunting hard at the effort and her choking- throat milks my coming- cock as she struggles to swallow the load down. Her head pops up as soon as I let it go, she coughs and tries to catch her breath. I see a dribble of my come on her chin– her lipstick- smeared lips adding to the beautiful picture, making her look thoroughly fucked.

I don't know if I've scared her so I'm hesitant to say anything. I've not had the privilege to do something like that to anyone's mouth. I don't know what she's feeling right now. So, I take this moment to tuck my cock into my pants and wait patiently for any hint of her thoughts.

I know she's ok when she starts to giggle.

My neck snaps at the sound. I catch her eyes immediately and I'm struck by the huge smile on her face.

"Well, you really like head, don't you?" licking the last bit of the milky white dribble

I don't know what to say to her, so I put the car in gear and take us back on to the road, peeking occasionally at the advances she's making at cleaning the makeup from her face. No longer looking like a clown, she goes about reapplying it.

"There, good as new," she says suddenly, announcing her job is done.

I turn the radio down and take a look at her efforts. "Very good," is what I say. Back to the boring girl she was before I face- fucked her.

"I've never done anything like that before."

"Could've fooled me," I joke.

"I mean I've sucked a dick before, but never like that and never for a ride. I am not a hooker."

"Didn't think you were although, you'd make a pretty good one if you ever change your mind." I look over to see how she has taken my joke.

She just smiles that shy smile from before. "Where are you going?" she asks.

"My father just died, I'm going back to check on my mom and talk about the Will and shit."

"I'm sorry," is all she says. I don't ask her any questions, we're just about to her drop off and I don't want her lingering.

"Anywhere in particular you want me to drop you?" The signs are announcing her destination now.

"There's a convenience store right after the exit... if you don't mind."

"That works," I say, looking at the fuel gage and realizing I should fill up while I'm there. My stomach growls to remind me that it's empty as well.

I pull up to a pump and she grabs her bag from the back, throwing the strap over her shoulder. "Thank you for the ride, Tyler," she says.

"Any time, doll," I respond back to her, giving her a wink.

She blushes before turning to go inside the store.

I put my debit card into the slot at the pump and watch as the numbers tick upward until they come to a stop once it's full. Then I pull the car into a spot and head inside to see if they have some sort of deli. They don't, I realize quickly. It's too small in here for much of anything. I grab a candy bar and a coffee to hold me over until I stop again and wave at April as I go.

She waves back, looking around self- consciously to see if any one notices.

Back on the road, I'm lost in the thoughts I was able to keep at bay with that girl next to me. I regret not taking her into the restroom and fucking her, but it's too late now to turn back, I'll just have to live with the 'what if'.

I laugh at the thought of her screams echoing in that small store. The old clerk would have lost his shit at the sounds that would be coming from her as I fucked her, her hot little pussy wet and dripping for me, pounding into her from behind.

I let out a frustrated breath. I don't want to work myself up any more than I have so I take my hand from my hardened cock and inhale deeply, pushing the thoughts those away along the long and slow exhale. I have not masturbated in years, too much time was being wasted on that, when the real thing could happen effortlessly enough. I'm not going to start now, not for that girl.

I turn up the radio and let my mind get lost in the lyrics, singing along when I know them.

It gets dark quickly, considering I hadn't left my house until late afternoon I'm not surprised, but it is annoying to try and navigate the desolate highway that is poorly lit. My eyes feel heavy and my head is pounding with my hangover. I should stop, eat and sleep for a while. I know there is a motel coming up— I'll check in, grab drive- thru food and take it in the room with me then catch some sleep.

The motel looks exactly like I remember it, a run-down row of rooms on either side of the parking lot. The brightly lit office sits behind a floor to ceiling wall of windows. As I pull up, I can see the clerk— a red headed girl about twenty. She sets her book down as the door chimes my entrance.

"How you doin' tonight?" she asks in a friendly tone.

"Pretty good, now," I say, noticing her chest as she stands behind the tall counter top.

She smiles and gives me a look that says she appreciates the view as well.

"You got a room for me?" I sidle up to the tall desk and rest my elbows on top of the cool top.

"Sure do."

"Great, I'll just need it for the night." She hands me a key; it has the number 12 engraved neatly into it.

"You have one closer to the office?" Since I have my eye on her anyway, I'd like to see where this could go.

"Number one is open, it's right next door."

"I'd like that one."

She gets that key and has me sign a log in book. After collecting the money from me, she hands me the key.

"I'm going out for some food, could I bring you something?"

"Oh, you don't have to do that. I'm off in an hour— I could just get something on my way home."

"How about I go get us something and you come eat it with me?"

She giggles, and sucks her lip into her mouth, dragging her teeth as it makes its way back out. I can see that she will accept my offer, maybe before she knows, so I ask her what she likes.

"I'll just have whatever you're having, and a chocolate shake." It sounds like she's asking if that's alright, and I think it's adorable that she is shy. It makes me want to make her let loose and get free of that.

"I'll be waiting for your knock then. Kelly. I add after reading it from the nametag she has pinned to her top.

"Ok, Tyler." She must have read it before because she doesn't look away from my eyes to confirm it with the paper I've signed. I'm surprised that it was possible for her to make out my chicken scratch signature.

I leave with her watching my back as I walk out. I can see in the reflection of the windows that her eyes never leave my ass. I smirk at her audaciousness.

I unlock the door to my room; a straight out of the 70's style décor hits me right away. The mustard yellow bedspread and avocado carpeting clashing just like the good 'ol days. It hasn't been remodeled to look retro either, this is very much original to the period.

The shower looks like its seen better days and those days were decades ago. I strip out of my clothes and take a chance with the germs permeating the filth in the stall and stand under the hot stream washing away the night of drinking and the hours of driving.

I feel refreshed– and slightly disgusted– as I wrap a stiff towel around my waist. I shake my head, flinging water droplets all over the mirror and let my shaggy hair dry naturally, as it's what looks best on me.

After dressing, I grab my keys and head back out, making sure I have the room key to let myself back in. I killed most of the hour in the shower so I rush to the 24-hour drive thru of the closest burger joint. The night is cool and I crack the windows slightly to enjoy the night's air.

I come back to the room and set the bags of food down on the circular table with two chairs. I kick off my shoes and get comfortable in one of them and not a full minute later the knock on the door excites me.

"Come in," I tell her, having left the door unlocked in anticipation for her.

It opens a crack and then slowly reveals her standing there on the other side. She looks even better now that I can see all of her. Her tiny waist makes her tits look even bigger it her tight black tank top– she's not wearing a bra so I can see the hard nipples not hidden underneath. The tattoos along her arms I hadn't seen before, hiding under a light sweater she conveniently left somewhere else. Her round ass hugged tightly by her skinny jeans.

Fuck, she's going to be a good time.

"All the way in."

She looks like she's only just realized she hasn't exactly entered the room. "Oh." She joins me at the table, going right for the shake I put in front of her food. "Thank you," she says after taking a hard pull on the straw, the effort sucking her cheeks in.

"Dig in." I'm starving now, the room is full of the smells of fattening food and a hot red head sitting across from me who's totally willing to fuck, tantalizing all my senses.

I unwrap my burger and take a huge bite, it only makes me hungrier, I hadn't realized just how ravenous I'd let myself become.

I watch her as she eats—much more slowly than me, and when I'm done, I just sit and stare. It would seem creepy for a man who is not me—who doesn't look like I do, but I'm able to get away with it. I've been described as 'hot' more times than I can count and when I look in the mirror, I can be happy with what I see. My deep blue eyes and blond hair that frames a chiseled jaw, lightly dotted with fuzz. Full lips women enjoy kissing and a tight muscular body they love to get their hands on.

I don't look away when she catches my eyes, she dares to hold my stare but is unable to for any length of time. She's trying to be daring– it's adorable.

I finally speak, pulling myself from my imagination. "You're fucking beautiful, you know that?" I mean it she really is stunning.

She laughs, not like the giggles I've heard come from her, but a real from- the- gut laugh and it makes me laugh.

"Thank you," she says when she remembers her manners.

"Do you have someone who will be wondering about you?"

She gives me a look I can't name and says, "Why? Are you planning on doing something horrible to me?"

She's joking, I can tell, but I see it become a realization to her quickly. I laugh and tell her I have nothing untoward planned for her. "I only want what you want."

"And what is that?" she says flirtatiously.

"You want me to tell you what *you* want or what *I* want?" I ask, pulling myself to the end of my chair.

"What do you think I want?"

I put my hands on her knees and push them apart until they are stopped by the armrests of the chair. "First, I think you want me to run my hands up your thighs until I can feel the heat coming from your little pussy." Her gasp tells me I'm on the right track. "Then you want me to drag your pants down your legs and bury my face inside of you."

She doesn't stop me when I get on my knees in front of her so I go about doing what I've said, reaching for her zipper I slide it down slowly. I grab the waistband of her pants and tug them down; she lifts her ass to help me. I pull off her shoes to get rid of her pants completely.

She tries to bring her legs back together, probably feeling exposed, but I don't let her. I put one leg on either of the wooden armrests and look at her glistening slit. I blow slowly on it watching her reaction to me. Her nipples are hard and her breath is coming heavy.

"You want me to taste this beautiful pussy of yours?"

I wait for her to answer, it takes longer than I think it should, but she finally nods and that is all the confirmation I need to dive in there. I slide my tongue up her cleanly shaven lips.

God, she tastes delicious.

I dip my tongue inside her and lap it up. She moans loudly when I reach her clit, sucking it into my mouth hard and then tickling it with my tongue, alternating gentle and hard— it drives her crazy. I pull back when I feel her tightening for her orgasm only to bring her to that point again moments later.

My cock is harder than it has been in a long while, I can't wait to get in to her delicious cunt. I push my fingers inside and the tightness of her hole grips my digits, I have to make a real effort to fuck her with them.

I lift her top with my other hand and bare her tits to me. Perfect, like I knew they would be— full and perky with soft pink nipples that are hard from being turned on while fucked. I pull one into my mouth and her already tight pussy clenches tighter around my fingers. "God, your pussy is like a vice grip." I say, switching sides, giving the same attention to her other tit. She arches her back and her hips start working in tandem with my fingers to get her off.

I put my mouth back onto her clit and I finally let her come. Before Kelly has a chance to recover, I pick her up off the chair and toss her onto her back on the bed– she climbs into the center of the mattress on her elbows and spreads herself for me, again.

I undress slowly, letting her watch as I reveal myself to her. She squirms with excitement, waiting patiently for me to fuck her.

"Now, you want me to put my cock inside of you. Don't you?"

She nods.

I take my hard dick in my hand and stroke it in front of her, alleviating the ache that had grown from ignoring it. I slide a condom on and climb in between her legs, pushing her knees up to her ears as I go– folding her in half. Then I line us up and push the full length of my cock into her, giving her no time to become accommodated with the girth, I start fucking her deep.

Her panting and yelps are being cut off by the next cry. She sounds like a porn star, but I know she's not faking. I can see in her face the pain of having me inside her at this angle– with this relentless rhythm. She is enjoying herself– the wet sounds coming from her pussy are enough proof of that.

I tip her ass up off the mattress scooting underneath her, resting the back of her thighs on top of my bent knees then drag her up by her arms sitting her on my lap– never breaking our connection.

She rides me, bouncing fast enough to get her tits jiggling. "Fuck, you look good." I say, gritting my teeth.

She likes the compliment, flipping her long hair over her shoulder so I can see more of her chest, which is what I wanted. I lean in and trap one of her nipples between my teeth, biting harder than is comfortable, but she doesn't pause, if anything it makes her hungrier for my dick.

I take the length of her hair in my fist and pull her head back exposing her neck, which I slide my tongue along until I move her mouth to mine, forcing her lips open with my tongue; I fuck her mouth. She kisses me back with my same hunger. We're not moving with any sort of rhythm—both just needing to fuck and be fucked.

I flip her over, "Get on your knees."

She does what I tell her, round ass in the air—at this angle it looks even bigger and rounder. Her tight little ass hole calling to me but I don't want to have that conversation right now, I just want to nut inside of her.

I stand at the end of the bed and drag her toward me. Pushing my way into her wet hole. I pull her up by her hair— her back flush with my front— and I thrust into her, resuming the frantic pace from before.

"Touch your pussy." I whisper into her ear.

She does as she's told and I feel her fingers work her pussy quickly, bumping into my cock occasionally from the frantic way she's rubbing her clit.

"I want to feel your orgasm, I want your pussy so wet it drips down your thighs." I thrust deeper, slapping our skin together.

I use her tits as a grip hold to keep her in place as I fuck her for my own release, quick and hard. I feel as soon as she reaches hers, holding my cock tightly, the friction is enough to do it for me. I pump everything I have into the condom and bite my teeth into her neck to muffle my groan.

I slide out of her; my cock misses her warmth instantly. She flops forward onto her stomach and I climb up next to her to lie down myself. I take the fully loaded condom off and toss it in the direction of the trash. I'm sure I didn't make it inside but I don't have enough energy to care. I wrap an arm around her waist, pulling her against me; my hand falls to her ass. I give it a squeeze.

She moans.

I smile.

I fall asleep before I realize I'm going to.

CHAPTER FOUR

I awaken sometime in the early morning hours inside of her again. She must have taken it upon herself to take advantage of my morning wood. Both of us are on our sides, her ass is grinding into me. I feel right away that I don't have a condom on but that can't stop me now.

She must realize I am finally awake because she starts moving quicker, backing her ass into me. She feels so good unsheathed— so wet and warm, too late, now, to worry about the consequences.

I pull her up onto my lap, facing away from me. I watch her round ass jiggle as she fucks me, mesmerized by my thick cock going in and out of her tight hole.

I suck my thumb into my mouth to wet it and without warning push it inside of her tight ass hole. It drives her wild, she fucks me fast and hard, milking my cock until it's spurting inside of her and she comes seconds later, falling back onto me.

"I'm on the pill," she says by way of an answer to that question that was right on my tongue to ask.

I rub my hands up and down her tummy, loving the feel of her covering me. I cup her tits and pull her nipples hard between my fingers.

"I should get cleaned up," she says and tries to leave.

I roll her off me and push her back into the mattress, spreading her legs. "I want to see my come inside of you."

She bites her lip, that fucking lip that makes me want to fuck her mouth. She spreads her thighs apart and I can already see the creamy white dripping from her hole.

"*Fuck* it looks good in there." I push my fingers inside of her and work them around, smearing my come across her slick pussy after taking them out. Then I tell her she can go get cleaned up.

She goes shyly to the restroom, coming out a few minutes later looking a little less fucked, although still completely naked, she walks over to her clothes and gets dressed. "Check out is at 11:00," she says

"I'll be out before then," I say back.

"Ok."

And she fucking leaves– just like any good whore, she's out before it gets weird.

Fuck, I'll miss her.

I want to go back to sleep but I don't let myself, I need to get back on the road. I take a shower instead. I change into a fresh pair of jeans and a new tee, slip into my shoes and do a quick glance around the room, making sure I haven't forgotten anything.

I drop the key at the office with an old man I'm glad wasn't here to check me in last night, it wouldn't have been nearly as fun a night if he had. He asks me about my stay and I tell him it did the job.

I get back on the road, stopping at a coffee shop to grab a large cup for the road and make quick work of it during the next leg, stopping once for food, which I eat as I drive.

I see the lights of the town just as night falls. The familiar glow of my hometown brings about memories I had forgotten along the way.

I call the attorney's number back and let Mr. James know that I've arrived. He tells me to go ahead and come up, that he will be in his office.

I do just that as I come to the familiar building, which has changed a lot yet somehow remained the same, the rustic red brick colored façade now covered over with a white washed paint, giving it an updated look in this grungy town. He must do fairly well for himself here. A brightly lit sign adorning the entry leads the way.

He has me sit down before starting his spiel. "Mr. Rydek, again, I'm so sorry for your loss."

"It's fine, I'm fine, let's just get on with this. I've had a long drive and I just want to get to my parent's house and settle in for the night."

His expression tells me I've been too blunt so I ease up on him. He has also lost a good friend in my father— so he says.

"I'm just going to read his last wishes for you. Then you can be on your way."

"Great," I say, leaning into the chair, settling in for what I imagine is going to take a while.

"Basically, your father has left you everything, the house and all its contents. The car lot— he would really like it if you would run it. He says here if you'd rather not he would like you to sell it and use the money for something useful, not to throw it away."

I roll my eyes; I can practically hear my father in those words. He had always been so worried about where my money goes. Which is ridiculous— I've never given him any reason to think I'm a frivolous spender. I own my house outright and my college loans have never been in default. I'd never asked the man for a dime.

But he had come from a family that was scraping by most times, a drunken father who'd plundered most of his earnings, so I let it slide, knowing he meant well. "Is that it?" I ask, trying to mask my irritation.

"He's left a large sum of money from a life insurance policy. $250,000. That will be yours to do with as you see fit."

The money sounds good to me; although I'm sure my money hungry mother will think I should do something for her with it. "Did he have one for my mother as well?"

"I have you labeled soul beneficiary."

Well, that gives her even more reason to hate me. My father never really liked her, even as a child I could tell he wasn't fond of her– her bitching and complaining about any and all things he did drove him away even before I left. Her incessant nagging pushed us both away. Only he had stayed for whatever reasons he thought outweighed the life he'd have without her. Now he's gone and never gets a second alone without her, I'm sad he never got away. As bad as that sounds, it's more truth than anything I've ever thought.

"Great," I say, and even I can hear that it sounds like a bad idea for him to have done.

"He restored three vintage cars; those titles will be transferred over to you, and the contents of a safe deposit box he held at the bank here in town."

I know the one he's talking about– it being the only bank in town, I assume it's where everyone has to do their banking business. "What's in that?" I ask.

"The contents are not labeled– I have no idea." He hands me a key along with the paper he'd been reading and reiterating to me. I look it over and see that he has missed nothing.

"Is that everything, then?"

"Yes, it is. Thank you for coming on such short notice. I know it must be a hard time for you. Your father was a great man. I'm sure you know that though."

"I do, absolutely. Thank you for staying late to see me tonight. I appreciate your time."

"Not a problem at all, it was nice to finally meet you, your father had nothing but kind words when speaking of you."

"I'm sure that's true, he never spoke of the bad things about anyone. Thanks again." I fold the paper, sticking it into my back pocket and leave before he can rope me into one of those 'remembering the good old times' conversations.

It's too late to go to the bank tonight, I'll have to make that trip tomorrow. I head in the direction of my old house. Something I'd never thought I'd do again, unless of course my father died… but only then.

I'm surprised the house is dark when I pull up, my mother never kept late hours but I assumed she'd wait for me to get here. I don't ring the bell; I grab the key I know to be under the fake rock in the flower bed by the door and head inside.

It looks as it always has— like my drunk mother decorated, nothing really going together or fitting in the space it was intended for. I never did like the look of this place. It has great potential, being an old farmhouse style layout, long and brick, with a wraparound patio area around the entirety of the bottom story- the brick whitewashed and beautiful. But when you walk inside it's a huge contradiction.

Since its mine now, I have a quick thought of gutting the whole thing and starting over. I could really turn this into something great. But I have my fucking mother to worry about now. Where the fuck would I put her? I don't know what my father may have done to ensure she would be ok without him, nor do I care really, other than how it will affect me. Which is an awful thing to say about the woman who gave me life, but I can assure you if she were your mother, you'd have the same thoughts. This is one fucked up woman to grow up with.

I look around the rest of the bottom floor before heading up to my old room, no sign of my mother anywhere. I walk past their—her—bedroom but the door is closed and I don't really think I'm ready to see her yet so I let her be. I catch myself actually tiptoeing passed the door, I must really be dreading seeing her.

I push the door closed quietly and flip the light on; throwing my bag on the bed, I look around. It all looks as I last left it. It looks like I'm sixteen again, which is the last time I'd done anything in here to spruce it up. The half-naked pictures of women I'd jacked off to hung on the walls next to more trophies than I ever had room for.

I'd always been into sports, learning early on that the girls always wanted the boys that played. And I wanted the girls. I liked to play, don't get me wrong, but the incentives were better than the actual sport. I was good at most things I put my mind to, sports came easy, then the girls came even easier.

I flip on the TV just for background noise. I text Cammie, letting her know I made it. Then I call her a few minutes later when I don't get a response. "Cam... where the fuck are you? I could use a little comfort right now, my fucking dad just died. What the fuck are you doing that's more important than that?" I leave those words as a message on her voicemail and fling my phone onto the bed.

I get undressed and slip into the covers; my parents have always kept the thermostat a tad too cold in this house.

I fall asleep quickly, still not having caught up on my sleep with this whole ordeal.

CHAPTER FIVE

I wake early, it's still dark out, but the birds tell me it's morning, I haven't been woken by nature sounds in a long time. It's actually nice. I've finally replenished my missing sleep; I can feel it in my bones. The weariness is gone and my brain is able to focus despite the dreams of younger me being home, the times I try hard not to remember, the times my mother was not a mother, but the devil.

The urge to pee is what finally has me up and out of bed. I relieve myself and plop back onto the mattress, arms tucked behind my head I let my mind wander to the girl at the motel. *Fuck*, she was cute. Maybe I'll stay there on the way back. Maybe get into that tight little ass next time, she had enjoyed my finger in there, little ass slut.

Her perfect tits make me hard again. I'm not usually a chest man, but those were perfect, and they had bounced like mad while she had ridden my dick. I tug my cock a few times before I stop myself. Although I'd love nothing more than to leave a nut stain right across the sheets I don't give into that urge, instead I wrap my hand around my cock unmoving until I feel it softening. Focusing my thoughts on the impending errands I need to get done today– starting with the bank, I need to get over there and get the contents of my father's box. I should do that before my mother wakes so I don't have to see her first thing this morning.

I dress quickly and sneak passed her still- closed door.

Relief floods when she is not downstairs. I leave quickly, climbing into the car and heading for the bank, I'm curious to see what my father had kept in there, I knew nothing of a safe deposit box, I didn't even know my father to be the type to keep one.

The town, overall, looks as I remember, old and a little run down, full of mom-and-pop shops run by the town's residents, the two stop lights are still functioning and no more have been added. I guess the population hasn't grown enough to warrant an additional one. If I'm being honest, I don't remember a time I actually used the stop lights as they were intended, more like a stop sign, just double check no one – or police, are coming and just drive on through. Anyone around here knows that to be how they work; people even stop at the green lights to make sure the person with the red light did not have the right of way.

I pull into the empty bank parking lot, for having the business of the entire town it's not as busy as every as one might assume.

I reach for my cell and call Cammie, she's really pissing me off now, why the fuck won't she answer? I call four times before giving up and texting her that she needs to get ahold of me. *Bitch*. I toss the phone into the passenger seat and head for the entrance of the bank.

Andrea, who I went to school with, is the teller that calls me over. "Hey," she says in a too- chipper voice. The girl always had a crush on me, like, in a way that creeped me out and never let me use her. I kept far away from her; her chubby body helped with the task. She looks better now, trimmed down, but her face is still that of the girl that I recall watching my every move and asking me to every dance that the school held. Overtly throwing herself at me at every party we found ourselves at together.

"Hey, Andrea," I say and a shock crosses her face, maybe she was expecting me not to recall her name, but one does not simply forget their stalkers names– or faces.

"Oh, my god, you look so good, Tyler... I mean you have always looked so good, but now you're a man."

Oh, my fuck, some things never change.

"Thanks," I say with a small smile so as not to piss her off and make her go crazy stalker on me. I don't add anything about how she looks.

She asks what brought me in and I'm assuming she knows about my father because it's a small town and everyone knows your business, sometimes even before the person the news is about knows. I've found out plenty of things about me and my family through the grapevine rather than actual facts from the sources.

"Just here to collect my father's safe deposit contents. Could you help me out with that?" I say it a little nicer than I need to, in case it's a hassle or too much work, she may be able to expedite the process.

"I'm so sorry for your loss, I always remember you two having such good times together." The look of pity on her face makes me want to hit her. I shake that from my mind and the fact that she was not an invited witness to any happy times with my father. You think she'd want to hide the fact that she stalked me, but instead she uses that information to recall 'memories' of me.

"I'm fine, thanks for saying that." What the fuck does a person say when people are apologizing for things they've had no part in? *Whatever.* "Think you could help me out with that box?" I hold the key up to help her focus... maybe she likes shiny things.

"Oh, sure, follow me."

I do, and as we reach the rows of boxes, she grabs for my arm and waits until I look at her before she speaks. "You want to get a drink or something?" She attempts a flirty smile, but it looks like a sneer and it's not flattering, luckily, I have an excuse this time and it is air tight.

"I'm just not ready to be social right now, you know, losing my dad sure did a number on me. Thanks for the offer though, maybe another time." I wink at her; I don't know why. I can pretty much hear the rush of wet flood her panties. I almost laugh. The whimper that escapes her does finally make me laugh. I don't mask it. I don't wonder if I've hurt her feelings– I just want his over with,

She hands me a metal box without another word and won't make eye contact again, the submissive thing works for her. I could do some things to *this* Andrea– and not nice things, well, not for her. I hold back that laugh, unlike what you might think, I'm not usually a dick.

"Thanks," I say, taking the box from her and setting it on the table. I open it with more eager curiosity than a Christmas present. It looks like a shit ton of paper work mostly, there is some jewelry and trinkets in here that look like they've meant something along the way. I don't remember them all. Most are my grandmother's things; I remember her wearing many of the pieces.

The rewritable CD that I see is confusing more than anything so far. I don't think of my dad as much of a tech guy. Not even techy enough to make a disk, I'll have to check out his efforts. I think maybe he's converted photos to disk. It might be interesting to look back at some of those times, even if they are not fond memories.

I take the paperwork out and dump the rest of the contents onto the table then load up my pockets with what will fit. Andrea must think I look foolish–mostly because I do. I should have brought something to carry this shit, but I hadn't thought about the fact that my father would be sentimental or a mild hoarder.

I thank Andrea for her help, not waiting for a response and head for my car, emptying the contents of my pockets into the seat next to me. I'll take them into the house when I get back.

I check my phone, no response from Cammie. I think about texting her something mean—meaner than I've already been to her. Maybe breaking it off, but I don't, instead, I head back home, stopping first for a breakfast sandwich that I eat in the driveway before going in. Whether my mother has cooked something is not of my concern, she has always been an awful cook in the kitchen. I'd have passed on her concoction either way.

I go inside finally, taking a deep breath to ready myself for seeing her; she will definitely be up now, although when I don't see her downstairs, I get a little excited to put off this reunion for a while longer. I decide to check through the rest of the house, calling to her, although I'm not eager to see her, the trepidation is killing me, better to get it over with rather than dwelling on it, I suppose.

"Mom," I call throughout the upper level. I knock on her bedroom door when I reach it, turning the handle when she does not answer.

The room is dark; the shades are drawn. I can't see the bed clear enough to say one way or the other if she is tucked inside, so I go forward. It's empty. She must have gone out. Relief floods, along with something else I can't name right now— something close to regret, even though she was an awful, selfish, whore of a woman she is still my mother and maybe a little comfort from her right now would be nice. She has never been the type to hug the sadness away, leaning more toward the 'oh, fuck he's crying again, I better avoid him' side. It might be nice to see if there has been a change in the way she might handle such things now that I am older.

I sit on the end of the bed. The room is so fucking flowery and feminine; my father never put much effort into fighting for what he wanted. 'Just let your mother have her way, it's just easier,'– that was his motto. It made me so angry to hear; knowing my mother took full advantage of that frame of thought— took full advantage of most things in this fucking house. I get angry at her all over again. She is such an awful woman.

I'm angry at my father for letting her win all of the time with him, and taking away my own choices in most matters. Forcing me to sit by and let her do whatever she wanted, not backing me up and helping me stand up to her.

My life would have been far better if she were not involved and now, I wish it was her being buried in a few days. I'm angry at her for not letting my father live a single day without her and her demanding ways.

I leave the room and slam the door shut behind me, rattling the walls. *Fucking bitch*. My anger rearing its ugly head, anger I've somehow tricked myself into thinking was behind me.

I have to be here through the day of the funeral, I'm not going to miss that just to avoid my mother. I think four more days of this sneaking around will not be too hard to handle knowing there is an end to it.

I'll just let her stay in the house until she meets her own fate and then sell it. Then we won't have to have that awkward talk about where she might live or how she would afford it. I don't even want to talk about the fact that my father has left me everything.

He had inherited this house from his family and my mother must not have gotten on the deed if he can hand it over to me outright without her permission. It's actually a shame that the house would leave the family. I may keep it after all, not to live in, but to pass down if I have children. I almost laugh at the thought of me fathering a kid, it's not likely, but who can say what the future holds.

I'm only 25, I can't know what will come down the line in a few years. I'm guessing nothing too much further with Cammie if she can't even be bothered to call me now. But there is a world of women out there that may love to come when I call. The thought excites me, having some submissive girl begging me to tell her what to do and fucking her silly.

Fuck.

That would be perfect; I think I may end it with Cammie after all. She would never be that. She practically makes me work for her pussy and it's often times not worth the effort.

I only had to lay a fast-food meal in front of the motel girl, Kelly, and she road my cock like a fiend and nothing was awkward with her, little effort for massive reward. I like that.

I go about unpacking my bag, getting a little more settled in, I wonder where my mother had run off to this morning. She hadn't left a note telling me what she may be up to. I know she didn't have a meeting with that attorney. Maybe the grocery store?

I call Cammie one more time, "We need to talk, I feel like we need to have a good heart to heart and this avoiding me shit has gone too far. Call me. Now!" I leave on her voicemail.

My phone buzzes before I put it down. A text. "We have nothing more to talk about."

What the fuck? Women and their fucking mind trips. "What are you talking about?" I hit send.

"You have some really big balls to think I'd want anything to do with you after what you did."

Well, I know she has no idea what I do. She has no idea about the women I fuck behind her back or the things I love to do to them. "Where's this coming from?" I feign innocence.

"Are you fucking serious?" She never swears, not so much as a damn, so I know something must really be bothering her.

"I don't have any idea what could have gotten your panties in a bunch. Please remind me of this awful thing I've done."

"Goodbye."

I hit call and wait for her to answer, she sends me to voicemail instead. "You fucking call me, or you'll regret it." I don't know what I'll do if she doesn't, but this fucking mind fuck has got to stop, I will have the upper hand. "You have until tomorrow to have a normal conversation with me." I hit end angrily.

Nothing comes from her end, but I don't really expect it right away, she will wait until the deadline before responding. I know her well. I tuck the phone in my pocket and head for the kitchen. I need another cup of coffee. Then

I'll get my hands on that disk, see what my dad thought important enough to save.

The coffee is dark and delicious, I take it up to my room and put the unlabeled disk into my laptop, as the images flood the screen, I realized it may not have been meant for me.

My father is ass naked, leaning over the table in what looks like the basement, pushing buttons on his recording device and setting the frame up. As soon as he steps away from view, I see my mother equally naked. It sends shivers across my body. I've seen her in this exact way countless times— spread eagle and waiting. I can almost hear her voice now, 'such a good boy, come love your mother.' That old familiar feeling of dread hits me in the pit of my stomach. For some reason I continue to watch. That is how fucked up she's made me.

He walks over to her and starts to fuck her. She doesn't move, much like a dead fish, just lets him fuck her. She is soundless as well, which as I recall is unlike her. She was always very vocal with me when she made me fuck her.

He goes at her vigorously; I've never seen them together like this. I know most kids wouldn't, but in my house, with a whore of a mother like I had, you'd think she would have liked having me catch her being fucked— try and make me jealous or some shit. The mind games I've encountered my whole life started with her. But I avoided a closed door like the plague, not wanting any more of her than I was forced in to.

My father's ass cheeks clench and unclench as he works her over. I'm not able to look away. I wish I could, the memories of myself standing where my father is now, between her legs, come flooding in– although it was never in the basement.

She loved me to come in her room at night when my father would work late. I'm not at all sure he was unaware of what was happening. How could he not have known though?

She loved living on the edge of almost being caught, loved to push the envelope. Calling me in only a few minutes before he was due home, insisting I fuck her, rubbing herself in front of me, knowing it worked to turn me on and make me hard. Rubbing me through my pants to make sure it happened. Being at a young and impressionable age, it worked effortlessly. She took advantage of teenage hormones and used them in her favor. She would suck me off in the garden after insisting I help her with the plants– my father in the house just a few feet away. She was my first at everything and insatiable with her demands. She couldn't get enough of me.

I watch while my father finishes, pulling out, I can't see much but his arm is pumping his cock aimed right over her mound. The first real sound comes as he grunts while coming. Then he leans over and grabs a towel, wiping his spunk from her.

She still has not engaged. Even as he walks away to stop the recording, she says nothing, just lies there. She never would have been like that with me. For some reason I take that as a win on my behalf. Some fucked up part of me has counted that as a victory. I fucked my mother better than her husband– my father did.

Woo fucking hoo. I am disgusting. *Thanks mom.*

I'm about to push the eject button, assuming that must be it, a simple recording for the spank bank for my father's keepsake, but another scene of my father in the same nakedness leaning over the camera, fixing settings for the video stops me.

I watch as he goes to my mother again, this time her ass is in the air, down on all fours. I remember her loving that. She loved it from behind. Her legs are wide and this time the camera is closer, my father doesn't last as long as the first time. He finishes quickly, after going at her hard and fast.

This time as he pulls out to come, I notice how wide my mother's pussy is— it's gaping, a perfect circle right through to her insides. I'm bigger than my father, cock and all... by a lot and I've never made her hole look like that, even after she made me fuck her with larger objects, her hole accommodating most anything she thought of. Her pussy always returned to normal after it was out.

My father must be working her over quite a bit. Maybe it's because her pussy is shaved, that's new, she always kept a little hair on there. Maybe it was always like that and I missed it, I doubt it... but it could be.

He wipes off the come he emptied onto her then goes to the camera to turn it off and this time another scene does not follow.

I don't want it to be true but my cock, which I've been ignoring, is achingly hard. Most people would be disgusted watching what I just did— their parents fucking, but my mother did quite a number on me, and my father fucking her was not as disgusting as I thought it would be to see.

Fuck.

I squirm in my seat, trying to situate my hard cock in a way that I could get comfortable, but unlike the times that I think about women and get hard this isn't going away by simply changing my train of thought. The more I try to ignore it the more I'm reminded that it's there and waiting for me to notice it.

I stand and stretch, hoping the flow of blood reaches other parts of my body, but it is no use, my cock is throbbing so hard I can feel my heartbeat in it. I reach down and do the only thing I can do. I fucking yank on it until I spill my come on the carpet, rubbing it in with my sock covered foot. I don't let myself replay the video, although some part of me wants to– the sicko part that she made for her pleasure. But I don't let her win, not this fucking time. I tuck my cock back into my pants and try not to give the video another thought.

The doorbell rings, interrupting me and I'm not sure what to do. It may be my mother with her hands full of groceries, thinking I should go help her with them. In case that is what's happening I walk slowly down the stairs, not overly excited about seeing her for the first time in this way, especially after watching the video and jacking off for the first time in years because of it.

I calm myself down, gripping the handle of the door; I pull it open unceremoniously, stepping aside to let her in. Only it's not her. It's Jamie, a flood of memories, all including her naked and sprawled out in front of me– the cock- hungry whore who would do anything for me at the drop of a dime. "Jamie," I say, looking at her from head to toe.

Nice.

"Hi, Tyler," she says as hungry for me as ever.

Fuck, I just might have to get in this. "What's up?"

"I just thought I'd stop by and see if you need... me." She licks her lips seductively.

"Fuck, baby, I just might." My cock jumps, thinking about her tight little pussy wrapped around me. "Come in."

She smiles at me; walking passed and then stands behind me.

"You see my mom in town today? Don't know where she is at the moment."

"No, I haven't seen her for a while." She comes up to me rubbing her hands down my chest, brazenly grabbing hold of my jean covered cock. "Does that mean we have the house to ourselves?"

"I guess it does. Why don't you go on up to my room and get naked?"

She does without a word, stripping as she goes.

I follow her up, taking my own clothes off as well.

"Get the fuck on the bed."

"Oh my god, my pussy has missed you so fucking much. Nothing makes me come like your massive dick."

"Put your ass up." I come up quickly behind her, spreading her cheeks apart to see her ass hole— my favorite thing about her. Her ass is always so hungry for my dick.

"You gonna let me in this hole?" I push my thumb against the entrance; it gives only a little.

"Anything you want. Take whatever you want." Her pussy is so wet, it glistens as I manipulate her back hole.

Music to my fucking ears.

I look into the side table at my bed and see that the lube bottle that has been in there since last time I used it is still there, right where I left it. I squeeze a small amount into my fingers then rub it into her puckered hole and down her pussy crack and then I push three fingers into her hungry hole. The wetness seeping from her pussy mixes with the lube, aiding in the effort.

She moans loudly and greedily tells me, "More." So, I give her more, adding my remaining digits into her juicy hole. She yelps when I slide into her up to my wrist and then she grinds her hips against me.

I push the thumb from my other hand into her ass and she goes crazy. Last time we fucked, I wasn't even eighteen yet, I've learned a few things since then.

Try as I might, I can't get the video out of my head. Although I don't want it there it drives me forward, making me so fucking hard— harder than I would be normally doing such things. I try to get angry with myself for it but that emotion won't come, instead I embrace it. I fuck her fast with my fist until she comes so hard her pussy squirts– that's not uncommon for her, she has always been a squirter.

I take my hand out of her and it's covered in her cream, I use it to stroke my cock to get it ready for her ass which I enter as I would a pussy, hard and relentless. I push against her ass's rejection and I fuck her tight hole as it squeezes me almost painfully.

If this were any other girl she'd be crying right now, but this one is unlike the rest, she loves this. *Craves it.* And I'm more than happy to oblige. It's been more time than I'd like since I've ripped into an ass hole and what better way to welcome me back to it than this girl.

"Oh, fuck, Tyler. *Fuck me.*"

I go at her harder than usual, I have to grip her tightly and pull her back against me to stop her from falling forward. Our skin slapping so hard together that it's turning hers a light shade of red. She is yelping and making nonsensical gibberish as confirmations for my efforts.

"I want you to come inside my ass."… "Fill up my hole."

That's what I can make from her, she's spewing all sorts of porn star phrases at me. It fuels me, I want to rip her in half with my cock, tear her open and come inside of her deeper than I have ever done.

I pump her until I my balls are ready to explode and when they do, I push into her deeply and fill her up as requested.

I pull out of her and she keeps her ass up for me but the rest of her body collapses onto the bed. I can't help but look inside of her, I've always been drawn to the holes I've come inside. There is a ring of white cream around her ass hole and I rub it into the red hole.

She whimpers, I can't imagine her ass not being sore.

Poor little slut.

I spread her open and peer inside.

Fuck it looks good in there. I love the thought of my come sitting inside of her ass, oozing from her after it warms.

"Your ass is so full." Even though I came only minutes before she showed up, I still had plenty to give her.

My mother did that for me, conditioned me to be always ready and hungry for more. I'm sure Jamie would thank her if she knew, she has been on the receiving end of my cock– letting me have plenty of use out of this hole, more than any other woman in this entire town.

Aside from good 'ol mom, she would never be in second place, she had far more years with me than any other woman.

When I'm finished admiring her asshole, which is now tightly closed, I tell her she can get up.

"Is there anything else I can do for you?"

I couldn't imagine what else she could have in mind; our interactions have never been more than me ordering her into a position and then fucking her. We've never even had a conversation about anything outside of sex.

"No, I think that really helped, I had a bunch of things to work out and your ass has helped immensely." To any other girl that may have been insulting, but not her, she takes it as permission to be done here.

"Ok, then, call me if you want me again before you leave. I'll be around."

"I will." I know that to be true, no way would I leave this town not hitting that again.

I show her out, she walks a little like she's just been on a horse– her ass must really hurt. I know my balls feel like they've taken a beating, smashing them into her ass has made them tender.

I go back upstairs, having come down completely naked, I don't have to undress to climb into the shower. I don't give it much thought; I know my mother could have been home after the time Jamie and I had spent in there. I can't help but think I wanted her to see I'd taken another woman into my room and made her howl like a virgin in a horror movie being torn to shreds from the inside out.

She may have been jealous, although she hadn't initiated things with me for a few months before I had left. I'd always wondered what made her stop. I kept waiting for her to call to me and when she didn't, I was relieved at first, then I was curious as to what may have made her change her mind about me.

I had this routine, well, my cock did. I went elsewhere fucking any hole that would let me inside, making my way through every girl who had ever looked my way, from my friend's mothers, to anyone who gave me that 'come fuck me' look.

I'd had other girls while my mother was using me, but she took up most of my time and then I didn't have that as an outlet so I needed to fill her demanding schedule, one she forced me to keep as well, with other women. No one ever being as hungry as her for cock, I had to have many girls in the mix.

CHAPTER SIX

I shower quickly, dressing in clean clothes. I feel tired, I could probably lie down for a nap right now, but I don't, instead I head for the kitchen, fixing a peanut butter sandwich.

It doesn't look like anyone has been shopping in a while, not much in the pantry to choose from.

I wander around the living room, spotting something out of place almost immediately; the lock on the basement door is new. We never had a master- lock keeping people from opening the door.

There is no access to the house from down there, not even a small window typical in most basements. I recall the small key from the things in the safe deposit box, if I remember right, it is a key that could fit this lock.

Tempted by curiosity, more than anything else, I run upstairs for the keys to the car and go retrieve it, along with the rest of the things, putting those on the counter, I bring the key to the lock and sure enough, it works to open it.

It is dark inside, always has been. I wonder if there is some sex swing set up down here, recalling the video of my parents again, my mother sprawled out on the table, maybe they'd upgraded into a real sex dungeon.

I can't turn the overhead light on, it seems to have burnt out, so I pull my phone out of my pocket and turn on the flashlight. It doesn't light up enough to see much, but I take a quick look around, seeing no real reason to warrant the new lock on the door.

It looks a lot like I remember it, the setup is the same: mostly boxes, Christmas decorations from years accumulated, my boxes, stacked neatly in the corner, I'd put them there before I left, promising to come back for what I couldn't take in one trip. I haven't given the contents much thought after packing them— must not be too important. Some old bikes, boxes labeled donations, the now infamous fuck- table covered in a white sheet, probably to keep it dust free for quickies, so they don't have to clean the area first.

I wander over to it and lift a corner, I don't know what compels me, I just simply want to see the spot my father fucked her in the home movie.

Whoa.

I'm shocked to actually see something under the sheet lying on the table. I've lifted only a corner and there is a foot. Toe nails painted red like I remember my mother doing, sometimes soliciting my help, 'come fuck me red' she had called it.

My father has some sex doll under here, I'm sure of it. I almost laugh.

Almost.

Instead, my curiosity forces me to lift it off the rest of the way. Slowly I uncover its knee, then thigh. I go to the other side, doing the same. I'm actually excited to see this; I've thought of getting one of these things. I rub my hand up its inner thigh, stopping just shy of the sheet. It feels smooth. They make them pretty life like, it seems. Next, I reveal the naked pussy, but I can't see it very well with its legs closed.

I continue to pull the sheet higher up, exposing the tits. They're soft and pliable as I can't help but give them each a squeeze. It's a thin looking woman full chested. It has nice flared hips, I'm sure if I flip it over the nice round ass would be there to match.

I reveal the face, I'm curious to see the mouth, I'm sure I'm going to see some sort of apparatus you'd stick your cock into to simulate a blow job. And I am right, but it's on my mother's face. There is a plastic ring encircling its lips, I push my finger into it and the cavity is hollow and ribbed.

How the fuck had he gotten a life-sized doll of my mother? And, looking more closely with the flash light I see how remarkable the recreation actually is.

Now that I know what to look for, I can see all the telltale ways this doll meets the standards of being a perfect representation of her. She really has always had a nice body; I can see why he'd gone too all the trouble.

All I can think is she must have stopped letting him fuck her– that this may have even been what he was fucking in the video, I knew my mother couldn't have been that quiet while being fucked.

I can't help myself— I bring the flashlight to the apex of its thighs and the same type of circular hollow cavity is there, two of them, one for the pussy and one for the ass hole. When I run my finger along the circumference of it, my cock does what it would if this were a real woman— my real mother. It fucking hardens.

I want a go at this thing for sure, the faux skin feels soft and the cavity snug, I could really have fun with this but that will have to wait. I can't have my mother coming home knowing her replica brought me to that. That is, if she even knows it exists. She could be the reason for the lock on the door, keeping her on the outs with his little sex- doll secret.

Maybe his little plastic fuck doll mistress is a secret. Sick as it sounds, I may take this thing with me back to my house.

I cover it back up, against my cock's argument that we could get in and out before getting caught.

I lock up the door and run up to my room when I don't see any signs of my mother having returned.

And since I've thrown out my no masturbating celibacy, I fuck my fist until I come, feeling only mildly satiated, but it does the trick. For now. I'm gonna need to get in that sick little fuck- doll if I'm to alleviate this hard- on.

I am having a hard time wrapping my head around my father's need for that little toy. He has my mother here, and although I'm not sure of their sexual habits I can say with first- hand knowledge that, if he wanted it, I'm positive my mother would have no problem opening up for him.

I lie down, exhausted from such a strange day, the realization of the video and what's down in our basement would be mind- fucking enough, but throw in the fact that I literally can't get that sex doll out of my mind, with all its resemblance of my mother set aside… or more possibly because of the uncanny way it is identical to her.

I bet if I replaced the bulb down there and saw it in full light, it would not have such a perfect look to it. It would show the flaws and the missteps in recreation. I close my eyes; I can't hold them open another minute. I fall asleep to the memory of how the doll felt under my fingers, the smooth texture of the skin.

CHAPTER SEVEN

There's a noise in the house that awakens me. My eyes pop open, I'm not familiar with my surroundings at first, it takes me a few moments to remember where I am. I realize I've slept until nightfall. The sun hidden away and the moon full in the sky, casting shadows in my childhood bedroom. Familiar shapes forming where they always had. I listen for the sound again, reacquainting myself with memories of this room at night.

I decide to chase down the noise. If it's my mother I'd like to be the one to initiate the meeting to cut down on some of the power she's always held over me.

I walk slowly down the stairs, avoiding the center of the steps where they all creak from age, listening carefully to the silence. I don't hear anything but my beating heart, sending blood rushing into my ears. I realize I'm full of anxiety for the impending reunion.

I crane my neck to look over the banister, hoping to pinpoint where she might be. The room is empty. I rush forward, finishing my descent down the stairs, finally coming to the bottom, I look around only to find nothing that could have been responsible for the sounds I heard.

I'm beginning to think I may have imagined it, possibly something in my dream sounded instead of in reality.

Relieved, I go to the fridge, hungry all of a sudden, it looks the same as this morning; empty. I really hope my mother is stopping at the grocery store tonight. I can only eat so many peanut butter sandwiches before I end up hating them. I devour two, making the second as I eat the first.

As I am taking the last bite of the second one, thinking I may need a third, I notice the papers from my father's safe deposit box on the counter, a diagram drawing my attention.

I thumb through a few of the top ones until I reach the one that had caught my attention. It's of a human outline, words scribbled in my father's handwriting covering the blank spaces around the form. I can't make many of the words out, he's been told a number of times he has the handwriting of a doctor.

I flip to the next; it has his scratchy lettering top to bottom, tiny cursive writing pinched together in the lines of paper. It looks like he was taking notes. The next page is the same, endless pages of scribbles. I come to another diagram in the midst of them. This one I can make out a little more clearly.

"disembowel... embalm... preserve..."

What the fuck? It sounds like notes an undertaker would be making.

I turn the page over and continue to try to make out the scattered ramblings. He says something about failed attempts deteriorating before arriving at some sort of sanitation regimen to aid in the preservation– killing off the bad bacterium that initiates decomposition and introducing an exotic cocktail of microorganisms to preserve collagen elasticity and cell structure. He seems to think he may have mastered the recipe.

I didn't know my father was interested in such things. He owned a car dealership, never being the type to open a book, let alone practice things you'd find in medical journals.

The term 'failed attempts' has me wondering what he may have practiced on and what could possibly motivate him to try such things.

Making my way further through the stack I find the recipe, a page headed with the words 'aftercare instructions' with a list detailing the procedure.

-wash with step 1 (follow recipe exactly when reproducing)

-liberally apply step 2 (bottles marked)

-clean cavities thoroughly

The list goes on and is very detailed. I can clearly make out his words here; he seems to have taken extra care in the printing of this sheet. The last thing says to make this a daily chore.

Who has time to complete so many steps... every day? And for what? What kind of taxidermist wants to spend countless hours following endless steps to preserve their specimens?

I flip through a few more pages and what catches my attention next is a letter addressed to me.

Tyler,

I know that if you are reading this I'm gone. I want you to know that you have always been my favorite person, I was proud to call you my son.

I had not always been the best father; I know things were not always good for you. I didn't know at the time what your mother was doing to you. I'm sorry I was blind to it. I didn't know I had to be on the lookout for such things. It came to light recently; she felt a strange need to confess. I was shocked. I didn't handle the news well.

That being said your mother is no longer with us. I let the altercation get out of hand and I am at fault for her death. I hadn't told you before this because I couldn't bring myself to admit the truth.

I know you loved her; I know she loved you... a little too much. She shared with me things I can't rid my mind of. She admitted the only reason she stopped sleeping with you was her hysterectomy, there were complications that left her in severe pain on a daily basis.

We were no longer having sex. I was left to my own devices; I had a sort of epiphany. I needed a substitute. A surrogate.

I perfected the process, I'm sure since you've made it this far you've seen the notes, maybe even assumed what I'd been up to. I'm probably not the man you thought you knew while growing up. I've not always been a good man, in my search for a surrogate I'd done awful things to get the right specimen.

What the fuck does he mean by '*specimen*'?

This whole thing has me confused. My father is talking as if he means a *sexual* surrogate. I realize it must have been hard for him after my mother was no longer able to perform in that part of their lives, but what awful things could he have done? I continue reading for the answers.

It came to me one night, lonely and in need of something, I got to thinking. I won't bore you with the details— you can read them for yourself in the notes. I will say that I found a way to preserve the human body so it wouldn't decay. I used that to create a sex doll.

It was through many failed attempts that I arrived at the right process to make it a success. I learned along the way what worked and what had not.

It is simple now looking back; rid the body of the bacteria that feeds on the flesh after death. That was step one— and the hardest. You have the recipe in my notes; you must follow exact measurements.

The bioorganic gel derived from algae was the answer to keeping the bodies soft and malleable after the fat and muscles deteriorated. Injected in just the right spots it's able to keep the shape of the person you are working with.

My 3D printer came in handy to create posable joints capable of locking into place, attached to the major bones, the faux-joints will keep them mobile and flexible to suit your preferences.

Add everything together and you have the perfect woman. I must say that what happened to your mother the night of the fight was a happy accident; I no longer had to search for a new woman. I had her now. I have preserved her. She is in her new home in the basement.

Please don't be alarmed. I don't want to overwhelm you right now. It must be quite a shock to learn all of these things after hearing about my own departure.

I want you to have her.

She is yours now.

What the fuck? The doll downstairs is my mother?

I can't breathe.

What is going on here?

My whole life is fucking twisting and I'm not able to see straight.

Not only is my father dead, but my mother is as well. And a fucking sex doll?

To top it off, I can't even be disgusted right now. My stupid fucking aching cock is throbbing, begging me to go back down there and fuck that fucking doll.

I am so fucked, and it turns out, I came from two crazy fuckers who have very little morals to share between them.

What fucking hope did I have?

I read the rest of the letter, resisting the urge to run. To where?—I'm torn between the basement and my home a thousand miles away.

I finish the letter with shaking hands, but I can't tell if the shaking is from disgust or excitement.

Do with her what you will, to be fair she always did what she wanted to you.

I love you son, please don't think of me any differently for this.

If you choose not to accept this gift, I have left a list for you to follow for disposal of her body.

Dad

CHAPTER EIGHT

I lay the stack of papers down; my head is swirling and the thoughts trapped inside are confusing and twisted. I know I should be upset that my mother is dead. And I guess I am, but only because I never stood up to her. It sounds like my father did it for me though; he killed her in light of her confession about her depraved appetite for me. I don't know how far she went into detail about what had happened throughout the years, but it was enough to send my father over the edge.

I feel vindicated, and a little angry all at the same time. I feel so dizzy with excitement, I'm so fucked up.

I don't even realize my feet have taken me to the basement door until I reach it. I'm torn between opening it right now and following my father's list to dispose of her. My shaking hands work the lock. I let my mind wander around the implications of both choices. Of course, my cock wants to weigh in. Of course, the anger at her fuels my perversion, making me want to fuck her silly.

She did this to me, and I wouldn't be held accountable for anything I ended up doing to her, she made me the sex crazed man I am today, the man who is giving real thought to fucking his dead mother, preserved for just such a thing– by his father, no less.

I take a bulb from the lamp in the living room, remembering the one down in the basement is out, after screwing it in light floods the room, sending the shadows to the furthest corners.

The video of my father down here fills my mind as soon as I see the sheet covering her body. The feel of what's under it calling to my hands. I want to touch it again; I want to know it's my mother and really see it for what it is.

I pull the sheet back quickly, whipping it off her body, she looks beautiful, she looks like she is not dead, looks a mixture between sleepy and aroused. I'm sure my father was able to make sure this was how she should be remembered.

I rub my hands up her body.

God, she feels so real.

She feels so soft and I can't get enough of it. She looks just like I remember her; my father hadn't taken any liberties with her– not making one change to enhance her or make her look younger than her 43 years.

She really is beautiful, her dark hair and blue eye combination was coveted by most her girlfriends, her fuller than average lips making her look almost pouty, the straight- lined button- nose with a smattering of light freckles perfectly centered, making her doll- like.

Her porcelain skin preserved perfectly, not a single flaw to ruin the look or feel of her softness, which feels like heaven under my hands. I am compelled to touch her, to spread her.

I'm taken aback by my own actions, watching me do things in a sort of out- of- body way. I watch as my hands run up the inside of her soft thighs, stopping just short of her fleshy mound and back down, the second trip up I don't stop, I can't go another second without touching it.

My fingers are shaking as I touch the folds of my mother's familiar pussy. My cock is achingly hard and pressed against the fly of my jeans, my heart pounding so hard its sending rivers of blood into my ears.

Before I know what I'm doing I push my fingers into the circled cavity. It is warm and tight, it feels like the flesh over the rest of her body, the only difference is this hole has small gripping ribbed bumps the depth of it, I'm assuming he has done it for friction.

I pull my fingers out and then back in again to test my theory. Oh my god, it feels so good. I can't help but imagine my cock is in here instead of my fingers, the grip of this hole would have me coming in no time, and I need that. I need to come so bad right now. My throbbing cock is drooling pre- come in anticipation of what I know I'm going to do.

There is no question anymore.

I let my pants down; they fall heavy to the floor. My feet pull me forward, I stop to spread her legs, true to my father's claims, the locking joints hold her legs up, and open, I stare right into the wide hole I need just before I plunge into it.

I almost explode before I can draw out, I'm like a fucking teenager losing his virginity right now, it's unlike anything I've ever felt.

I am consumed with the thought of this being my mother's existence now. She is here purely for me to fuck at my leisure and the control is overwhelming. Fate has dealt her the hand that she dealt me growing up; I was simply a means to an end for her, to be used as she wanted, when she needed to get off. Now, I would be the one using her and the shear depravity is sending me over the edge.

I slow my shaky breaths, and rest my quivering hands on her breasts, squeezing them at the peak. I move slowly inside her, trying to bring myself to the here and now instead of rushing this, I want to remember it, not look back on it as a blur.

The pussy is practically milking my cock and in only a few more thrusts I can't help but come, I explode harder than I can ever remember doing before. I collapse on top of her, my cock still convulsing inside the ribbed pussy hole, my breath slowing, no longer heaving. The blood is able to flow to other areas of my body.

I don't feel one hint of shame for this, I thought I'd get it out of my system and regret or some other form of self- hating would take over but it doesn't. I'm excited to be the new proud owner of this perfect sex doll.

I pull out of the pussy hole and look for the ribbed tube to pull it out of the socket; my father's instructions told me how to remove them for clean- up. I follow the steps precisely, knowing I want to preserve this fuck doll now, knowing I'll need it for as long as I can think.

I pour some of the solution onto the sleeve and clean it free of my come, leaving it out to air dry.

I pull my pants up, finally, after almost tripping over them, still wrapped around my ankles. I take one more look at my new inheritance and head up the stairs before my cock thinks it needs a second round.

CHAPTER NINE

I had run right up to my room after my interaction with my 'mother' doll, I stayed away physically, but my brain couldn't focus on much else, the excitement swirling around my head was almost constant. I had to take a sleeping pill and go to bed early or I know I would have spent the night in the basement fucking myself dry.

This morning I'm groggy from the pill and exhausted from a night full of weird vivid dreams about my mother, both alive, and the new basement version of her.

I wake to the sound of my phone ringing, still plugged into the wall across the room. As I make my way to it to return the call I missed, I wonder if it's Cammie.

I hope it is Cammie, we have things we need to talk about, like the fact that she *won't* fucking talk to me.

It is her and I hit redial, waiting for her to answer. I hear Cammie's voice right away say hello, she sounds irritated despite the fact that she had been the one to call me.

"Hey, how are you?" I ask, trying hard to start us off on the right foot.

"Fine," she says flatly.

"You missing me?"

She chuffs a laugh, "not really,"

"What the fuck, Cammie? Why can't we just get over this? Why are you being so hard on me?" I spit the words into the phone; this bitch sure can hold a grudge.

"Are you sure you need to ask those questions? You can't just know that what you did to me the night before you left was way too fucked up?" There's more of those swear words she's throwing around lately.

"I do think it was fucked up, but as I tried to explain, it was just that you were so fucking sexy in that little skirt, I got carried away, men sometimes do that when a woman looks sexy, maybe you shouldn't wear that sort of stuff anymore." I know that's not true. If I were a gentleman like she had always thought I was, I would have kept my hands— and cock—away from her after she'd told me no. But I know it works sometimes to turn it around on her and make her feel guilty about not giving me what I want, so I give it a try now. "You are just so hot, and I love you so much, you know I didn't mean to hurt you."

"You tore my clothes off and didn't even care that I was begging you to stop. I was crying and you wouldn't listen." Her voice is cracking, I can tell reliving that night is hard for her to be doing right now. "You hurt me."

I know I should not be turned on right now, but the memory she's sharing with me to get a response of shame is actually making my cock hard.

Ripping her skirt from her body and slamming her on the bed facedown, I remember pounding her so hard my balls ached the next day. I fucked her while she lay there crying and then came on her face, mixing my come with her tears.

I had gone into the bathroom to clean up, and when I came out with a wet towel for her, she'd already gone. I knew she would talk to me again, even though she's a fucking prude she does want me to be happy and in her own stupid way she fucking loves me.

"I know baby," I put on my best apology voice; even to my own ears, I sound sincere. "You know I'm sorry, right? You know I didn't want to hurt you."

"Yes." That simple three- letter word means that she has forgiven me, found enough reason to blame herself and is now back in the palm of my hand.

Stupid fucking girl.

"I really need to see you; I have been missing you."

"Me too."

"But I have to be here for a few more days, I can't miss the funeral."

"I could come." And that's the exact response I needed to hear.

"You sure you want to?"

"I think I should be there for you."

"I think so too, how bout you get your stuff packed and head over right away."

"Ok, I'll see you soon, Tyler. Thanks for the apology."

"I *am* sorry, babe. You're such a sweet girl, I'll see you soon."

I drop my phone on the bed and head downstairs, I feel a rush of excitement thinking about her being here. My throbbing cock takes me down the next flight of stairs to the basement- sex- dungeon and my pants are off before I know what I'm doing. I am so hard right now and the sight of the sheet- covered table sends my dick into an impossibly harder state.

I crave what's under that cover and it drives me crazy to be able to use it whenever I see fit. I waste no time inserting the pussy tube that had been drying since the night before and slipping my cock into the cavity, the warmth is there right away and the tight grip around my cock lessons some of the need.

I spread her legs wide, fuck it until I'm dizzy and need to come. This time I pull out and spray come all over her full tits. She'll be ready to fuck again sooner if I don't have to clean the tube- insert each time. I remember my father possibly sharing the same idea in those videos from his safe deposit box. He had pulled out, too.

Although there is really no need to worry about running out of holes, there are two others I could use as back- up. I almost have the energy to give one of those a go, as well, but I want to hold off for Cammie– pound that bitch into submission. I'm not the perfect boyfriend, but I do like to make sure she gets off when we fuck.

I figure I'll go out and see the town while I get some fucking food for this place, since my mother is most definitely *not* grocery shopping.

I chuckle to myself, she's not doing anything but being a fucking come receptacle, but that's how I always thought of her. I can think back on those days where she was warping her young son, turning him into a deviant– a degenerate, she was so hungry for me, and now she can have her fill, I'll feed her load after load of my nut.

***

The grocery store, and everything in this town leading up to it, is exactly as I remember it, the same people walking the same streets, the same houses looking exactly the same. I'm feeling a little more nostalgic than I was when first arriving. It feels comfortable, like the hometown I grew up in– familiar. I think I like it.

On the way home from the store, I stop at my father's– now my car dealership. The man behind the desk is Bill; he has been here since I was a kid and loved to come hang out with my father while he worked.

He recognizes me right away. "Tyler! You're looking great, a real man you've become."

"Thank you, Bill. You're looking well; my father must have been treating you nicely."

"As always, the best man I knew." He seems to become lost in the fond memories.

"I'm just going to take a quick look around." I'm not sure why I've come, feeling more and more like I belong here, maybe?

"Will you be staying... taking over for your old man?" He seems hopeful.

Like many in this town relying on one of the few jobs with benefits, working for a man who actually gave a shit about his employees. I'm sure he must be worried about losing his job if I were to sell the place, not knowing whether the buyer would keep everyone on board or hire a new crew, or simply start over and make it something completely different. The lot is prime real- estate, overlooking the most beautiful parts of the town, right off the highway; it gets a lot of drive by traffic.

"I'm not sure enough to say quite yet." I see the hope in his eyes die a little; he knows that I ran from here long ago. Maybe he assumes I'd still be in that frame of mind. Maybe I am. I feel almost sorry enough to say yes, just to ease his tension, but I can't—not until I'm sure.

I wave to the familiar people I pass, a nice smile that says I'm here on business plastered to my face.

My father's office is the same— the man absolutely loved routine. I sit behind the desk for no real reason; I only want to see what it feels like, mostly. What it would be like to step into my father's shoes and be the younger version of him in a career I only know enough about to skate by.

I know I am capable enough to learn along the way before anyone would notice I don't know a fucking thing about it. That eases my mind a little, although I'm not really so much stressed out about this leap as maybe anxiety-ridden about leaving the old life I built all by myself and trading it in for the life of my father. I don't want anyone to think I couldn't make it on my own. I could and I did it fucking well.

I shuffle the papers sprawled across his desk, not finding anything amusing enough to focus on, I stand and head back out the way I came. "See you later, Bill. Got somethings I need to sort out. You will be the first to hear my decision." I look him in the eyes and say it with feeling.

I see relief in his eyes as I speak, he knows he will have a heads up about my choice before some head honcho waltzes in and starts barking orders.

I think the whole way home about what life would be like living here. Maybe I *could* do it and even if I couldn't hack it, I know I'd be able to leave with no issue and start over. I have done it before with far less resources.

My house appears before I'm ready to be home, I sit in the driveway staring at the structure I have so many fond memories of and so many horrific things buried here that it repulses me almost equally. I'll have to reflect on those the next few days to see if the good outweighs the bad— if I'd be able to erase the negativity from this house.

CHAPTER TEN

The day goes by slowly; waiting for Cammie to show up is taking forever. The girl is always in her own world, on her own time. The long drive has me impatient. I can't wait too much longer to get my hands on her. I know some may think I've ruined my chances with her, but I'm a great manipulator and I'm confident in my ability to change her mind about me.

I kill time reading my father's notes again, I'm shocked that he has come up with this idea, let alone executed it perfectly. I'm proud of him for being more than just a business man, he has proven to be quite ingenious.

It makes me wonder what I'd be capable of if I wanted something bad enough— if I put my mind to something like my father had, would I be smart enough to do it? I'd like to think so.

Cammie's text comes in; telling me she's about an hour out still, her GPS is leading the way here. She's so awful at directions, barely able to distinguish her left from her right.

I decide to go to the basement, I don't know when I'll have another chance to get down there with Cammie here, and though I'm confident in my ability to fuck her the second she walks in, I know she won't let me inside her ass, which is want I want right now.

My cock is rock hard, a mind of its own driving me forward to the tight hole I'm thinking about. As I lube up my cock with the bottle my father has created to be used in conjunction with my mother's body, I'm thinking of all the times she had me do this to her while she was alive.

I slide into her back hole effortlessly, not having to worry about the pain it would be causing. I thrust deep inside, forcing my way into the deepest parts of her ass. It feels like I remember it feeling, tight and warm, the friction building my release, my balls tighten and I let myself fill the cavity with the pent-up nut they have been carrying around.

Fuck... I will never get enough of this thing. Best fucking invention ever. The feel of a real woman— her being one and all, coupled with the fact that she is silent and won't deny me anything I'd think to do to her.

I tuck her back under the sheet, flattening her limbs I pat her on her thigh, telling her 'thank you for being such a good sport', and am still chuckling as I lock up the basement again.

I'm hardly done with the task when the doorbell rings. I must have been down there longer than I thought. I really get lost in that thing.

"Tyler! I'm so sorry I wasn't here for you when I first heard the news about your dad, I feel awful that you have been dealing with this alone." She kisses me hard and I let her.

"It's ok babe, you're here now." I squeeze her ass as she presses herself against me. If I hadn't just come, I would bend her the fuck over the couch and take her pussy hard, but I did, so it will have to wait.

She's grinding herself against me like she wants me to.

Fucking idiot.

Girls like her are so predictable, it almost makes me want to send her right out the door again, turn her around and get her the fuck out of here.

I'd have more fun with Jamie than her, she likes the way I fuck her and she's not complicated. I huff and pull her up the stairs to my room; taking her bags with us, I set them on top of the comforter and leave her quickly to unpack so she doesn't think I've brought her upstairs to fuck her.

I know she should be hungry and I take the fresh groceries from around the kitchen and prepare a meal I'm sure she'll be likely to finish– macaroni and cheese, it is practically the only thing she likes.

I put a ground up pill in hers, step one in my father's process, I have to empty her and the laxative should do the trick. I made the decision the second I saw her; I don't want her like this anymore.

She comes down just as I'm finishing up, I hand her a bowl and make one for myself. We eat in relative silence, my excitement keeping my thoughts elsewhere. I watch captivated as she takes bite after bite of her contaminated food.

We start a television show and shortly after, she excuses herself, saying only that she has a stomachache.

My cock throbs, waiting for her to be done; I can hardly keep my hands off it. Luckily, she comes back down awhile later interrupting my internal debate. She says she is too wiped- out to finish the program and wants to go to bed. I follow her up and lie next to her sleeping body, finally falling asleep myself hours later with the thoughts of what is to come in the morning swirling around my sleepy head.

The morning comes quickly, I'm not very rested, Cammie spent most of the night in the bathroom. Step one should be done now, she couldn't have had too much to get rid of– her small appetite can't have her full of too much.

She rolls over and wraps her arms around me, I follow suit and hug her for a few moments before saying we should get up. She seems disappointed but comes downstairs with me.

I hand her a bottle of water and brew myself a single cup of coffee. I watch as she drinks until it's gone. I don't want her having too much more than that. I just need to make sure she is flushed out and then we can begin the next step, the one I'm more excited about than I thought I'd be.

I didn't know that this would be so much fun... the plotting and manipulating. She has no idea what's in her future, and I can't wait to see her in mine– lain out and spread wide– ready to take me. First step will be fucking her virgin asshole– primed and ready for me like my father did to his homemade sex doll.

I ask her how she feels this morning.

"I'm ok, I feel much better than last night... must have been all the stress I felt over leaving you alone over here."

"Well, you can make it up to me right now– if you want," I say in the tone I'm sure she knows by now as the flirty- guy- who- wants- to- fuck.

"Ok." She licks her lips and I know she gets the message.

"Come on." I grab her hand and lead her to the couch; I really meant it when I said I wanted to fuck her bent over it. "Take your clothes off. Let me see you."

She does as she is told.

Fuck she has such a tight little body, high, perky tits with nipples that make my mouth water. The gap between her thighs coupled with her meaty pussy makes it easy to see the lips from where I sit in front of her.

I pull her over to me and spread her thighs wider, one on either side of my own naked thighs; I sit her down on top of me, pushing my fingers deep inside of her. I plunge my fingers into her like that until she's clawing at me, the wet sounds of her pussy filling the room.

I pick her up by her armpits and push her down onto the couch, shoving her face into the cushion. She goes to make a noise of argument but bites her tongue, knowing she shouldn't voice it right now, not with her feeling so bad about my dear 'ol daddy passing and her leaving me to fend for myself.

I take advantage of that, going a little rougher than I know I'm allowed. Even after her having a valid excuse to push me away– *fuck*, I practically *raped* her last time we fucked. But she stays where I put her, spreading her thighs wide enough to accommodate me. Her pink little asshole calling to me– *that* I'll wait for though, I have proof that it will be better when we're done here.

I slip right into her wet hole, all the way in, my balls pressing right against her soft mound. I don't fuck her yet though, instead I reach around to the front of her and work her clit like I know will have her lost in an orgasm in no time.

She moans and fucks herself on my cock, I don't help her, I just hold my pole in place for her pleasure. And, just like I knew would happen, her pussy tightens and convulses around my cock. That's when I finally fuck her, I go hard and fast, pounding her until she can hardly hold herself up. I am shoving her body hard into the back of the couch, grunting hard– almost missing my moment and coming but I'm able to pull back in time to hold off my nut.

I reach for my 2- inch chisel I had tucked into the cushion and align it with the base of her neck. She's so lost in what I'm doing to her pussy that she has no idea what is happening right behind her back.

Finding the exact area indicated by my father, I draw my arm back and thrust it hard into the spot, I feel right away that it has worked, her body goes limp, I keep fucking her until I'm done– which is only seconds later, the feel of her lifeless body under me practically forces the come from my balls.

I recover quickly and drag her tiny body to the basement where I'm told to hang her upside down by her ankles. I feel for the spot on the neck to sever her jugular vein, which should pull the blood from her body. My father has the perfect set up– a drain in the floor under the ankle holster makes for easy clean up.

That should take a while I'm told, so I go upstairs to shower the smears of blood covering my naked body.

I can hardly wait to get back to the basement. I rush my shower and am back in no time, just a pair of boxers on.

EPILOGUE

The next few days I followed my father's instructions to the letter, going between creating my very own fuck doll and making time with my father's creation. I feel like I've never felt before, I'm exhilarated. I fucking love this, the two most perfect fucking specimens— mine to fuck when and how I want. There is no other way to explain it but to say I am content. That's what I am right now, perfectly content.

My father's funeral went off without a hitch and I'm back in the basement now, finishing everything up with my little 'Cammie' doll, inserting her very own fuck tubes and sponging both bodies off for the day. She looks as good as my 'mother' doll.

Not too bad for my first try.

I told Bill at the shop that I'd be staying on and keeping everything as my father had set about doing. I gave him a promotion to general manager, knowing his knowledge will come in handy along the way.

I redid the house, redecorating it to fit my style, gutting most of it to accommodate me. I absolutely love it here now; the town feels like home.

They think my mother ran off with a new man, something my father had been telling them for a while now. It was an easy lie, the town knew my mother couldn't keep her hands to herself, she fucked many of the men in town while still alive and 'happy' with my father. While keeping our activities a secret she still had a need for more.

Fucking whore.

There is a new woman in town, she caught my eye the first time I saw her in the shop, she came in looking to trade in her old car, fresh start and all, she had to upgrade her wheels. I think I'll grab her and add her to my collection.

My father may have been happy with just my mother, but I have a need for variety that hasn't been quenched yet. Our first date is tonight. I guess we'll see how it goes.

The End

RETALIATION

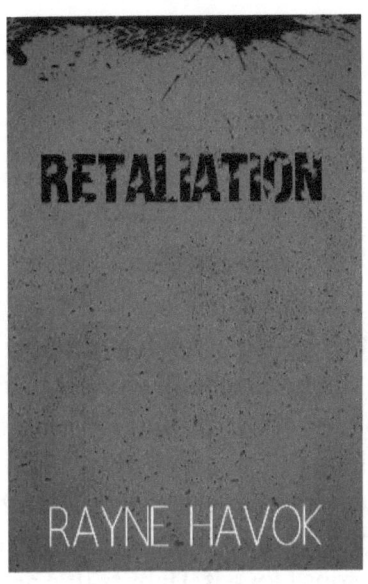

MILLER NEEDS TO UNWIND SO HE GOES FOR A
RIDE DOWN THE LONELIEST HIGHWAY IN
AMERICA. ONLY TODAY HE COMES ACROSS
SOMEONE—A COCKY ASSHOLE WHO NEARLY
RUNS HIM OFF THE ROAD.
TIRED OF PEOPLE WHO THINK THEY CAN DO
WHATEVER THEY WANT, MILLER RETALIATES.

ONE

I woke up this morning feeling just how stressful my week had been. The headache of working far too many hours was threatening to take over, and the only cure for that I have found is a long ride along Highway 50. The highway that cut right through town goes the length of the U.S. They've dubbed it the loneliest highway for obvious reasons, which are the reasons I love it. Light traffic and anyone who travels this road often knows the ins and outs of how to get through it— as fast as you can.

I decided since I'm up early anyway, to get on my bike and put as many miles between work and me as I can.

A shower and a quick breakfast is all I give myself time for before hitting the road. I feel the excitement building as I anticipate the high speeds that the road allows.

As I leave Lake Tahoe behind me, the stress falls away. I can feel it practically breaking free of my shoulders and the weight of it gone has me breathing again.

I don't have one of those classy jobs– the kind people brag about. I manage a casino; it's about as glamorous as scraping shit off your shoe. The pay is decent, but I have to work more hours than god to achieve it. I stay only out of shear hatred for the idea of looking for something else.

As long as I can take a day or two every once in a while, for a nice road trip like this, I can get back in there and start building up all the things that drive me crazy, until I do it all again.

The mother fucking American Dream.

It's a beautiful day; the road is as empty as I need it to be to avoid yielding to anyone. The scenery is flying by in my periphery and all is perfect.

When I come to the town that I usually pull off the Highway to refuel for the return home I decide to stop and eat as well. There is a diner here that does breakfast the right way– big and greasy.

I pull my bike into a spot, deciding to eat first, shaking my hair free of the helmet shape that does nothing to compliment my good looks. I say that only because I am sure not every woman who has told me so could be a liar. I'm tall, thick chested, rugged and hung like a horse. What else could I be blessed with to add to the package? I'm forgetting my sense of humor– ladies dig a man who can make them laugh, but only so long as they can make her scream later– which I'm told I also do well.

Mostly I'm just an all- around nice guy, I have friends who can count on me and women practically lining up to have a chance with me. That may sound cocky and counterproductive to have you believing what I have said— but it's true nonetheless.

The waitress who comes to my table to ask about my order has an adorable face, she is young and seems to be shy. It's hard for her to make eye contact, I'm sure it's because, in mine, she can see how deeply I can read her. I have a good sense about people; I can generally tell a lot about them in a few seconds. The years spent running the casino have given me such skills.

I let her off the hook when I realize I'm not going to get anywhere. She is not one of those girls who feigns shy and then turns into a fucking porn star in bed. She seems to be the real deal, and when I realize there's no shot at a quickie in the bathroom I back off.

I give her my order, which may seem like more people will be joining me, but they're not. I'm just fucking hungry. She turns and leaves without so much as a single word and I'm happy to see her go. She has a nice ass that shakes as she walks. She is so naïve that she may be totally unaware of what it does to the men in here.

I watch the other people in the diner enjoying their food and conversation with their companions. Just a typical Saturday lunch for them— for me too, but I'd rather it be alone.

I have to deal with enough people in my job, nobody comes to me unless they have something to complain about and then they just want me to fix it... *instantly*, which I'm not always able to do and then *I'm* the one at fault for keeping them unhappy. For that reason alone, I usually enjoy my solitude.

The waitress sets a cup, along with a carafe of hot coffee, on my table. This time, as I look up to meet her eyes, they are already on me. She bites her lip, as I'm sure she is nervous about my attention, but walks away again without a word.

She is a strange one, that girl.

My food is brought out shortly after by two women— neither of them her, taking quite a team effort to deliver my complete order all at one time. I thank them and dig in— my god it's all so good, I have no complaints.

Once I've eaten my fill I lean back into the booth and take a moment to let my food settle. I sip a third cup of coffee slowly before I head back out.

I pay my tab and leave a tip on the table for my favorite new shy girl. It's larger than is expected and I'm happy to do it, she gave me somewhere to focus my mind and get my head somewhere else. I'd never tell her where those thoughts actually went— mostly with her bent over hard surfaces with my cock buried inside of her. It's a shame I don't see her before I leave.

I take the ride home slower; the dread of returning is building up those tensions again. I can almost feel the weight of my life bogging me down. I'm wallowing in that when one of those big trucks— you know the ones, smoke stacks and black shit billowing out of them, polluting everything it touches. A true measure of a man's cock— the bigger the truck the bigger his cock– we are supposed to believe.

Anyway, this fucker decides to not only pull out in front of me, causing me to narrowly miss him by inches after having to veer off the road onto the dirt berm to avoid his taillight, but to slow down to an almost crawling speed after doing so. Then after coming back onto the road, looking to clear out of his way, I speed up and just when I'm about to pass him he accelerates, unleashing a black cloud of shit that I get lost inside.

Something inside of me boils, he's done this on purpose for his own enjoyment, I'm probably not the first to be on the receiving end of his little- dick truck's performance.

I am under some sort of autopilot as I follow him. He's racing as fast as his truck can go now, and I'm keeping myself at a distance. I don't even realize what I'm doing until I turn my bike off the highway where he does. It doesn't dawn on me that I've also turned off onto a dirt road behind him. I can see the trailer that will be his destination– it's the only thing down the desolate unpaved street.

I stop my bike and watch him proceed until he does, in fact, pull in front of the trailer. I've been glaring at it for more time than I can recall. Like the house had wronged me, but it wasn't the house, it was the man *inside* that fucking house.

I am carried forward by my rage and am off my bike before I can think my plan through. My fists pummel the door until I hear the man behind it call out to me.

"What the fuck do you want?" he shouts repeatedly until I've heard him.

He hasn't opened the door– I don't know why I thought he would. Mr. Fucking Big Man when he's in his smog machine, but not so tuff when it's man on man, I guess.

"You fucking idiot, pulling out like that in front of me, you could have killed me, then blowing that shit in my face... are you fucking *crazy*?"

I hear this fucker laughing behind the door, but he says nothing in return.

"What the *fuck* were you thinking?" I'm getting angrier than I have ever been– my blood is boiling.

"Fuck you."

Are you fucking kidding me?

Fuck me?

My fists fly at the door again, leaving blood smears on the white panel. I'm furious. "Why don't you come out here and let me show you 'fuck you.'"

More laughing.

I try to calm down, I really do. I try to search for somewhere to shove this rage but I have nowhere to channel it, my hands are shaking and the rush of blood pumping in my ears is deafening. The laughing is driving me insane. Like the sounds of an asylum echoing in my head. I literally am losing my *fucking* mind on this dude's doorstep.

I try to make my feet move but I can't. My brain is not focusing its attention on my commands.

"If I ever run into you again, or hear of this happening again, I don't care if it's you who is behind it, I will string you up by your balls and rip out your asshole."

Whoa, I've never even thought such words before, yet they come very willing out of my mouth.

The laughter stops and what is said behind that still-closed door drives me crazier than I thought possible. "Fuck you, I do what I want."

Everything around me fades and I become hyper focused on those words. 'I do what I want'– they play over and over in my head like a fucking mantra.

That is exactly how this fucker lives his life, he wants to cut a bike off in traffic... he does it. He wants to blow black smoke into the face of a stranger... he does it. He wants to hide behind a fucking door and shout bullshit through it... he fucking does it.

Maybe I need to be taking a lesson from his book. I want to fucking kill him right now and since he has so kindly shown me the ways of life... I *will* fucking do it.

And, with that thought comes the calm. A Zen sort of flush happens and the rage is gone, my feet happily take me away this time. I don't even care that once I've reached the road, he finally opens the door and shouts at me something to the effect of how big a pussy I am. It doesn't faze me.

I get on my bike and I fly home. I have some things I need to do to get what I *want*.

TWO

The next few days go by in a flash. I thought that maybe my anger would dissipate, but it has not. I thought that man might fade from my mind, becoming just another of the jackasses along the way, but instead, he has become *the* jackass. The one in which I will measure every future jackass by.

I'm actually quite happy to have it be in the back of my mind. I have been feeding off it for the last few days. Every time someone irritates me, I push it back there to sit and fester with the other things.

The plot of retaliation is coming together and excitement for the weekend is almost more that I can take. It feels like what children must feel when an impending trip to Disneyland is nearby. I'm giddy with the anticipation.

Recently, a few people have asked me what I'm so happy about, and all I can say is murder plotting must look good on me.

I go home at night and lie in bed, thinking of all the things that I could do to this man to squash his little psyche, to bring that fucker to his knees and show him that he fucked with the wrong guy. I'm not missing the sleep that I'm sacrificing for these thoughts. I wake up refreshed and ready to face the day ahead, knowing I'm one closer to exacting my revenge.

Friday morning comes and I'm practically jumping out of my skin. I have energy I didn't know I could call upon sitting right on the edge, waiting to be used. The day goes slower than I want it to, but I'm able to focus on it in small increments at a time.

The problems people are bringing to me to fix cannot fuck up my plans; I don't care one way or another if any of them get solved. In two hours, I'm out of here and not a single thing in the world will stop me.

When the watch on my wrist hits nine I walk with an eager step to the front doors, pushing them open like the high school just released for summer, the crisp air hits me and all my tension evaporates. A giggle escapes my throat as I climb onto my bike, forgoing my helmet, as I want to feel everything right now. I wouldn't dare miss a single second of this night.

I get home quickly and grab the bag I've had packed after arriving home the night of the incident, adding a few things to it as my thoughts took a far darker turn as time passed. It's your basic murder kit, I'm sure you can guess what is in it and if not, you may be in the wrong place for story. Knives, rope, tape and other fun things to keep us occupied for hours of fun... doing all the things I *want*.

I load the bag onto my bike and head out in the direction of his trailer. I drive straight through and stop only when I see his street. It looks slightly different in the cover of the night, but I couldn't forget this house if I had been struck in the head and come down with a case of amnesia—it's burned into my mind.

The dead grassed- lawn that he had parked his truck on is empty now, so I know he is not home— which for some reason is exactly as I knew it would happen.

I need to slip inside and be waiting for him when he returns. The house is dark and no outside lights are on, lending me a perfect cover.

I try the knob when I reach the door, hoping to save myself the time of having to pick it, but it's locked and I have to use the skills I've picked up from google over the last few days of researching lock picking. I became pretty good, although, I've only practiced on the locks in my own house. His doesn't look too much different so I have faith I can get in without a sign.

It goes off without a hitch and I'm inside in less than five minutes. Pretty good time for an amateur— let's face it google knows its stuff.

The interior is much like the outside, from what I can see. His truck is the newest thing he owns, probably sinking all his money into it. The couch looks second hand and the rest of the living room is scarcely decorated. I sneak through the house finding a dining table with two chairs, one that looks to be newly broken, sitting in the corner of the dining room. The kitchen is bare, the pantry empty. There are generic take- out containers in the fridge overflowing the space.

There is a bathroom right off the living room and the ring inside the toilet tells me he's not much of a housekeeper. The mirror has splattered toothpaste covering it. The faucet dripping.

I could leave right now and know I have a better life than he does, living in a slum like this could be punishment enough. But that's not what I want to have happen and he said those magic words that have since changed my life. 'I do what I want' so here we go.

There are two rooms at the end of the hall, one on either side. I go to the one that has the door open and peek inside; it's empty save for a plastic lawn chair tucked under a small desk with a hundred-year-old looking computer sitting on top of it. There is a pile of laundry in the corner stacked high.

I go to the closed door and turn the handle slowly; the creak that the door makes as I push it open is nothing I'm concerned with until I see something alarming. There is someone inside, laying under a blanket on the bed. The light is not here for me to see who it might be— the moonlight doing nothing to lend a hand; I have to creep inside to get a closer look.

It's a girl, I can tell right away as I'm confronted with a set of tits that would make a man blush, the comforter having slipped below them. But her arm is thrown over her face so I can't get a good look at her, which is a shame; these are not the tits of an ugly girl.

I have to take a few minutes to think through my options. The dude was such a fuck wit I didn't have plans for what to do if he had a girlfriend at home. How this guy landed these tits is beyond me.

I have the essentials to restrain her, which is what I'll have to do. I'll figure out what to do with her after that, but I can't have her running off and alerting anyone about me.

I take the bag off my shoulder and set the tape on the nightstand. She doesn't have one of those handy beds that has posts or a frame of any sort to trap her with, so I decide quickly that it would make such a nice picture for Mr. Fuck Head to come home and see her restrained first thing. And what better place than the kitchen table?—considering my options are not ripe for the picking, it will do just fine.

Luckily, the girl is not heavy because when I opt for the scoop- technique to get her off the bed, she instantly wakes up and throws herself around, frantically trying to escape. I am able to subdue her quickly enough to avoid injury in the process, flinging her over my shoulder and grabbing the tape before I go, heading straight for the table.

She's not only topless but completely naked and the softness of her body under my hands is creating a turmoil inside of me. I am not a man to take things from women they are not offering but before last week I wasn't the man I am tonight, breaking into the house of an idiot I plan to kill. Therefore, we will just have to see what else has changed inside of me.

"Sit on the table." I say it firmly enough that she starts, but she does so grudgingly. "You move or try any of that funny shit again and I will fucking hurt you."

She nods. It's hard to see in the darkness but I can feel her body shake with the frantic motion of her head.

I tape the first ankle to the table leg, keeping my eyes on high alert for any sudden movements. I move to do the same to the next after I see that she's going to behave.

"Lie back." I take her wrists and tug her the rest of the way down attempting to secure them to the last two legs of the table. And that's finally when I notice her face, it dawns on me that she is the girl from the diner, the waitress who caught my attention.

Well, fuck.

If I wasn't already in the middle of a murder plot to kill her boyfriend, I would consider the rape-y thoughts running through my head to be the worst thing a person could do to another.

A flash of me going around and sticking my swelling cock into her completes my hard on and I struggle to complete the task of getting her arms affixed to the posts.

Oh, my god.

"What do you want from me?" she asks.

"Oh, honey, you do *not* want to know the answer to that question."

She gasps as the recognition hits her. "You're the guy from the diner."

"I am."

"I thought you were a nice guy. You left me such a nice tip." She seems to be disappointed in herself for being wrong about me. Well, she was right at the time, I used to be a nice man who would leave a nice tip and be a gentleman who might have asked her out on a proper date, but today we meet again after I've become someone else.

I lift my shoulders in a shrug to let her know I don't really care about her perception of me.

"My boyfriend will be home soon," she says by way of a threat.

"Oh, I know, that's why I'm here."

"What do you mean?" She is frantic now.

"I came here for him. You've just become a side project."

Her face has comically fallen, her jaw drops and her eyes bulge. "What do you want with him?"

"Everything." I say it matter-of-factly. It's the truth— I want everything.

"He doesn't have anything, well, nothing but his fucking truck; he loves that thing more than anything."

I look around the room, reminding myself of the slum he lives in and I laugh. "I can see that."

"So, why don't you just take that?"

She doesn't understand what I meant by everything. I scrunch my nose at her and shake my head. "That's not enough— it's not *everything*."

"Well, he doesn't even love me, so you're wasting your time with me."

"We'll see." Something has come to me and I think I know just how this is going to go down now. She's made an even better plot unfold in my mind.

I walk around the table and stand a few feet away from her to admire the view; she's spread wide by the restraints and lying on her back splayed out on the table. I get the perfect look at her clean- shaven pussy.

I hear myself moan and it surprises me again that this is turning me on. I'm tempted to touch her but I refrain. I don't know how I hold myself back honestly, I want nothing more than to slip my fingers inside her right now, instead I push my hands as far as I can into the pockets of my jeans and go back up toward her face.

"So, you're not going to hurt me?" She seems to think that since I've held back, I'm not going to do anything to her.

Ok, she can think that for now.

"What are you going to do to Jimmy?"

Fucking Jimmy... of course that's his name. "Whatever I want." I answer her.

"Oh, god," she cries now, tears fall down the side of her face, collecting in her blonde hair. I think it makes her look even prettier. I don't usually like a woman crying; in fact, I do anything in my power to stop it from happening. But on her, right now, it looks like heaven. Her chin quivers as she tries to hold back more tears and I want to run my tongue along her lips and up her cheek to collect the wetness.

"So, when is Jimmy supposed to be home?" I ask, sidestepping her suffering.

"What time is it now?"

"That's none of your concern; I asked you when he should be home."

"He's home about 3am most nights. He works late."

"You sure he's working and not out fucking some stupid girl? Doesn't look like he brings in a lot of money."

"He spends it on the truck mostly. I don't think he's cheating; he wouldn't do that to me."

"You said he doesn't love you, what's to stop him then?" I look at my watch and conveniently, he should be arriving any time now. I feel the adrenaline hit me and my heartbeats quicken.

"He doesn't, but I still don't think he could cheat." Her face tells a different story and it makes me sad for her.

"Well, either way, he may be coming home any time now and I need you to be a good little prop while we wait for him, got it?"

She nods.

"You even *almost* say something to warn him and I will take all of this out on you."

"I'm not going to do anything, but you have to promise you won't hurt me."

"I don't have to promise you shit. You do what I say or there will be consequences. Do you *fucking* understand?" I didn't know I had it in me to speak to a woman like that— but here it is... the new me.

After more time and tears pass, there is a loud rumble outside and I assume it's his fucking truck roaring home. It's confirmed when she mutters something about that being him.

"Great, you want to behave, right?"

"Yes," she says, pitifully.

"Then just lie there and wait for him to come in before you so much as move a muscle. Got it?"

"Yes."

THREE

Jimmy's key hits the lock and the sound is like music to my ears.

I am in position behind the door so I can get the jump on him before he knows something is up. And it goes exactly like I think it will, I wrap my arm around his neck and force the blade of my knife into his throat. He stops instantly, and I shit you not, begins to shake uncontrollably.

I hadn't gotten a good look at him at all during our first introduction, but he fits what I figured a shithead who hides behind a door, talking a big game would look.

He is about 5'10"– a few inches shorter than I am, and plump with a round belly. How he got a girl like the one on the table is beyond me. He doesn't seem to have much to offer her, not even the ability to quiet her doubts about his love for her.

I push him forward into the dining room and he instantly sees his girl sprawled out on the table, she is crying again— of course, which I'm sure she wouldn't be doing if she knew how it affected me.

"Starla!" he shouts.

I direct him to the only non- broken chair in the dining room, it becomes quite difficult to maneuver him around as he tries desperately to escape, although I'm not sure if it's to save himself or Starla. Doesn't really matter either way.

"Sit the fuck on the chair," I push the blade deeper into his skin and the droplets of blood flowing out alarm poor Starla. She squeals and cries more openly now.

Jimmy does as he's told and I'm able to secure him without too much more trouble.

After he is strapped in at the ankles and his hands behind his back, I take a deep breath to organize my thoughts.

"How the fuck did you get this girl?" I ask, seriously wondering.

"Fuck you," is all he says.

"Do you remember me?"

"Yea, you're that pussy on the bike that ate my smoke."

The look that crosses my face has him regretting his words instantly, seeing his girl turned into a tablecloth and being trapped to a chair himself did nothing compared to the crazed look in my eyes. I make sure he watches his mouth in the future by hitting him square in the jaw. The startling crack is almost too loud in the small room.

"So, I'm sure you may be surprised to see me here tonight, although you couldn't be too shocked that someone would hate you enough to do what I'm about to do."

"What are you about to do?"

The fear in his eyes is laughable; he was such a big talker when I showed up to his door last week but nothing about him presently seems to help support those words. You'd think a man who would cut someone off and risk their life would at least be strong enough to fight back if such things were to bring upon a physical altercation.

Poor fuck isn't gonna know what hit him. He's one of those men who think they're big and bad until someone big and bad comes along and proves him wrong.

I'm glad to be of service.

I walk over to Starla, who has been wide- eyed, watching the shit hit the fan and I run my hand up the inside of her thigh, which has the intended effect on Jimmy, he struggles against the tape. I go higher still, only stopping when I touch the warmth of her pussy lips.

She gasps, letting poor Jimmy know I've hit home.

"So, Jimmy, you said to me last time we met that the reason for doing those things to me was because you wanted to. And if I were going to use your logic, I'd have to say that what is going to happen here tonight is what *I* want.

That must seem fair to your flawless way of thinking. Am I right?"

"That's not what I meant. You can't have my girl because you want her. She doesn't want you."

"Oh, I'm sure of that right now, but what's say we try and change that?"

He's confused, but he laughs anyway. "She will never want you, you're just some loser biker who comes into people's houses and acts like a fucking dick.

"I'm about to act like a dick, a big dick that's about to get into a nice tight hole." I push my fingers inside her pussy and they glide in easily. I don't want to get excited thinking about her being wet for me, but my cock doesn't know the difference or care for that matter— a wet hole is a wet hole to him.

I massage the inside of her, working my fingers the way I know women love. Her eyes are closed tight, not like she's enjoying it, but like she is trying to go somewhere that this isn't happening. I couldn't care any less where her mind goes, so long as this hole stays here.

"Does he make you come, Starla?" I ask.

Her eyes fly open and then go right for Jimmy. "Yes." She says in his defense.

"How does he do it? Like this?" I fuck her harder with my fingers slapping noises fill the room. Her nipples harden as she obviously becomes aroused.

"Jimmy, do you ever see her face look like this? Look at it, she fucking loves this."

"Fuck you, she doesn't want you, I already told you."

"Starla," my fingers stop. "Do you want me to keep going? Do you want me to make you come?"

She catches my eye through hooded lids and I know her answer without her speaking, so I continue. I move slower this time, rubbing her clit with my thumb while I push my fingers deep inside of her.

Her breathing is becoming loud, I know the second it's going to push her over the edge, and that's when I stop.

She whines, trying to mask it with a belated coughing sound.

"Starla, I'm going to need you to tell me how that compares to Jimmy. Can he read your body like that? Does he know the second your little pussy is going to come?"

"Of course I do!"

"Is he telling the truth? Be honest, he's a grown man, he needs to know if he's doing it right. It would only serve you to tell him that he needs to change something in his technique."

She bites her lip nervously and I know then that Jimmy doesn't know a thing about this poor girl's body or how it works.

"Do you have to fake it for him?"

She shakes her head, obviously lying.

"So, he knows what you sound like when you have an orgasm, a real one that lights your insides on fire and makes you scream?"

She nods.

"Let's see about that."

"Get the fuck away from her," he spits.

I get down on my knees in front of her, running my fingers up her slit parting them as I go, burying my mouth into her pussy.

She yelps.

He growls.

And I lick.

At a frantic pace, I make short work of it. Letting go, she begins moaning and thrusting against my mouth, taking full advantage of my expert tongue and in only a few minutes, I hear that scream I was talking about. It lingers longer than I'm down there and by the look on Jimmy's face he's never heard it before, from the look on hers, after she's able to focus on the present moment, she's never either.

"You're welcome." I say to her.

She blushes, a real full-on blush, as if she's embarrassed that she liked what I just did. I can't blame her; she went pretty wild just then and in front of her beloved Jimmy, no less.

"So, Jimmy, you're sure you've heard those sounds from her before?" I'm mocking him and he knows it.

"Fuck you. She's a slut anyway."

"Oh, I doubt that, she didn't even look at me in the diner when I met her there last week."

He looks at her for confirmation but she doesn't meet his eyes.

"Whatever." He pouts.

"You ready for round two, love?"

She looks panicked and excited all in one brief expression.

"I want to fuck you. I want to tear that pussy apart." I come around the table to where her wrists are bound then take her hand and press it up against the swell of my cock. "You feel that? You want that inside of you, stretching you wide?"

Jimmy hisses but says nothing.

I unzip the fly of my jeans and take my cock out, wrapping her fingers around it. She squeezes it of her own volition and I can feel it jump with excitement. "I want you to tell Jimmy that you'd like to fuck me."

"I can't."

"I want you to say those words right now or I won't do it."

She hesitates, but only for a moment, "I want to fuck you," she says, barely above a whisper but I hear it.

Those words hit me right in the dick. "I said I want you to tell Jimmy." My hips start moving, fucking her hand.

"I want to fuck him," she says after a full minute.

"You don't have to do it. He said he wouldn't fuck you." Jimmy is whining now, his voice pleading with her to put a stop to this.

"Is my cock bigger than Jimmy's?" I ask, knowing the answer already, I'm bigger than average, it would be a surprise to find Jimmy hung like me.

She doesn't verbalize her answer but her head nods, telling me I'm right.

"Fuck you, Starla; you know I'm not small." He's pouting, I'm crushing his poor little ego that he thought was big and strong enough to withstand anything. And *that* is exactly the route I wanted to take; nothing ruins a man like him more than a bruised ego.

I take myself out of her hand and come around again to her pussy. It's definitely wet now, there is a small drop slipping out and running toward her asshole. I intercept it with my finger and walk over to Jimmy to show him. "You ever make her pussy so wet it drips?"

I want nothing more than to make him eat it, so I do, I pinch his cheeks together and squeeze them hard as I paint his lips with her juice. "She taste good?"

His reaction is priceless and it makes me laugh.

I am still laughing as I wrap my cock with a condom from my wallet, feeling grateful there is still one in there. I look at her pussy again before I enter her, its glistening. She is soaked. "You want this, don't you, Starla?"

She nods, unashamed now of her dirty little wanton ways.

I slide my cock up and down her slit, distributing the juice around for easier penetration before going for it. I push hard into her, my balls smashing into her ass. And, no joke, I feel her constrict and come around my girth. I fuck her hard before she can come down, pounding straight through her, burying the entirety of my swollen cock into her tight pussy.

She's making sounds only wild animals could decipher and I stop myself before I come, regretfully pulling out of her. I admire her now swollen pink hole, having taken more of a pounding than she is used to, I'm sure it will be sore for days.

"Would you eat it again?" she begs.

Are you fucking kidding me?

I bend over and suck her puffy clit into my mouth and only seconds later, she's howling again.

I watch Jimmy, who despite being furious, is also strangely enthralled by what I'm doing to his girl. Possibly trying to pick up pointers he has no clue he'll never be able to use– as he will have no time left to practice his technique.

I come back up to Starla, "it's only fair that you reciprocate." I say, pushing my cock into her face. I pull it away before she can do anything though. "Do you want to hurt me or make me feel good?"

"I want to make you feel good." Her tongue darts out in search of my cock and I believe her so I let her have it. "Open wider."

She does as she's told and I push my dick into her mouth far enough to feel her tonsils. Her gag reflex kicks in and she begins to cough, I don't stop though, I couldn't even if I wanted to. I continue to fuck her as tears roll down her cheeks, thrusting as hard as I was doing inside of her pussy. Her teeth scrape a few times but I can tell she is trying to avoid that.

"I'm gonna come but I don't want you to swallow it... I want you to hold it in your mouth... do you understand?" I say in between pumps.

She nods as best she can and with a few more thrusts, I let loose inside of her mouth. I slow my pace until I know it's empty, letting her milk it completely before pulling my cock from her mouth with a pop.

"You have all my warm come in there?"

She nods, cheeks puffed out to accommodate the load.

"Keep it in there until I tell you, got it?"

Another nod.

I cut the tape from her wrists and help her sit up. She has a question in her eyes that her mouth is too full to ask.

"Now, love, I need you to spit that right into Jimmy's face." I whisper into her ear.

She looks at me pleadingly, begging me to not make her do it.

"I want you to show him what a good girl you are for me." –this I say so Jimmy can hear, it confuses him not having been privy to the earlier statement.

Her head nods barely and I get excited to see his face when it hits him.

She takes a deep breath through her nose and holy fuck that girl can spit; she sprays the entirety of what was in her mouth right across his face. Thick gooey come landing in gobs on his cheeks and mouth.

"Good girl," I say into her ear. "I like you."

She licks her lips, collecting what she can from them and then spits a second time at him, keeping her eyes trained on me.

"Is that your way of telling me you like me, too?" I ask.

She nods.

"Tell Jimmy that you like me."

"I like him."

Jimmy doesn't dare respond, I'm sure mostly out of fear that some of my come dribbling down his lips will make it into his mouth if he does, but I can see the hurt in his eyes– he really may have love for her after all.

"Starla, you told me that Jimmy might not love you. Do you still think that's true?"

She nods.

"Is that the only reason you let me do what you said I could do tonight?"

"No."

"Why did you let me do all those things to you?"

"It felt nice."

"Jimmy, do you love Starla?"

He nods.

"Use your words, Jimmy," I say.

"Yes." His mouth opens just enough to let a dribble fall between his lips. He tries to spit it out but I am sure not all of it leaves his mouth before he seals it back up.

"This man just took a giant load to his face, which you spit onto it– I might add, and he just said he loved you, risking my nut's entrance into his mouth. I'd say that is love. Wouldn't you?"

"Yes."

"So, now you know he loves you, right?"

"Yes, I do."

"Do you love him?"

"I did, but I don't think I do now."

"Really? What's changed?"

"You... maybe?" She doesn't meet my eyes when she says it, instead she looks down at her folded hands on top of her lap.

"You are telling me that a man sneaks into your house, takes you from your bed and straps you to a table, tortures your boyfriend's poor little ego and *that* man is what changes your mind about you're loving live- in boyfriend?"

"Yea, I guess so." She looks at me finally, a question in her eyes, as if she's asking me for permission to concur.

"Prove it," I say.

"I...I don't know how I would do that."

"Oh, I'm sure we could come up with some way for you to prove it." I pretend to think; really, I already know what I want to ask her to do. It would torment poor Jimmy for the last few moments of his life. But I want to... so I will.

"What? Anything." She begs for me to tell her.

Perfect.

"I need you to tell me first if you'd be willing to do all these things, we did here tonight all the fucking time. Let me fuck you, as I want when I want. Would *you* want that?"

"More than anything." She practically looks ready to jump on my dick again right now. I just rocked this girl's world and turned it upside down. I knew I was good but surely, I can't be *this* good.

"That's what I wanted to hear. Now, what I want from you to prove to me you want me over Jimmy is to help me out here tonight... even more than you already have." I indicate with a nod of my head in the direction of her pussy just what I meant by that.

She pulls her bottom lip into her mouth and it makes me want to bite it. "Just name it."

Jimmy finally risks more come- filled words to plead with her. "Starla, stop this." His mouth closes quickly.

She doesn't look at him though, and I know that I have this in the bag. This girl would do anything for another of those screaming orgasms.

I walk over to her and stand between her thighs, still spread wide by her restraints, and push my fingers back into her pussy. She melts instantly, grinding hard against my hand. I pull her face close and whisper into her ear, "I came here tonight to kill Jimmy, you know that right?"

She nods.

"I want you to help me with that." My fingers work faster, pushing her over the edge.

"Ok," she squeals as she climaxes.

"Jimmy, Starla has something to tell you, it looks like she'll need a second to recover first though." I laugh at his reaction.

"Starla," I turn her face to look at me, her eyes slowly open, regaining her composure finally. "I want you to tell Jimmy what you just agreed to do."

"I said," she looks back at me, unable to hold his eyes. "I told him I'd help him with what he came here to do tonight."

"Tell him what that is, Starla." I say, as if I'm talking to a toddler.

"He came here to kill you," she blurts out quickly.

"What the fuck? You were going to kill me because I cut you off? That's the stupidest shit I've ever heard!" He no longer cares that my salty fluid might still be tasted. I take it as a sign that he finally knows I'm serious about what's happening here tonight.

"You never know how your actions will affect people. A simple apology hand wave could have saved us all the trouble of what has gone on here this evening."

"But…"

I don't let him finish; it wouldn't help his case anyway. I turn my attention back to Starla, "I'm going to cut the tape away from your legs now. Are you sure about this?"

I know that there is a chance she could turn on me—be planning something shifty to try to take me out instead, and I'm prepared for that, in fact, I'm anticipating it. It would be really fucked up for her to be on my side after what I've put her through today and what with the history they share together, I'm the interloper.

She, however, nods indicating that she is, in fact, ready to kill her boyfriend.

I crouch down and cut the tape away from her feet; she hops off the table and stumbles on wobbly legs from the time she has spent immobile on the table.

I push the 6- inch knife into her hand and instruct her to cut him.

She looks me right in the eyes and nods.

I can see a hint of nervousness in hers and I can't tell if it's from the thought of killing him or the thought of killing me to save him. Either way, I let go of the blade and watch curiously to see how this will play out, pulling my gun from my hip holster for my own protection.

She does the thing I expect least, she walks up to him, and puts it right into his gut. It only goes in about half way or so, she must not know how hard it is to push a knife into someone. Fuck, I don't either, I've never done it before. I am absolutely shocked by this action.

As is he. He must have been aware that it could have played out the other way and worked in his favor, probably even assumed I could not have been on the winning side of this ordeal.

"Do it again." I say, and fuck; I'm so fucking hard right now, I could rip the zipper from my jeans.

She does as she's told; covering her hand in blood as she removes the knife, there's a weird suction sound as she yanks it out of him. This time when she pushes it into him, she buries it up to the hilt. She turns and looks at me for approval. I give it to her with a slow smile.

"One more time, baby, this time look him right in the eye and tell him it's over."

"Jimmy, it's over."

I'm sure he'd have something to say right now but he is in a lot of pain and the screaming he's doing is occupying his vocal cords.

She gets the knife out and back in swiftly this time, her confidence growing.

I call her over to me and let Jimmy bleed out of the holes she has made. "Listen, I'm going to be honest with you, I really didn't think you were going to do that. I'm really shocked that you did that for me."

She smiles, proud of herself.

"I have met a lot of women, some single, some married or in some way 'involved' I would love to find a girl who is ready to settle down and do nothing but try her hardest to make me happy. Some pretty blonde waitress I could sweep off her feet and take away to a fairytale life." I tuck a strand of hair behind her ear.

"Really?" she seems so happy to hear those words.

"Really," I nod. "I'm a stickler for loyalty, love."

Her smile goes wider.

"I need a girl who is loyal; it is the only thing I ask of anyone. And what you've done here tonight has me questioning whether you are loyal."

Her face falls a little as she waits for me to finish.

"I think you're lacking in the loyalty department. Fuck, I'd be worried the whole time we were together that some douche bag would sneak into our house and fuck you silly and you'd be stabbing me next. And that just won't do." I pull the trigger and her sad looking face explodes as the bullet tears through her head.

I turn my attention back to Jimmy before her body even hits the floor. "I hope you saw that, Jimmy, my friend."

His eyes flutter as he struggles to look at me and when he finally does, I pull the knife out slowly from his wound and drag it across his throat, finishing the job his lady started.

That went better than I could have ever hoped; I got exactly what I wanted. Jimmy's stupid philosophy about doing shit just because he wanted to has really given me a new outlook on life.

I hope that you can get all the things you want in life, as well.

The end

Devour

THEY CAME TO MY DOOR AND I KNEW RIGHT AWAY THAT THAT WAS IT. I KNEW THAT DAY WAS COMING AND STILL MADE NO ATTEMPT TO HIDE WHAT HAD BEEN DONE.

THE POLICE ASK THEIR QUESTIONS AND I DON'T ANSWER. MY ANSWERS WOULDN'T MAKE THEM UNDERSTAND… MAYBE YOU WILL.

1

Today...

"Mrs. Winthrop, I need you to initial at the bottom of this page, stating that you've heard and understand your rights as we've gone over them."

I can't for the life of me understand how I let myself end up here, how this cold dark room in the police station is where I've spent the night, interrogated by two asshole cops who look dumb enough to pee against the wind. I wish they would, it could give me a smile that would last a lifetime. Instead, their cocky, shit eating grins are going to be ingrained in my mind.

I feel so tired. I wish this whole night was over and that I was sleeping, whether it be in my own bed or some shitty mattress they set up for people here— I wouldn't care either way. I would sell my soul to the devil, right now, for a three-minute nap. But that's how they do things around here— I've seen enough television to know that they like the suspect to get so tired they start blurting shit out and confessing.

I can't say that I won't do that, but I haven't yet. So, there's that.

"Ma'am, please, I just have to get this initialed, it's a formality, you're not confessing to anything by doing so." This is from Mr. Good Cop, he's been pretending to be on my side the whole night, telling his partner to ease up on me and offering to get me a glass of water. Again, I've seen this before. T.V. shows these days really give a lot away about how cops operate, they must get some old retired dudes to tell all their secrets and the rest of them are too dumb to switch up their routines.

I know it doesn't mean I'm confessing to anything—and I won't be. I just don't want to do anything they ask of me; I don't want to interact one minute with these dicks. They've gotten to choose the setting for this little powwow they want to have with me and I will obtain the upper hand somehow in this matter. Even if it pisses them off. Let's see how long Mr. Good Cop can keep up his role.

2

In the beginning...

Let me start by saying we had an unconventional start to our relationship, I met Matthew in high school, I was a senior that year, and he was my English teacher.

I had shit going on at home and was contemplating dropping out, getting a job and getting the fuck out of there. That was, until I laid my eyes on his beautiful blue ones. My god, I can see them in my memories just as vivid as they were back then. I think I fell in love with him that very instant.

It took him a few weeks for him to notice me, but I knew the moment he did, I saw him see me and then there was this jolt in my soul that would forever change me.

He swept me off my feet and never set me down.

One day after class, he told me that he needed to see me, and my heart swooned. I had imagined those words coming from his mouth every time our eyes met, which was frequently, both of us getting lost in the others for what felt like hours, but really only a few moments would pass before he'd look away. Which would send me into a path of self-doubt, thinking I'd imagined the intensity of our connection, but it would happen again and wash all of that away. He had a way of reassuring me in a second flat.

I sat in my seat and awaited further instructions from him, petrified that what he would say to me would not be that of my fantasies; rather, it would shatter the illusion I had of us. I had to know though, for good or bad, I was ready.

"Please come here, Collette." He sat back into his chair and waited for my stumbling legs to move me forward.

I sat in the seat directly across from him, the desk at his side, our knees practically touching. My hands shook, waiting for my life to change.

"Can I speak frankly with you?"

Oh, *fuck*, this was not going to go in the direction of what I wanted, he was about to tell me that I'd crossed the line and made him uncomfortable, that I was imagining the shit between us.

Still, I nodded, readying myself for the biggest rejection of my life, unable to look at him as he took a deep breath to speak.

"You are a very beautiful girl."

I closed my eyes tightly, afraid that I'd say something so stupid that I would fuck it up somehow by actually acknowledging him. I swallowed my words so hard it hurt my throat, my heart beat so fast I thought it would pump right out of my chest.

"I..." he put his hand on my thigh, just below the hem of my short skirt, well above my knee. "I haven't been able to stop thinking about you." His thumb rubbed my goose-bumped flesh, slipping under the fabric.

I dared, then, to look at him; the ferociousness in his eyes sent a heat through me to my bones. I'd never been more on fire in my life. I parted my legs as my way to confirm that we were on the same page, my voice still unable to speak.

He looked hungry as he pushed his hand between my thighs. "Do you want me to touch you like this?"

All I could do was nod.

"Has anyone ever touched you here like this?"

I cleared my throat, hoping my words would come out stronger than the puddle of lust I felt. "I'm not a virgin, but nobody has touched me like this before."

His fingers rubbed against my panties, sending shivers down my body. I couldn't hold back the whimper that creeped forward as he moved them rhythmically.

"Collette," he waited until I looked at him before continuing. "Do you want me to be inside of you?"

"Uh huh."

"Stand up."

Oh, fuck, I couldn't remember how to use my legs, my knees were so weak, but I had managed, after pulling my attention away from him for a moment, to focus on the task.

"I look at you sometimes and I think of how good it would feel to be inside of you— buried so deep that I'd get lost in you." He pulled my body against his and wrapped his fingers in my hair, pulling my face upward to his, his kiss so hard it almost hurt, but I welcomed the pain— it took some of the focus away from the throbbing ache inside me.

I dragged my hands across his body, touching him everywhere. The fantasies I'd had of him were nothing compared to the way he felt in real life.

He was only a few years older than I was, this was his first-year teaching, but his hands knew what to do with my body. He took his time kissing me before progressing, and when he finally did, it excited me through to every nerve ending. I felt exhilarated when he slid his hand between us and into my panties. I'd come in only minutes.

He took my hand and placed it against the hardness in his pants, it felt so good to touch him there.

I was so naïve then, but in that moment, I felt just how it was supposed to be between two people. Unable to contain any ounce of dignity, and not caring to try, I got onto my knees, pulled his hardened cock out of his pants, and took it into my mouth.

I watched his face for his reaction to my efforts; I would never be able to forget just how excited he looked, moving my head in harmony with his bucking hips to get himself off. "I want you to taste me so bad, I want to fill your mouth up," he pulled my head away and left my mouth empty and hungry still. "But I need to be inside of you."

I thought I couldn't get more thrilled by anything at that point, but those words drove me crazy.

He lifted my feet up off the floor and directed me to sit on the edge of his desk, the very desk that had been a fixture in my dreams of him.

He spread my legs apart and sunk into me, I was so wet he was able to fill me in one attempt.

"Fuck, Collette, you feel even better than I thought you would, you're so fucking tight... and wet. I never want to leave here."

He moved slowly at first, and just when I'd thought I would die from his patience, he started to pound me, pushing harder and harder until I felt myself fall over the edge, crying out with my orgasm.

He wasn't done though, he slowed again, kissing me sweetly across my neck and down to my tits, after he'd lifted my shirt to expose them. I wasn't wearing a bra– I never did, he moaned his approval. "I didn't think you were wearing one, I've been lost in the sight of these hard little nipples since you walked in today." He took turns with them, biting each one hard and then sucking them into his mouth, taking the sting out of it.

He gathered me into his arms and shoved my back against the wall behind us. He continued fucking me until I almost couldn't bear another second, and that's when he came, he filled my pussy with his warm come and it felt like heaven to know a part of him would be inside of me even after his cock was gone.

He put me on my feet and situated my panties to cover me again. "Are you on the pill, Collette?"

I nodded.

"Good girl, I won't be able to come anywhere else after feeling you around me."

"Mr. Winthrop?"

He leaned into my ear, "after having my cock inside that sweet little mouth of yours, you'll need to call me Matthew, unless of course you'd like to keep this more professional?" He sucked my ear into his mouth, nibbling the lobe.

I gave some thought to what it would be like after that day, and professional was the furthest thing from my mind. "Matthew?"

"Yes, Collette?" His kisses didn't stop.

"I need to get home, I'm so sorry, but my mother is strict and she'll be wondering where I am if I'm not home soon." I looked up at the big clock on the wall and realized she'd probably already be expecting me.

"Ok, Collette, you may go, but I'll need to see you tomorrow, tell your mother you have a project to work on, have her call me if she needs verification."

"Ok."

I did just that, and we were able to keep our relationship a secret for the rest of the year– through to graduation, fucking every chance we got, risking his career every time we did.

And he was never concerned about it, he told me he wanted me more than his job, he wanted me more than *anything*. I, myself, couldn't stop if I tried, my body was addicted to his, craving him only moments after having him.

I left my mother's house the day of graduation, moving into his condo across town and I never looked back. We were married in December that same year.

I couldn't think without him near, wasn't able to function unless he was inside of me, and the same could be said for him, he was just as hungry for me.

We spent those first few years in a sort of limbo, dividing time between the 'real world' and the next time we could fuck. We spent every moment together fucking until sleep took us for the night, waking to do it all over again. We were like nymphos, craving more and more of each other. It never grew old, I never lost that need for him and I could see how ravenous he always was for me.

But, after the accident things were not the same. They weren't happy times anymore.

3

Today...

"Mrs. Winthrop, despite the fact that you refuse to acknowledge that you've been read your rights we still must proceed with questioning. We have it on video when Detective Patterson read them to you." This is coming from 'bad cop'– even his tone is condescending.

I still say nothing; I don't want these assholes to even know I can speak, let alone hearing what I would have to say on this matter.

"Ma'am, we found your husband dead. Your silence is confusing us, if you had nothing to do with his death, why won't you speak up so we can clear you of any wrong doing?"

Sadly, me speaking would not rule me out. I didn't kill my husband, not directly, anyway.

"We found him in his wheelchair, in your house, with you at home. Surely, you knew he was dead, it looks like it has been weeks since his passing. The worst you could be charged with is 'accessory after the fact', being that you knew he was dead and didn't report it, that's only if you knew nothing of how he came to die.

"I could overlook that and not charge you if you can prove you weren't at fault, but the only way to do that, is for you to speak with us. That's a deal I wouldn't pass up, your husband is badly decomposing and the smell is noxious, we have no doubt you knew he was in there festering. So bad, in fact, that it's hard for the M.E. to confirm cause of death just yet, but trust me, Mrs. Winthrop, he will find that out. And it would behoove you to help us in the meantime or reap the consequences your silence brings."

Wow, that was quite a spiel; I'll take my chances with my silence. They do say it's golden.

I stare at him for more time than my eyes want to focus, but I want to show him how steadfast I am in keeping my silence. Not even to ask for an attorney. I have nothing to say.

The knock on the door concludes our staring contest, and I'm glad for the interruption, until I hear the words that I know mean they've found what I'd been waiting for them to see.

Some guy, I've not had the 'pleasure' of meeting, peeks his head in and glances my way before quickly averting his eyes to look at the detective. "Sir, there's something you need to see." He avoids my eyes on the way out.

4

The accident...

Matthew was coming home from work one night, the fifteen- minute drive he would usually spend watching me via his phone on a webcam he had set up at home when he couldn't be nearby. I would get started before he walked in, putting on a show for him so he could make the drive better and build the anticipation.

I would do a little strip tease for him or fuck myself with his choice of toys, this particular day he wanted to watch me finger myself; it was his favorite. Occasionally, he would join in and jack off, knowing he would be ready for me again when he walked through the door.

I remember being so lost in my show for him I hadn't realized he was no longer responding. A lost connection was nothing new. The minutes ticked by until I realized too much time passed. I stopped immediately and called him.

Voicemail.

Fuck.

I became instantly worried, panic hit me in the gut like a fist. I knew something had happened to him. I felt it in my core. I paced the floor until I got a call, the call I knew was coming, not from Matthew, from the hospital.

"Mrs. Winthrop, this is Kate, I'm a nurse at First Presbyterian Hospital, your husband has been brought in, he's in surgery right now to repair some of the damage resulting from a car accident he was in earlier tonight."

"Thank you, I'll be there as soon as I can."

"I doubt he'll be ready for visitors, but if he asks, I'll tell him you're on your way here. Do you need the address?"

"No, I have it. Thank you."

I had no emotion; I had known something had happened—at least I knew then that he was alive. I could deal with anything else but death, which I could not have gotten over. That, whatever shape he was in, I could deal with that. I would make sure he was ok; I would help him heal from that.

Getting to the hospital that night took more out of me than anything I had ever faced. Dread weighted me down as I trudged along to the waiting room the nurse directed me.

He was still in surgery, although they said he would make it, most of the damage was to his legs and back. They had to rush him in with a specialist to remove some of the swelling that was happening on his spine. They were worried about nerve damage, which they said, could lead to paralysis.

After he got out of surgery, almost eight hours later, the doctor came out to talk to me; I knew it was bad by the look on his face. The words that followed were as bad as they had feared. He would be a paraplegic; they had determined that most if not all feeling was gone from his chest down, narrowly escaping becoming quadriplegic. The doctor told me if the nerves damaged were slightly higher, he wouldn't have had control over his arms.

I sobbed there, in that waiting room, for hours before being told I could go back in and see him. I dreaded the sight of him, or more so, him seeing me for the first time, my pity would be evident across my face. I've never been one to be able to hide my emotions, my reaction would set a precedent for how this would go, how he would see himself through my eyes from that day forward.

I didn't want him to feel anything but loved, so I set my face in the most loving way I could and I opened his door, and my god, it was the worst thing I could see. I almost ran out of the room— for his sake not mine. I couldn't let him know how sorry I felt for him, how badly I wished it hadn't happened. That was our life now and I wanted him to think I was strong enough to handle it.

Luckily, he was not looking at the door as I came through, I was able to fix my expression and call to him before he looked at me.

"Matthew..."

"Hey, love." He sounded like himself, even if he didn't quite look like himself, not that there was damage to be seen, but just the machines he had to be hooked up to and the way that I could tell it wasn't the same man lying in that bed, my heart was breaking.

"Has the doctor been through your prognosis with you?" I didn't really want to be the one to tell him, but I couldn't sit here another second not knowing whether he knew.

"Yea, seems I really fucked myself up." Those are the same words he would have used before this calamity, but the inflection of those words was different, they didn't hold the same humor.

"Do you need me to get you anything?" They said he'd need a while to recuperate, a lot of internal damage took place in that car.

"Could you just sit with me? I've missed you more than I thought possible." Those words melted me to the core, maybe not all was lost and maybe I could find him in there again.

I did sit with him that night, for hours, in silence, neither of us knowing quite what to say.

5

Home...

We had gotten home from the hospital, where every moment I could feel things becoming awkward and strained, however that did not measure up to how it was once I had gotten him back.

I had put all my hope into that moment that that time would be behind us and right away, I could feel that things had not changed.

Almost a month spent getting him ready for that day so he could return, but he was no longer the man I had married, a new version of the man I had fallen head over heels in love with had snuck into him, wearing his skin, changing him into a fucked-up version of my beloved.

"Matthew, I got everything set up for you, everything is wheelchair accessible now, but if you need help, I'm right here for you."

"Thanks," he grumbled.

I could tell he was angry, although I couldn't pinpoint if it was at me or the predicament, he was in. I blamed myself for his accident; I didn't know how he could *not*. There was a lot of guilt building inside of me for what happened that night, thoughts running wild inside my head, circling around, all of the things that could have happened differently; they played on a continuous loop through my conscience.

Had we not become so engaged in the sex- play he may not have lost focus and driven head first into that telephone pole, which, as luck would have it, hadn't stopped the car's momentum, he flipped the jeep countless times after.

With no witnesses on the scene, it was hard to know for sure what happened. It had knocked him unconscious and it was a while before someone stopped to phone police, his nerves were dying while he lay there waiting. I was the source of the distraction and my guilt wouldn't let me forget that.

I regretted my decision to not go out and check on him after I had realized he was late and possibly in trouble. I had never really been clear headed in times of stress or worry, that was always Matthew's job.

I went about making him as comfortable as possible, bending over backwards to accommodate him. Going forward, I chose not to ask him if he did blame me for what had become of him.

I could only serve him for my penance– every meal, every bath, every time he had a fucking phantom itch, I was there to ease the burden.

We had settled into that routine quickly– me his servant, and him the poor man who had lost the ability to function from the chest down. Luckily, he hadn't lost the use of his arms, although sometimes the nerves inside them made it very painful to use them.

I was just grateful for his life– he, perhaps, was not. I knew he would have preferred death over what he got that night. He said sometimes, that he wished his broken and useless body would wither and die, but the doctors all had hope for him to have a normal life– whatever the fuck that was.

Days went by, I tried so hard to love this new man, the grouchy, and often times, mean and cold shell that my sweet Matthew used to wear, this stranger had taken over and begun using it.

The night I knew it was over for sure was about three years after the accident; I was trying, as I often did, to satisfy the man he was in bed. He still had a voracious appetite for sex. He had the sex drive of the man I remembered late at night in my fantasies, the man he was before. He said he couldn't feel it like he used to but his cock worked and, in his words, "it's the only thing that could get up from this fucking chair". I, being the dutiful wife to a paralyzed man who had become so low and depressed, wanted nothing more than to satisfy him.

This night I lay him back onto the bed, rubbing his legs to stimulate the blood flow, sometimes it helped, and I always tried my hardest to do everything I could to help ease him through that time of our lives. I still loved him, despite the miserable man making himself at home inside my husband.

We had always been at our best when we were fucking, I knew we were meant to be from the first time he had taken me inside his classroom, the chemistry had always been there. It had fizzled a little after the chair, but not so much so that it wasn't still the hottest sex. Or so *I* thought.

I put on a cute little tee and some barely- there undies, slid up his body to kiss him, then made my way down his chest to his hardening cock, he was still so responsive. I took it onto my mouth and sucked it hard, making sure to keep my eyes on him the way I knew he liked.

I pulled my panties over to the side and sunk down onto his slick cock, grinding on the top of his lap. He groped me, grabbing my tits– his favorite part of me.

"You feel so good, baby." I told him, completely lost in the feeling. "Rub my pussy for me." It's something he loved to hear me say, it always turned him on to have me hungry for his touch.

I saw something flash in his eyes, something I hadn't noticed before, I saw hatred, it had me regretting my words immediately, although I couldn't understand why. "You need to make sure you're getting me off, too." His words were so full of anger.

My chin quivered, holding back tears that were right on the edge of falling out. I hadn't realized how selfish I might have sounded.

"Of course, Matthew." I made my best attempt at a smile, but I knew it wasn't a success.

"Get off of me, you whore. You don't even care about me; you only want more and more. I can't even feel *anything* and you want to feel *everything*– you greedy slut."

I ran from our room, leaving him naked on our bed. I couldn't bring myself to come back in for hours. I sat in the bathtub, the hot water turning cold, crying all the tears I had been holding in so I could show a brave face to my husband.

I began to feel bad for leaving, those words were harsh, meaner than I've heard him ever speak, but I realized he was frustrated and what kind of wife would I be if I couldn't support him in his condition. Our vows very clearly stated that it was for better or worse, sickness and health. And although this wasn't quite sickness– it was *worse*, and I had made him a promise. So, I stood and dressed, then made my way back into our room to tend to him.

I feel utterly embarrassed to say the next part, but I need to explain the progression his anger was taking.

I walked in the door, tail between my legs, ready to apologize, but what I was met with was him fuming. "Get the fuck over here, Collette." He pushed his words through gritted teeth.

I walked to him hesitantly. Against my better judgement, I sat next to him on the bed. He reached up and grabbed me hard by the hair. "You think it's ok to leave me in here to fucking piss on myself?"

Shame flushed through me, radiating more pain inside me than his hand fisted inside my hair. "I'm so sorry." I truly felt so bad for causing that to happen.

"You want to make me feel like a piece of shit? You want to degrade me and show me that I'm scum? Well, it fucking worked. I pissed all over."

He pulled my head down and I could do nothing but follow him, he tugged hard until my face was level with the wet mattress and he shoved my face into it. He didn't let me up for long enough that I began to panic, I couldn't breathe, which made me gasp, forcing the urine in through my nose and mouth and into my lungs.

His arms were the only part of him that hadn't been deteriorating, they'd actually gotten stronger from using his chair. I couldn't escape, not without ripping the hair from my head. So, I just lay there, struggling to breathe, feeling that was going to be my end. I was going to die there with my face shoved in a puddle of my husband's piss.

I couldn't help but think it was my fault, so when I forgave him for it, I thought that I could avoid things like that happening again if only I was good enough. But no matter what I did, it wasn't good enough, not right enough. I still suffered his wrath. Where before the accident he could see no wrong in me, afterward he could see no right.

It broke my heart, shattered it to pieces on an almost daily basis– until I had no heart at all. It was an unrecognizable thing that stopped feeling and had become something that just pumped blood. I couldn't find an ounce of compassion for him. I couldn't find a flicker of love.

On our tenth anniversary I had realized I'd spent more time with him in this condition, (I'm not speaking of the wheelchair– I could have loved him forever in whatever shape I was blessed to have him in) I mean the cold, heartless, and hating man he had become after. The weight shifted inside of me when I realized I'd been with him happy less time than I'd been with him miserable and mistreated.

I felt something take hold inside of me, some vengeful thoughts that hated him for taking the man that I loved and morphing him into this man– if I could call him a man, a real man wouldn't do the things he had done to the woman he supposedly loved.

6

After that dawned on me, I couldn't help him anymore, I couldn't keep waiting around for him to become something else– the man he was before. I felt I had given him enough time to change and become accommodated to his new life. He'd taken enough from me and I was done giving.

I went about my duties as if I was a nurse; I made sure he had everything he needed: food, shelter, bathroom, showers. Everything else fell away and he didn't ask why. He did not attempt to inquire and I gave no answers to him.

On this particular day, he had taken it upon himself to get out of bed alone; he had done it on occasion with my supervision– he really had become quite strong and self-reliant. It would have been impressive if I still cared.

I heard the crash from the kitchen, the walls shook as if a bomb had gone off, and I ran so fast into the room. He was lying on the floor in a crumpled heap.

It's hard enough for me to maneuver him when he is in his chair or on the bed, it is nearly impossible for me to deadlift him off the floor. I tried and tried until the sweat was mixing with the tears streaming from my eyes; he called me names, made me feel awful, and blamed me for that happening, saying that I had left his chair unlocked.

I felt like I wanted to curl up into a ball and drown my pain in a big bottle of some mind- numbing alcohol. Instead, I took a deep breath and heaved him up until he could grab the arms of his chair and help me the rest of the way.

I practically fell on top of him as I released his weight and plopped him down, having exerted all my strength. I regretted it instantly as he used his favorite move– grabbing me by the hair– it incapacitated me right away.

He didn't speak, his breath was coming as hard as mine, but he hadn't exhausted all his energy, he still had some reserved for my face, which he struck repeatedly until I couldn't feel my head, it was swollen and bleeding freely from more than one gash, swelling my eyes shut almost immediately.

There was so much blood coming from my face that I hadn't noticed he was also hurt. I didn't notice until that night, when I undressed him to shower, that he had cut his back on something left on the floor. It was a fairly deep laceration and by the time I found it, it had not closed.

I put him on the bathroom chair and sat on the toilet seat to tend to it.

He seemed really annoyed at me for neglecting to find it earlier, like I wasn't busy enough with my own shit.

With my eyes still swollen shut, I attempted to clean his wound. The anger in me was growing, he didn't feel his pain and I was struggling to overcome mine. I was growing resentful, even more so after having to care for him while he was the cause of mine. It didn't seem fair.

I wiped the blood without a care; he, of course, didn't feel it either way, so to get back at him, I didn't do it nicely.

I wanted to gouge him, dig my finger inside of his cut, to make him feel it and, before I could stop myself, did. I pushed my finger along the incision and I felt vindication, I felt stronger inflicting him with that. I didn't care that he couldn't feel it.

"Hurry the fuck up, how fucking long is this going to take you?" I hated him so much, I couldn't even respond.

I didn't care that he was impatient, I just pushed deeper into his flesh until blood poured out, dripping down his back. I crooked my finger and slide it between his skin and the meaty flesh underneath; it went easily, like I was skinning a chicken breast. I did that around the perimeter of the cut. My hands were shaking, and the excitement of the mutilation gave me quite an exhilarating rush.

I slowed my breathing and calmed myself so I could carry on, cleaning and bandaging the cut quickly after I was done. He was none the wiser and I had felt great. It almost made up for what he had done to my face.

Almost.

I slept great that night, lying next to him with my little secret keeping me company.

7

Today...

"We found some questionable marks on your husband's body. Before we get started with those things, do you care to explain what you think they might be?" he walks through the door asking, setting down a manila folder, which I assume to be photos of what he's talking about.

    I say nothing; nothing could explain what they have found. I can't explain why I did those things, even to myself. How would I be able to form the words to say it aloud to him?

8

What they'd found in the photos...

It didn't stop there. His abuse or mine toward him. A part of me looked forward to him hurting me so I could retaliate. His evolution of abuse and mistreatment of me fed my own.

He would call me over to him, and expected me to stand there as I took his punches, and I would, I would stand there and let him hit me, let him manhandle me. After a while, he kept them aimed away from my face, learning quickly that I couldn't still leave the house to run the errands he demanded of me.

If he was able bodied, I'm sure rape would have followed, he had gotten hard on more than one occasion. It repulsed me— fed my hate.

I had waited for that beating to be over, then I went over to the kitchen sink, grabbing the first knife I saw, and jabbed it into his back. He hadn't even moved, so I'd done it again. Three times in total, three slits half an inch wide and about an inch deep, dripping blood down his shirt. I didn't

even bother bandaging them or the ones that would follow—
I couldn't necessarily let on about what was going on
literally behind his back.

At night, while he slept, I would push my fingers into
them or trace along the scars of the older ones.

Once, I had become so angry with him for sleeping so
peacefully, that I pushed a thumbtack into him; a blue one
that was on my nightstand, in and out to my heart's
content— the popping of his flesh each time I did it seemed
to calm me. There must have been hundreds of little tiny
little blood dots.

He woke me up that morning, not in the usual way,
not demanding I take him to the bathroom so he doesn't
have an accident, no, that morning I woke up being
suffocated with his hand. It surprised me more than
anything else that he got the leverage to prop himself up
into a position to do it. He rarely let on about his strength,
unless he was using it to abuse me. He had always
demanded I do everything for him, claiming he wasn't able
to himself.

I pulled free of him easily by simply sliding off the
bed away from him. "You are so fucking stupid. Who the
fuck were you going to call for help after you killed me? Not
thinking too smart, you dipshit."

I left the room, not letting him respond. I put on my
coat and left the house to escape him. Whatever happened
after that was completely on him— or on the mattress, so to
speak.

I regretted it the second I walked back into the room that evening. He was lying on the floor again, having fallen from the bed again, in a puddle of piss. He was furious.

I was scared to go close to him; I knew that it would be a bad beating for sure. So, I avoided it as long as possible. I turned and left him; walking into the kitchen to make dinner. I thought that maybe he would be thinking of food and want to eat; maybe it would postpone the inevitable.

I brought the plate of food into him, setting it on the nightstand. "If I pick you up off the floor, are you going to hurt me?"

"No. Just get me the fuck up."

"If you so much as *think* about hurting me, I will throw your food away and leave you on the floor."

"Just pick me the fuck *up*, you bitch."

"You're lucky that didn't hurt my feelings."

"Whatever," he mumbled.

I got Matthew into his chair without incident and rolled him over to the stand so he could collect his plate. I turned to go make one for myself when the plate hit the back of my head. I fell to the floor before I knew a reason for the pain. I passed out; I remember waking up without knowing right away my reason for being on the floor.

"What the fuck?" I shook my head and felt more pain than I ever had before. I had landed face down on the hardwood. The blood seeping out of my head dripped down my face, flooding my eyes and drying before I woke.

"It tasted like shit." He shrugged his shoulders, completely un-phased by what he'd done.

I felt the back of my head and my finger landed along the gouge. It was deep; too deep to close itself, I knew I needed stitches. I got myself ready, without a word to Matthew and drove to the emergency room where I sat fuming, boiling over with rage. I needed to hurt him.

If it was bad before, after that it was worse, I couldn't even stand the sight of him. I returned home with sixteen staples in the back of my head. I had to make up a lie to tell the nurse when she looked horrified while questioning me about what had happened. I felt embarrassed. I know I could have gone to the police, maybe I should have, but I'd done some things to him as well, things I couldn't explain away.

I returned home and he instantly began shouting for me. I couldn't bring myself to go into the room just then, so I sat on the couch and listened to him until he stopped.

He could have simply come out of the room, if he really wanted to, the whole house was accessible to him, but he chose not to. So, I left him.

The night came and went, still nothing from him. I didn't sleep, my head hurt too much. My mind was spinning with thoughts of the old days, the before times that were so good that they made me really know what love was. Hate took my feet toward him; he was asleep in the bed.

I glared at his sleeping body, boiling with hatred. I walked up to him, grabbed him, and pulled him off the bed; he hit the floor with a thud. I took him by the arms and dragged him to the basement door, then opened it, and against my desire to roll him down the stairs, I instead, eased him down one by one, his feet crashing down on each step.

"What the fuck are you doing?" he asked when struggling and fighting against me weren't working.

I didn't answer, my voice wouldn't work. Plus, I didn't really have an explanation as much as a compulsion to do that. I turned and left him lying on the cold and dirty floor, alone in the dark room for hours before returning to check on him.

He was shouting when I opened the door, demanding I put him back in is his chair and feed him. He didn't say anything about taking him upstairs, probably knowing his attempts would be futile.

I went back up to retrieve his chair and brought it down the darkened stairs to him. I thought about just killing him. Not like the times I had done so before, this time, I had a clear image of me walking over to him and gutting him.

The thing that stopped me was unclear. I don't know why I didn't go through with it then. Instead, I loaded him onto his chair, he had no idea how close he'd come to drawing his last breath just then, if he had, maybe he wouldn't have done what he did next.

As I was walking away from him, he grabbed onto my thigh and I fell face first onto the floor. That was the last straw, as I picked myself up for the last fucking time, I vowed to end him. I didn't have anything left holding me back, that thread that tethered me to him snapped the second my chin bounced off the concrete floor.

"I'll be back down in a minute with your food." My voice sounded strange, even to me, it wasn't the same as it had been all those miserable years, it was the old me, she came through just then, and it felt like she was saving me, rescuing me from this shithole my life had become.

I welcomed her as she joined me in making his food, uplifting me in a way I hadn't been able to myself in all that time.

He treated me like a fucking dog, worse than a dog, the shit that comes out of a dog, and that was how I wanted to repay him.

I made chicken marsala that night, served over noodles, it was delicious, what I brought to him were the scraps of my own food: chicken bones mostly, like I said it was delicious, I nearly ate it all.

"What the fuck is this?" he said, when I handed him the plate.

"Shut up and eat it, there won't be anything else tonight." I responded politely as my alter took over again.

Matthew didn't get hungry like you would imagine hunger. He had explained it to me one time– his brain sort of told him it had been enough hours and he craved food, there would be phantom pains he would feel but not like the old hunger pains, so when he threw the plate across the room shattering it on the wall, I left. He probably wouldn't miss it anyway.

I went down in the morning to find him on the floor; he had fallen over reaching for those bones and eaten them where he fell.

"I see you decided to eat."

He didn't respond.

"Do you want back in your chair or not?"

"Yes."

"Yes, what? You lost your manners?"

"Yes, please."

I reached over and patted his head. "Good dog." My tone was belittling, he said nothing, just sort of growled at me. I let it go.

I pulled him up into his chair, noticing some serious cuts on his back and arms from the shattered plate– you would think I'd have learned my lesson about those fucking things, but that was the last plate I gave him so there wouldn't be a third time he could chuck one at me.

"I'll be back down in a minute, don't go anywhere." I sing- songed.

9

Today...

"Where you Matthew's primary care giver?" They brought back in Mr. Good Cop; I can tell his opinion of me has changed, where he used to look at me with mild confusion and maybe a small amount of pity, now I see a mask covering his disgust. I can't blame him; I was waiting for it to happen.

"Well, as you may know, the M.E. has been giving your husband's body an examination, since you've been no help what so ever by way of answers to what happened to him.

"He found some marks, looks like some older than others, pretty deep lacerations covering his back, you're not going to try and convince me he was just clumsy, are you?"

I don't say anything.

"Upon further investigation he found some larger chunks missing, it was really gross; I looked... wish I hadn't.

Some of those pieces are a match for what he found in his stomach."

10

Devoured...

I left Matthew down there for weeks; checking on him became far less frequent as the days passed. I couldn't make myself care anymore, everything he said to me added fuel to the fire. He got weaker; I could see him withering away. I didn't feel an ounce of regret for that. I knew the moment I took him down there that I'd never bring him back up, I knew inside that I was sending him away for good.

I snuck down there one night, he was sleeping, as he had been most the time, he became very lethargic, not having energy left.

He was hunched over in the chair, his head nearly touching his knees, wearing the same pair of boxers he'd been wearing when I dragged him there weeks ago.

I went upstairs in a trance, coming back down with the paring knife in my hand, I sort of watched myself cut a moon- shaped half circle into his back, slipping my finger inside it, I pulled the flesh from the meat and cut a palm sized chunk from him.

There were festering wounds covering him, they looked awful: infected, rotting and stinking.

He didn't even move. I would have thought he was already dead if I hadn't heard his shallow breath.

I did the same thing on the other side, pulling the skin back down to cover the crater, then headed back upstairs.

I took out my cast- iron pan, and I fried those pieces of meat, plating them next to green beans and mashed potatoes, and then brought it downstairs for him.

"Eat," I said. I watched as he ate hungrily; choking to get it all down. It must have been longer than I thought since last I fed him something other than my scraps.

"Finally, a decent fucking meal." I watched him eat until he popped the last piece of himself into his mouth.

I think a part of me knew that that was the last time I would see him, I don't really know when he died, I didn't go back down there after that to confirm. He got his last meal and I felt that was all that was required of me.

I set about living my life again, doing all the mundane shit that was required of me.

The next thing I knew, about three weeks later, the cops were at my door pushing me aside and claiming they had a search warrant. I wasn't nervous, or scared like you might think I'd be with a man downstairs that I only assumed was dead.

One of the officers that stayed behind told me that some kids found something suspicious in my basement.

I wanted to ask questions, the first being why the fuck were kids poking their noses in my basement, but I didn't. I let him speak.

"They threw a ball and it broke your window, instead of bothering you at your door they snuck in to get it. Creeped them the fuck out to find what they claim was a dead body. We are just here to check it out, can't be too sure. Seemed legitimate though– most kids don't confess to a crime like breaking and entering unless they're really freaked out, you know?"

There were shouts coming from the basement, and I knew what was coming, he took my wrists and cuffed them behind my back.

"Looks like those kids were right." He started in on my rights, leading me to the back of a cruiser.

11

Today...

"That is the sickest most disgusting thing I have ever seen; you are one sick lady. You really aren't going to want to take your chances with a jury, they'd feed you to the wolves," Officer Bad Cop says.

"The M.E. says he must have died from infection, says that that was some of the worst conditions he could have been in. You would have to be pretty heartless to leave a man in like that."

I am heartless. Wheelchair bound Matthew stole my heart, ruined my life and tore me apart repeatedly. I don't feel bad, in fact, I don't feel anything.

epilogue

My punishment...

Prison is fine, I have no complaints. The women in here know what I did to Matthew— news travels fast around here, and they mostly avoid me.

When I hear anyone talking about me, they use the word heinous a lot. I guess I am a kind of monster. I wasn't always, and I miss that girl sometimes. I don't know how to get her back though, I think we both died in the car the night of his accident, neither of us were really the same after that.

The end

XXX

XAVIER: "I ESCAPED FROM PRISON, HAULING ASS IN A STOLEN CAR, PUTTING SPACE BETWEEN ME AND THAT BARBED WIRE FENCE, WHEN THE DAMN THING RUNS OUT OF GAS.
LUCKILY, I COME ACROSS AN OLD FARMHOUSE THAT LOOKS EMPTY, EVEN LUCKIER, IT IS NOT. THE THREATS ABOUT DADDY COMING HOME DON'T SCARE ME... MAYBE THEY SHOULD HAVE"

CHAPTER ONE

The gas light had just come on, I figured I had a few more miles to look for a station, but that's the thing, when you steal a car, you don't really know all the ins and outs of its mechanics. This one seems to have a malfunctioning gas gauge.

Fucking thing leaves me stranded on the side of some shithole road with nothing in sight but trees on either side. I haven't seen another car in a hundred miles. The hour of night doesn't help, 1:00 am— I shouldn't expect much.

I've been hauling ass through this town and now I'm trapped inside of it until I can figure something else out. I need to find a place to hunker down, hopefully get some shut- eye so I can do this all again tomorrow. I need even more miles between me and the high walls of that fucking prison.

I choose a path that looks the easiest to hike through and go into the forested area. It's a cool night and the breeze is refreshing. I can't see anything in front of me but the trees, tons and tons of fucking trees, what a shitty spot to get stranded.

I have been walking for what feels like miles, but really it can't be, it's the terrain that makes it feel that long. I trip again and catch myself before I fall another time– I am getting really irritated by this shit.

I look up to survey my options now, thinking I may just save myself a broken ankle and crash here for the night, when a glint from the moon's reflection catches my eye and I thank my fucking luck that something is here.

I can make out the rest of the window and as I walk closer, the rest of the farmhouse comes into view. It's an old run-down building that looks at least a hundred years old. A wrap around porch that's missing most of the banister, shutters hanging on by the skin of their teeth, and the siding dirty and dilapidated.

I can't imagine it's occupied, but I walk carefully around it to investigate the likelihood. I can't see anything that alarms me so, I grab a rock and knock it against one of the small panes of glass near the door. I spend a full minute listening before reaching my hand in to find the lock.

The door creaks as I push it slowly inward. The kitchen is right inside and from what I can see of it, it's dirty and dusty, looks like no one has cared about it for some time.

I'm riffling through the cupboards to find some none perishables when movement catches my eye, and for fuck's sake, it couldn't be a more welcoming site. I move my head slowly in the direction of the girl in the white top– I say that only because it's the only thing she's wearing, well, that and a tiny pair of pink panties. I can't take my eyes from that little V of fabric.

It's been so long since I've been in the presence of a young woman— *any* woman actually, and my god, she is young. She looks fresh out of high school. My blood is instantly hot, my cock so hard it could push through the zipper on my jeans.

"What are you doing in here?" she says in a sleepy voice. I probably woke her breaking the window.

I creep forward slowly, so as not to alarm her, "I got turned around out there, I thought this place was empty." I slow my pace even more, creeping like a hunting cat might do, and inch by inch, my feet get closer to her. "Is there someone here that could help me?"

She shakes her head.

I can't imagine this girl is alone out here all by herself. "Your parents aren't here?" I'm almost close enough to grab her now. I can smell her sweet scent, something floral, and it is calling to me.

"My mom is asleep; I can go get her if you want." Her voice is full of innocence— just what I like.

"No, sugar, you don't need to do that." I reach out quickly, seizing my opportunity, one arm wraps around her small waist and the other tightens over her mouth. She tries to get free, but I lift her up and keep her from being able to run. It doesn't stop her legs from flailing about, kicking wildly in the struggle.

Her back is pressed to my front and she's squirming against me, rubbing her little ass against my cock. I almost can't breathe; it's been so long for me.

Eight years in the Pen, with each day feeling like a hundred, eight fucking years without a woman– this poor little girl doesn't know what she's doing to me right know, how she is driving me wild with her struggle.

I've been a 'free' man for nine hours, most of which were spent jacking a car and fleeing from police who gave chase for a while until I could evade them. No time really, to enjoy my freedom, yet. And this little lady is just ripe for the picking.

I look frantically for somewhere to take her, somewhere, that if she makes noise, she won't be heard so easily. "Stop squirming, little girl." My voice is raspy with lust. My grip tightens around her, trying to calm her movements but it only makes her struggle more. "Oh, fuck." I lose it, I fucking come right in my pants. I grind my cock into her ass, jerking the rest of my release.

I think she knows what just happened because she stills. I wish she would have done that when I asked her to before so I wouldn't have to walk around with this load in my jeans, but I'm grateful either way, it's made it easier to haul her around.

The house is dark, but my luck holds true, and I am able to find a spot for her. I push open the last door and it is a bedroom– looks like it hasn't been used in long time. The bed is a welcome sight. My mind becomes a kaleidoscope of depraved images with her being the star.

I plop her on top of the comforter and the dust dances in the moon light. I cover my mouth to avoid choking; giving her the time she needed to squirm off the bed. I grab her by the hair and rip her back toward me. She yelps and goes stick straight from the pain. The tiny tears pricking her eyes feed right into me– I want more of those.

I get her back onto the bed, using the weight of my own body to hold her down; then I sit on top of her and straddle her waist, ripping open her tee- shirt. Her round, young tits are beautiful, but before I let myself become too distracted by them, I make long strips from the torn shirt and restrain her with them, wrapping them tightly around her wrists and through the slats in the bedframe, immobilizing her.

I wrap a thick one around her mouth, securing it tightly behind her head. It muffles her enough that I don't worry about the noise she might make. The house is huge, and from what I've seen of the bottom floor, no one else is nearby.

I shimmy down her body. God, it's been so long since I've smelled a woman, I bury my nose into her panties and breathe in her scent. I get so fucking hard, harder than I thought possible, my adolescent cock has nothing on me now.

The last woman I had was on my last night as a free man, a saggy- titted- fatty that I caught while she was getting into her vehicle; I fucked her in the backseat of her minivan. She wasn't even worth it, just another tally to add to my list. She had some panic button she was able to push to alert the cops. I was zipping back up when I heard the sirens approaching quickly. No time to run, they were on me in seconds, cuffing me and tossing me into the back of a squad car.

I went down for the string of rapes that they were able to tie me to after getting my DNA. They'd said I was an atrocious monster for what I did to all those girls. Photo after photo of all the woman who'd come forward for my trial. Their little snatches all scared up and on display for everyone in the courtroom to see, some photos of the fresh cuts crisscrossing on top of their pussies coming from the ones who ran to the emergency room to get a rape- kit done right away.

I had been at it for years before being caught; there were a lot of women I marked with my X, that's what I've always been called, X, it's short for Xavier. These bitches should have been proud to wear my name etched into their skin, a constant reminder of being chosen. Instead, were sending me off to a lifetime in prison.

The jury threw the book at me, and with twenty-seven confirmed cases of mutilation and violent rape I wasn't surprised. What did surprise me was the small amount that had come forward. I always knew not every woman came forward after a rape, what I didn't know is that number is huge. I should have had one hundred and eighteen, by my count– and I *did* count. That's exactly how many women I'd raped at that point– all bearing my X– all my whores. An overwhelming majority must have been satisfied with our time together since I didn't see them at the trail complaining.

My first notch being an old woman in the neighborhood who asked me for help in her yard, which was commonplace in a neighborhood like the one mine was growing up. You helped each other out. And I helped myself to her. I was young and inexperienced– it was over quickly. I'm surprised still, to this day, that she didn't rat me out, she knew who my mom was and could've just told her, I actually waited for them to haul me off to jail for it. But the days past and nothing ever came of it. The worst that happened was I was never invited to help with work for her again– not a punishment, if you ask me.

Although, it wasn't as gruesome as the later ones she did still have my mark crudely engraved into her fleshy old woman mound.

I had finished with the work and she offered me a lemonade, I took it from her graciously, the woman's chores had worked me into a sweat, sipping it and talking to her, my eyes wandering to her fleshy thighs. I lost all restraint and my compulsion took over. I took the knife she had used to cut a piece of pie for herself and I put it to her throat. Before I knew what I was doing, I had my virgin dick inside of her, I had nothing to compare it to and it felt so good. It took only a minute before I exploded in her, the second minute past and I was rocking inside of her again.

The knife got lost for a moment, and before I knew it, I had cut her. A long, jagged slice right on the top of her hairy pussy, the blood lubricated us, excited me, and while I fucked her, I cut across that line and made an X, marking her for me.

The only sounds she had made were the cries from being cut, other than that, she was silent and unmoving. I finished inside of her a second time with a mixture of her blood and my come oozing from her hole. From that day on I knew what I needed. And by not going to police, she helped me do it to four more woman that summer before my senior year.

I had served eight full fucking years of my sentence before exacting my escape. It had been a plan in the making since day one. Now, I'm a 35- year- old man getting back on the horse, so to speak— if by horse you mean hot, young, piece of ass. This girl will be a 'welcome back to the real world' prize. I'm practically salivating with lust as I touch her.

CHAPTER TWO

I run my fingers up and down her tight little body, firm in all the right places, juicy in the others. It's been a long time since I've touched something so smooth.

I cut away her panties with the pocket- knife I found in the hot- wired car and spread her legs apart. The smell of her hits me again, young and fresh. I push my fingers into her tight hole and it barely gives at all, she is so fucking tight. I pull my fingers out to taste her– so sweet it makes me lightheaded.

I get rid of my pants and shirt, tossing them onto the floor then come back to her. Pressing her knees to her chest I bury my face in her pussy, licking and tasting her, sucking her tiny little clit into my mouth I eat her pussy like a ferocious mad man.

She squirms around but is unable to escape my firm hold on her. I know from experience I can make a girl come against her will and I feel her on the verge, driving me wild with control, I taste the warm juice that seeps out of her as she quivers under my tongue.

I flip her over, twisting her arms painfully above her head then pull her up onto her knees with her asshole pointed right at me. I push into it, tearing it open. I have to catch my breath; my excitement is overflowing my lungs.

When I regain control of my own breathing, my shaking hands grip her by the waist and I fuck her. Using her hips, I push and pull her away from me as I watch my cock disappear into her hole.

I smack her ass and her roundness jiggles. God, it looks so good. I hit her repeatedly until her ass is on fire, heat from my palm's marks radiate. I tug her harder and faster, excited to unload in her back hole. I come loudly, grunting like an animal.

I hear a loud crack and she screams through her gag. I don't stop to investigate what might have broken; I'm too caught up in the aftermath of my much-needed release.

I twist her back over, she lets out another scream, and I know it must have been her shoulder that had snapped. I put her legs together and sit on top of her knees to hold her in place while I carve my X into her, it's deeper than I usually do them, but I want this one to stand out.

I saw during the trial that some of them had faded. I want this one with her forever, I stab into her and slide along her skin, an inch or so deep, until the letter is gushing like a geyser, pulsing between her legs. I slip my finger inside the X, up to the first knuckle, and then I trace it.

That one is going to look good forever.

I leave her tied up tightly and go in search of her mother whom she said was home. She may not be as young and hot as her daughter, but I still want a go of her.

CHAPTER THREE

I pull my jeans back up, not bothering to zip them, and head back out in the direction I came, passing the kitchen as I go, I grab a glass and fill it with water from the tap. I'm so thirsty from that work out.

There is a huge staircase in the center of the living room, it has about eight steps and then a landing that forks off and goes in either direction with another eight steps, or so. I choose left and ascend to the top. I don't hear any noise, so I sneak quietly with my hand along the wall for guidance. There is a long hallway with many doors; I open them all as I pass, making sure to clear each one. The second is a bathroom and I take the opportunity to empty my bladder.

The next, and last door, is a bedroom; a nightlight helps aid in my investigation of the room. There is a girl sleeping, not the mother as I was expecting, but a girl to be about the age of the other one. It's hard to tell with people just how old they are, and if you ask me, if they have titties and a little hair on their pussies, they're legal.

She is blonde and small; I can hear her breathing, slowly in and out. I look at all the things she has decorating her room with, getting a better feel for the sleeping beauty in the bed.

Trophies line the walls on shelves made to display them all. I read one and it tells me she is a gymnast, which may explain her slight frame. She's won over a hundred of these by my estimated count. Her high school diploma framed along with other certificates she must be proud of.

Her name is Eliza by the name printed on everything.

She stirs in her bed, her white lacy cover gets tangled in her legs, pulling the blanket down a bit, she's wearing a little, lose fitting, yellow tank top and one of her tits is hanging out. Small little pink buds, only big enough to be called 'puffies' making my mouth water.

I let my pants fall and tug my cock a few times to alleviate the ache before walking over to her and ripping the covers away from her. I hold my hand over her mouth then I grab both of her wrists and lie down on top of her warm-from- sleep body. I pull that little titty into my mouth, licking around in circles and sucking it hard.

Her eyes are wild— as they should be, a naked man lying on top of you as you wake is something that would freak anyone out.

I do the same to the other, leaving both breasts wet and glistening from my saliva, then I pick her up out of her bed and carry her around with me as I go in search of restraints. I really should have done this a minute before, but I was too caught up in the sight of her. I could just

when I get inside and tear that little membrane the blood will do all the lubricating I need.

I line my hard cock up and I push hard until I fill her hole, I hiss as it grabs tightly and sucks my cock. I've had my fair share of virgins and none of them have popped like this one, my god she is tight. I can't move right away or I'll explode. When I am finally ready, I draw out almost completely then ram it back inside of her, a few more times and I see and feel the blood, now her hole is tight *and* wet. I watch as my bloodied cock fucks her, the red fluid covering my thick cock.

I pull out and taste her virginity, cleaning her fuzzy little bush with my tongue. I lap it up until I've had my fill. Then spread her legs wide and find that there is no stopping point for them, her limber, little, gymnast- body accommodates me in every way. I lift them over her head, her calves at her ears, I have folded her in half and her pussy is on full display.

I grab the ducky duct tape from the nightstand, wrap her ankles tightly together, and effortlessly tuck her feet behind her head before I lift her ass up, dragging her to the end of the bed I'm standing in front of, and set it on my thighs. If she chooses to look, she could watch all the things I'm going to do to her now.

I push my finger inside and wiggle it around; stretching her ripped hole, the tears streaming down her face are exhilarating, I love it when the bitches cry.

I lick her sweet and tangy flavor from my finger and then spread her pussy wide and slap it hard with my other hand. The sound reverberates throughout the room; I hit

disappears, having to shove harder toward the end as I reach the depths of her, and I fuck her with it hard, cramming it inside of her with my fist tightly around the base of the trophy with a stabbing motion.

Blood is pouring from her, as I am sure I've demolished her insides. When I feel like I've had enough fun with her, and the ache in my arm tells me to stop, I take the little trophy girl out of her and show her the bloodied figurine. She cries and cries, choking and struggling to breathe through her nose.

There are chunks of her insides caught a part of the trophy. I really ripped her apart, I feel proud knowing I did such a thorough job on her.

Hey, don't judge me, we all need to find pride somewhere in our lives. Me— I find it in the depths of a woman's pussy, bleeding and torn.

I carve my X into her so she can see she gets to wear my mark as her sister does. It is a little harder to manage as her hairs get in the way. It's been a very long time since I've had to deal with such an issue, even when I was doing this eight years ago it wasn't common place to have such a hairy obstacle.

It looks good in the end and I'm sure it will heal nicely... for me. Not so much for her, it will look horrid for her, a constant reminder of what I took from her. And to be completely honest I love when those women think about me, I love knowing I'm in their minds every time they fuck, knowing that even when their sex is consensual, it will trigger thoughts of me. I fucking *thrive* on that.

I leave her on her bed and click the door behind her; I need to find the girls' mom. I don't know if I'll have any nut left for her without becoming dehydrated, but a man's gotta try.

CHAPTER FOUR

I go to the other side of the house, passing across the giant staircase in search of dear mommy's room. Another few doors checked before I come to hers, left ajar, probably to hear if there is an intruder during the night. Not at all effective if that is the truth.

I sneak through the doorway; she is asleep in her bed, facing away from the door. I took the duct tape from little Eliza's room in case– mom is probably bigger and stronger than her little girls are.

I can see that she is a slight woman, blonde hair like her kids'. I take inventory of the room; it is certainly a feminine atmosphere, fresh cut flowers on each of the tops of tables. Floral coverings on her bed, she is sleeping in some pink nighty, long sleeved and ruffled.

Dear god, I hope she's not one of those 'old' moms, I'd hate to finish the night with that.

I pounce on her before she can learn that I am here. She squirms and struggles right away. I flip her onto her back and my god; she has the biggest tits, they're round and plump. I hadn't realized I was missing a set of giant tits until I saw hers. They jiggle as she struggles, and I don't try and calm her, the effect is working perfectly to get me in the mood again.

When she calms down enough, I chance a look at her face, she is beautiful, and the youthfulness of her daughters comes through right away.

She's breathing heavy when she tells me, "Don't hurt my girls please. Do whatever you want to me, I won't fight you, but please don't hurt them."

"Oh, honey, let me just say that the little gymnast one nearly sucked my soul through my cock." I lean in and whisper into her ear, "so fucking tight." I rip a piece of tape off and wrap it around her wrists. "Well... not anymore."

The horror of my words hit her and her face contorts as she cries, feeling the pain my words cause her heart.

I finish securing her wrists, pulling them up and over her head, wrapping the tape around the headboard.

"My husband is going to be here soon," she tries.

"I'm not falling for that." There's no way a man lives here, everything screams 'single woman' around here. I flick my knife open and she squeals.

"Please don't hurt me, do whatever you came here for and then leave. Please, you don't have to use that." Her eyes don't leave my weapon.

She pulls her tongue back in her mouth, fresh tears in her eyes. I don't take offence to them, in fact, I relish the sight of them. They mean I've done my job here.

I ease down the length of her body, and pull her legs apart. "I really want to see if that made you wet. I've been doing this a long time; you wouldn't be the first."

"You don't have time for this, please just go, my husband will be here soon. Please." She's grasping at anything to get me to leave, it only makes me more eager to play.

"Shut up." I lean my weight onto the backs of her thighs, pinning them to her chest, effectively giving me the best view of my target. I check her like a dipstick, in and then out. "Not as wet as I'd like, but for sure, wetter than both your girls were before I made them bleed. I guess being stuck out here in, in the middle of nowhere, would keep most girls virgins."

She's not as flexible as the second girl, Eliza, and I have to struggle to keep her legs out of the way as I push into her hole. I add finger after finger until I'm forcing my fist inside of her, punching into her hard and fast. She is crying, tears streaming down her cheeks and collecting in her hair, tormented by my hand.

"Please... please... please." She is sobbing and snoting all over; her face is covered in wet.

Her pussy is making all sorts of sloshing noises; it feeds my need to continue. "You're getting wetter now, you hear that. You want to come? I could let you come." I slow my pace in and out, letting her feel my hand inch by inch.

"Please just stop, I don't want this, please. He is coming, you'll regret this— all of this," she says in between her fit.

I rub her little clit gently at first until I feel it twitching. Moving in a rhythm along with my fisted hand, I manipulate her pussy to make her come. But more time passes, and each time I think this will be it, she stops it from happening. She won't let herself come. She's trying hard not to give me the satisfaction.

"I got your daughter off; she came so hard for me."

I knew those words would push her even further from the brink and I don't care, I hate her a little for not letting me win, for have such willpower to deny herself the orgasm.

I draw out my fist completely, but before she can recover, I slam it back into her with all my strength. She yelps in pain but I don't stop, I push and push into the barricade of her hole, trying to shove past it.

I get inside deeper than I've ever felt, pull out my bloody hand, then smack it across her face. Blood pours out of her, as I'm sure I've ruptured something in there, but still, I have things to do to her so I don't let her rest.

I dig my knife into her flesh and give her a matching X to that of her sweet girls— the night of the 'triple X', it will be my most prolific attack. I cut the tape away from the bed and drag her with me down the stairs to the bottom where I reaffix her hands, this time to the banister.

"You stay here, or I will do many more awful things to your girls."

I jog down the stairs to the first one's room and shove her toward her mother, who takes one look at her and sobs, her bloody tit is probably what does it for poor mom.

"One more," I say, coming back with the second one, my favorite little gymnast, Eliza. I found her in her room on top of a puddle of blood oozing from between her legs. I carry her to the first landing and then nudge her forward with my foot hard enough to send her down the second flight of stairs. She rolls down comically, as she is still in the pretzel shape, with her legs secured behind her head.

I pick her up off the floor and show her mother the mutilated hole I have given her, looking even more heinous than when I left her.

"My baby, I'm so sorry, honey." She cries and cries while I affix her daughter to the hand railing beside her.

I have all of them on their knees one on each step next to each other. Naked asses pointed right at me.

"Now, I'd like to play a little game."

"My dad is coming back; he is going to fuck you up." This from the first girl I took.

"Oh, sure honey." I do enjoy her gusto, but I can't believe a word she says, I've heard threats of this sort countless times before– so very unoriginal.

can't even tell that I'd stretched her at all, she's still so much tighter than the others.

I let them watch if they want, but I don't make them. I grab tightly to the small girl's hips and go frantically at her until I unload inside of her, grunting loudly as I come hard.

"God, you ladies sure do know how to make a man feel good." I wipe sweat from my forehead and take a minute to catch my breath. "You know, I might have to take this one with me." I say about Eliza. She could be a lot of fun for a while, and if I can get back to the group, I'm sure a lot of them would like a go at her too.

Men like me tend to stick together, to share, if the opportunity arises. I know that the eight years I've been gone will not have taken that comradery away.

It's not a really organized group and we have no rules. It's really just fourteen men, maybe a few more or less by the time I get in contact, the number is always fluctuating, who share in the same types of *hobbies*. When one of us brings a conquest back to share, it is usually crème of the crop type shit. Like a limber little gymnast, we could contort until her joints break.

Fuck. That would be real fun.

"You leave her the fuck alone," mom shouts at me.

"Shut up," I say back at her for interrupting my fantasy.

I'm feeling so tired suddenly, the long day has caught up with me. But I can't really end the game after only one round, so I stick with it. Heading back over to the first girl, I make a selection, and am very close to raping her with it, when I become distracted– as have the ladies.

They're all looking at the shadows on the wall, beautiful colors spring to life from the stained- glass window on the opposite side. They're shifting and dancing as the sun falls in the sky low enough to hit it. We all watch until it stops, the sun is gone and so are the colors, the shadows of the staircase blacken and morph into a shape.

"Daddy," the girls cry out.

What the fuck?

It's no longer a shadow, I watch until a form takes solid shape, going from grey and black to a man wearing a red plaid shirt and dirty jeans. The sound that comes from its direction, as he notices his family naked and raped, is that of a wild animal, he roars in anger so loud it shakes the walls of the house– rumbling aftershocks follow.

I have no idea what to do; I am frozen in shock that manifests as fear moments later as he rushes forward. His fists are huge, and as he rains them down on my body, I feel all his strength behind each hit.

My body crumples to the floor, and still he pounds. Harder and harder it feels, faster and faster they come. Then, I see from the corner of my bloodied eye, him draw his arm back and the last thing I feel is his fist plow into my face, crunching the bones that protect my brain and pushing into it. I don't feel anything after that.

CHAPTER FIVE

I wake up feeling groggy and sore, not altogether alert. I feel myself coming back, piece by piece I feel my body coming together, it feels like my whole body has those sleep needles, it hurts so much. I feel my face, preparing for the worst. I know that man did a number on me. But my face is fine, it doesn't hurt like I think it will. In fact, after a few more minutes, nothing physically hurts at all.

I can't help but remember the pain of being pounded on, I can feel it deep in my core. My bones remember being crushed and broken, my face knows it caved in, but I'm here and I'm healed— which makes no fucking sense.

My swollen eyes are finally able to open, and when they do, I see him here, hovering over me. I'm on the floor by the door I came through after breaking the window. I try to stand, but he doesn't let me.

"Welcome back," he says in the most sinister tone.

"What the fuck is going on?" I ask, not really thinking he will answer, but he does.

"Every night, I get you again."

"Uh, you might want to clarify what you mean by that." I've been locked up for enough years to know you don't back down or show fear to another man, especially when he is hovering over you menacingly.

"Well, every night at dusk, you get to come back, and I get you until midnight."

"I don't think that is how it going to go down." I scramble away and reach the handle of the door without him stopping me. I'm able to get it open quickly and I dart out of the house, running as fast as my feet will take me. Only, when I make my exit, it's actually my entrance, and I'm right back in the house, stumbling forward into him, his big arms wrap around me.

"I told you, every. night. you. are. mine." He grabs hold of me tighter, pushing his forehead against mine. "That's how this works. You die, and if you have someone here who wants you bad enough, you get to return to them from dusk until midnight every night, it can be love or hate that keeps you here— one man's heaven is another man's hell. Welcome to hell, fucker. Let the games begin."

CHAPTER SIXXX

He grabs me by my hair and whips me into the living room, I can do nothing against him, his strength is insurmountable. I go where he takes me, and no matter how hard I fight, I am no match for him.

He pushes me to the ground and I struggle to get free to no avail. He pounces on me and pummels me with his fists, the pain I felt last time he had done this to me comes back and I feel it stronger now. Each blow compounds and sends excruciating pain throughout my body. I black out before I know it.

***

I thought I had blacked out; turns out, he beat me until I died again. He caved in my skull and ruptured some vital organs; I know that for certain, as I feel it in my regenerating body. The pain sits in the back of my mind. I recall every moment he tormented me, even after I was gone; his fists flew at me.

I regretfully open my eyes now, it's dusk, I know, because I'm back. And of course, he is standing nearby... waiting.

He must have the hang of this death thing better than I do, I don't know how long he has been dead, but he seems to have a good grasp on it. Either that, or him not being beaten over and over and having to recover from it eases the arrival. I don't think I'll ever get a chance to know, as I don't see my circumstances changing any time soon.

I try to get ahead of him today, pulling to my feet quickly and running. Knowing the door to the outside will not be an exit for me, I run as fast as I can to the downstairs room I raped his daughter in and slam the door shut behind me, pushing my weight against it.

He turns the handle and I hold tight, then I am shoved all the way across the room into the opposite wall. My forehead slams hard into the sheetrock. I'm stunned, but recover quickly enough to scramble to my feet, hopefully this time I can go down with a fight.

I put my hands up to defend myself, but he pulls something from behind his back that is no match for my fists. He throws the knife with expert precision, it hits me in the chest, the wind is knocked out of me from the force, and my breathing is coming out with a strangled wheeze. I can't get enough air into my lungs. I choke and cough until it's all gone, then I take my last gasping breath before all the light fades from my sight.

***

Oh, fuck. I feel myself waking again, my lungs are sore and it's hard to breathe. I lie here, instead of moving, knowing he is with me already, waiting to attack.

He reaches over and grabs me; my eyes fly open just in time to see him hitting me in the face with a meat tenderizer.

"I'm going to make this one quick; I have to tend to my girls."

I just now realize they hadn't been around, too busy trying to plan my next move to notice.

"I bet they need time to heal from what I did to them. I raped your little girls right here in this…" my words abruptly halt as soon as I am struck again by the meat mallet.

***

More days go by, weeks possibly, each one has him rushing through and killing me quickly, wanting to spend as much time with his family as he can, I'm sure. I thought it was as bad as it could get. Torturing me and killing me over and over countless times.

It must have been months before I saw one of the girls. The first girl, the one I met in the kitchen, has gotten back on her feet first, joining dear old dad in the torture, she yells at me and tells me she hates me, hits me, stabs me. He stands by watching as she takes her vengeance. She's pretty tough, although he restrains me when it comes time for her turns.

A few more weeks and I see mom limp in. "Oh, you're looking a little worse for wear. You must still be recovering from the fucking I gave you, or have you always walked like you just got off a horse?" I taunt her, knowing I'm fucked either way, maybe if I piss her off enough, she will attack me quickly and it can be over. That is, until I have to do all of this shit again tomorrow.

I get so furious at that thought. I have to repeat this endlessly until who the fuck knows, trapped in this eternal fucking loop of hell. I'm not saying I wouldn't do it all exactly the same way– I had a damn good last hooray, but I would have left when that bitch told me her husband was coming. That's for damn sure.

Mom just looks at me, no anger in her face, it looks as though she might have a secret, a small sideways smirk appears across her mouth and it scares the shit out of me. I've seen a lot of things, I've never once seen a woman look more menacing than her huge ass, 'otherworldly' husband standing just next to her.

I step back without telling my feet to move, they're definitely on the same page as my brain, except that my brain can't talk right now.

"Honey, will you go get Eliza, I want her to be here for this." She kisses him sweetly on the cheek before he goes. I haven't seen her yet, I fucked my gymnast pretty good, she's probably needed the most time to recover.

"Don't start without me," he says.

"I wouldn't dare."

I fucking run, I head in the direction that always seems to be my first instinct and I'm distraught when I see the door still gone from the hinges of the room. I cower in the corner for nothing else to do and bury my face in my shaking hands. I really thought the worst was behind me. Being pounded until my bones broke and splintered, having my face caved in, is nothing compared to what this woman has in store for me.

She has a plan, I saw it in her eyes, and it isn't going to be quick like hubby. At least with him I could go back to the nothing, even if the time did move so fast that it felt like no time passed before I was waking again.

If the torture lasted longer though... I don't want to think about it. I close my eyes tight to focus on my surroundings, listening and waiting. I just fucking wait!

CHAPTER SEVEN

I hear the footsteps coming closer, the thudding of the large man as he approaches. He effortlessly drags me from my hiding spot and takes me into the kitchen, lifting me as if I weigh nothing, and setting me on the butcher- block- island counter top.

He takes my clothes off, and the smallest girl, my *favorite* girl, comes over to assist, but not with the unwrapping part— I wouldn't have minded that one bit— I am hardly able to keep my boner at bay with her around.

Instead, she takes tape and affixes it to my mouth, wrapping circles around my head and over my ears. Before she can cover my eyes, I see a contraption sitting off to the side. I know what it is right away; I just can't imagine what it could be used for in the kitchen.

Before I can wrap my head around the implications, tape covers my eyes. I can't see the rest, but I feel the very second someone has cut deeply into my thigh.

I hear the muffled voices of them all as they are talking through the next part. I hear the loud motor start and I scramble to get away.

Then the next piece of tape covers my nose and I can't breathe, which I think would the worst thing to happen tonight if I hadn't seen what I saw.

I feel the sharp, cool, metal object pushing into the hole in my leg, the noise gets louder and I hear the air compressor working, the rumble of the motor reverberates across my body.

My skin peels away, I can feel it separate, all my nerves are on fire, and although it only takes a few seconds, it's more pain than I have ever felt, every part of my body is alive and in pain.

***

I wake the next time still screaming and writhing.

The memory of being skinned alive is more than I can handle, I relive the feel of my skin balloon again and fill the gap between my flesh and bones as it separates. And my god, it is the worst thing to experience, but having to remember it in the depths of my bones is too much for me, I open my tear- filled eyes only to meet hers again, and I can't take it, I just know this is going to hurt.

The end

---

app

SALEM LOGS ON TO HER FAVORITE APP. HER AND KYLE ARE A MATCH. THE NIGHT STARTS OUT FUN, WITH BOTH OF THEM EAGER TO TAKE THINGS FURTHER.

THE NEXT MORNING, HOWEVER, SALEM WAKES WITH NO RECOLLECTION OF THE EVENING.

One

Salem

Wow, you're hot.

Favorite.

Nope.

Swipe.

Nope.

Swipe.

Gah, this online dating shit is hard. Generally, they take all the most horrendous people in the world and cram them together into online dating sites that value your appearance enough to make it your first point of contact, but we all know, even if you're ugly, you still want the cheerleader or quarterback. We're all thinking that we'll be different and special enough for them to not realize that we're ugly– or at the very least, not care. But seeing someone first, and not liking the way they look, is one sure way not to get to know their personality enough to give them a proper chance.

That being said, I'm not ugly, and this isn't an app for dating necessarily, it's more of a hook up thing. I don't care to get to know these men passed the point of initial attraction, I want drop dead gorgeous, I don't care if he's dumb as a rock, as long as he makes my panties fall.

None of the men on here are even ugly; we are all vetted and have gone through a rigorous sign-up process. We are all after the same thing– bagging a hottie.

Just because you're hot doesn't mean you're *my* kind of hot, though. We all have different preferences. And that's the way it should be. We can't all go clambering after one guy, he only has enough dick to go around for all of us to share before it would break off, or some shit.

I don't know, what I do know is my flavor tends to go toward big- kinda on the chubby side, tall, strong, and if I'm being honest– a little gingery. He's got to have an attitude in bed too, can't be one of those who doesn't take what he wants, he's got to be strong enough to handle what I want, mentally and physically.

I've been on this damn thing for over an hour, most of the men I've favorited are offline so they won't see that I've acknowledged them until they log back in.

There have been a lot of *no's* tonight on my end. A few have tried to talk to me that I put in the 'no' pile, and if I can't get a good one, I will just settle for one of them. I can't be too choosy on a Tuesday night, it's not really the night that brings the masses out. I just need something, and I can't wait until Friday– a more appropriate dating night, for it.

"Oh."

Favorite.

This one for sure is a keeper– best option of the night.

two

KYLE

Ping.

I open my app and see that someone has favorited me, it's Tuesday night, I wasn't expecting any action tonight, but that's how this app works, for the most part, they want something now.

I look at her profile; blonde, thin, huge boobs— gotta love that. Sweet, porcelain doll face and has been a member for more than a year. I like that, means she knows what it's about.

I don't respond right away; I have to let her dangle a bit. I scroll through some of the ladies who are online right now— nothing to write home about.

I hit the heart on one of her pictures, the one of her scantily dressed and showing off her most appealing attributes.

She sends a message.

"Hi."

Ok, not too much to it, but I like when they take a little of the initiative.

"Hello."

She doesn't say anything for a full minute, so I say something.

"Tuesday is not usually a busy night."

"I like Tuesdays."

I laugh.

"Ok, then, Salem, what would a great Tuesday be for you?"

"Dinner, flirting and…"

Nice.

"I like the 'and' part."

"You've never had an 'and' like me."

She might be right. I've been active on this app for a while, and from what I've experienced, it's all fun and games, there's a certain expectation from both sides that we are in agreement to what will happen.

I respond.

"You want to let me get through the dinner and flirting part of the evening so I can take you home and...?"

She sends me her address, which may sound strange to some, but this app does thorough background checks and vets everyone. Once you've been given a log- in it's just shy of a 'top secret' security clearance. We're all here for the same fun.

I ask. "What time?"

"Thirty minutes."

She logs off before I can confirm it with her.

Oh, well, time to get ready.

three

Salem

I log- off the app to get ready, Kyle looks great, he checked off all my requirements judging by the photos from his profile. And just that quick chat has gotten me worked up. I think this should be a fun night.

I jump in the hot, steamy shower, and clean away the day I've had, nothing like washing away a shitty day at work. I hop out, blow my hair dry then put my make up on. Going to the closet, I stand in front of it for more time than I should. I finalize my choice and pull up a pair of skinny jeans and my black Tool shirt I'd altered so it hangs off my shoulders, giving me just the right amount of cleavage for an evening like this, then slip into a pair of black heels that make me six inches taller. He's tall, by what his profile said, so I don't worry about emasculating him.

I check myself in the mirror, adding a few curls to my shoulder length hair, making it bouncy and light. Then I spritz a bit of perfume and I'm ready to go. Just in the nick of time, I hear my doorbell ring, letting me know he's here.

I open the door after grabbing my purse, and walk out onto the porch for our introductions. Then I see him, I mean I *really* see him.

Holy fuck. You know there are people who look really good in their photos, but in real life you know they aren't that attractive. Well, this guy is the opposite. I mean, don't get me wrong, he looked good in his photos, but here, in front of me... a thousand times better.

Everything about his well- over- six- foot frame screams man, right down to his scent. He towers over me, looking down at my upturned face and has this little sideways smirk, like he knows something that I don't, giving him a sort of cocky feel.

I pull my lip into my mouth to hide my own smile. I'm very happy about my choice tonight.

He says, "Nice to meet you, Salem." And my name coming from his mouth, as cliché as it may be, sounds like he was born to say it.

"Kyle." I put my hand out to shake his and that sideways smirk turns into a huge toothy smile, full of white shiny teeth. I can't help but return it.

He takes my hand, and instead of shaking it, he interlaces my fingers with his and holds it as he leads me away from my house.

I kind of wish he would tell me he wants to skip the other shit and go right for me, but I let him take the lead.

He escorts me to his car, parked in the bike lane in front of my house, and opens the passenger door for me. I don't know enough about cars to tell you what the emblem on it says it is. I do know enough to say it looks expensive; it looks like he spent a lot of money on this little toy.

I climb in and he pushes the door shut, the car smells like him, like that ruggedness he has.

I look over at him as he climbs in next to me and realize we look really cute together.

four

KULE

I walk up to her door, and as soon as she opens it, I get excited. The Tool shirt she's wearing is hanging off her shoulders and screams she's ready for a good time.

We didn't hash out anything about the evening, as far as where we were going, and I hoped she wouldn't be the type to demand lobster or some other fancy shit. Not that I couldn't afford it, I just don't like it, and I didn't feel like pretending through dinner that I did. So, I myself, dressed in a t- shirt and jeans. Her version, of course, looks so much better than mine.

She offers me her hand and I hold it; she doesn't pull it away so I know she doesn't mind it. I like the feel of hers; I like her long nails digging into the back of my hand as she grips it.

I can't help but take a peek of her round ass, stretching the fabric of her jeans, shaking back and forth as she walks. Her heels clicking hard on the sidewalk sends a spark to my cock. I love a woman in heels.

She watches me as I drive, I catch her and she doesn't look away, all I can do is smile. I'm so ready for this. Who knew a Tuesday night out would be with such a hot chick?

I pull up in front of my favorite restaurant, I have simple tastes and this place does burgers right.

"You ok with this?" I ask her.

"I used to waitress here when I was a teenager."

"You want to go somewhere you won't know everyone?"

She laughs; it's an adorable little laugh. "I don't know how long ago you think that was, but I don't think after all these years I'll know anyone."

"Ok, then. Let's fucking *do* this."

She laughs again and opens her door. I know a gentleman may have stopped her and opened it for her, but I like seeing her from the back. I'm a selfish man.

I meet her at the front of the car, take her hand in mine again, and lead her into the restaurant. This time I do open the door for her, ushering her forward, again, for selfish reasons.

fiUe

SaleM

As soon as he pulled up here, I thought he might have done some research on me. It has been well over ten years since I set foot in this place, but by his response to my comment about working here, I don't think he has.

The app does look at all your background in order to see if you are a fit, digging deeper than is common knowledge, but it doesn't share the findings with other users. And I didn't give him enough time to thoroughly investigate me, so I chalk it up to coincidence.

He asks for a seat in the back, it's not too busy, but I like that he wants privacy.

The waitress, who can't take her eyes off of him, leads us to a darkened corner booth. I slide in, and instead of going to the opposite side, Kyle sits next to me. I can't imagine I'll be able to think with him so near to me, all warm and close.

I take a deep breath to get the thoughts working in another direction– one more northern in location. It obviously does no good, just helps to get his scent deeper into my nose.

He leans over to me, we are far from prying ears and mere inches from each other, but he chooses to whisper into my ear.

"You are beautiful," he breathes. The minty-ness of his breath brushes across my neck; I get shivers across my body.

"Thanks." It comes out a little more demure than I would usually accept a compliment. He's just so hot, I can't grab my bearings.

Our drinks come quickly and I take a big gulp from my glass, I feel his eyes on me, and all I can say is, I don't mind it one bit. If only his eyes weren't so piercing, I'd be able to hold up my end of the conversation he keeps trying to start.

"What do you do, Salem?"

"I manage a bank."

He laughs, "You work in a bank? I must be going to the wrong one."

"What about you?"

"I own a garage."

"What's that mean?"

"You know, you take your car somewhere to have it fixed after an accident, that's me."

"Oh, that's cool."

The waitress comes for our order and I take a burger, like Kyle, only well- done because pink meat grosses me out.

"What are you wearing under that shirt?" Again, his hot breath skates across the hair on my neck. I know you must be thinking this is a little forward, but as I said, this is *all* I'm interested in. Just sex, plain and simple. My life doesn't need anything more and I don't care how hot he is, this is supposed to be an adventure for one night only.

"I don't have anything on under this." I answer. Finally, in a more comfortable element, I look into his eyes, daring him to confirm it.

"I didn't think so."

I feel his tongue graze my ear and I moan, unable to control myself. I close my eyes and tip my head so he has more access to me. Seizing the opportunity, he runs his tongue from my collarbone back up toward my ear.

My breath is coming quickly; my heart is pounding in my chest in- tune with the throb I feel between my legs.

I shudder a breath when I feel his fingers squeeze my nipple, hardened by excitement. I don't stop him; I don't want to. I want his hands all over me.

"You like me touching you?"

I nod, unable to control the shakiness in my voice.

"I like touching you, you have such a nice body. I want to touch it all over, cover every inch of you with my fingerprints. Drag my tongue up and down your body until you're covered from head to toe with me."

His hand finds the bottom hem of my shirt; he cups my breast, and kneads it roughly in his palm. I hardly notice the little waitress back with our food. I'm very nearly on the verge of something right now and I don't want to stop. Luckily, I don't have to make the choice whether or not I want to fuck him right here and now, with no regard for anyone else here, because he has chosen for me by removing his hand from my t- shirt.

He doesn't apologize to the waitress; he doesn't even acknowledge it. Just takes our plates from her and sets one in front of each of us. She smiles at me, like only a person who is completely uncomfortable does, and then turns to go.

"She probably won't be back to refill our drinks now," I say.

He laughs. "I don't want her to come back." His eyes look ready to devour me.

I watch him take a huge bite out of his burger and it makes my hungry for mine, so I join him and we mostly eat in silence. A few questions here and there getting to know each other on a basic level, but nothing more, which is typical. We are here for very superficial reasons.

I don't mind the lull, I'm actually a quiet person by nature, a little on the introverted side, hence why I choose the online dating and one-night stands.

He finishes first, the waitress came back and gave us each another drink in the mean- time, obviously seeing that we were only focused on eating. I finished mine quickly, thirsty from the excitement.

I put my own burger down and nibble on a fry when I see him looking again.

"I like the way you eat."

I look at him, raising my eyebrow in question.

"You're very focused," he chuckles.

"I wasn't the one who practically inhaled mine," I tease.

"What can I say, if I like something, I put it in my mouth."

I nearly choke. That was not only the most out- of- this- world thing to say, but also the hottest thing, I must be very confused... or very interested in him to find such humor in his weirdness.

"What? You don't like stupid come- on lines?" He feigns heartbreak, putting his hand over his chest.

"I don't mind it."

"Well, there's plenty more where that one came from, you just wait."

"I can hardly contain my excitement."

"How 'bout this one..." he pretends to think for a minute, tipping his head from one side to the other. "When I saw you at your door for the first time, I nearly took you right there."

"I would have let you," I say back, and laugh at his reaction. That's not the rules of the app, there are expectations that are in place that should be followed, it's part of the fun. Getting to know someone, even a little, can help with the trust part of sleeping together.

"Do you want to do that now? Or do you want your third drink?"

I know what he's asking me, do I want to break the rules or not. I tell him I'd like another drink, and he gets it, following the rules. If we make it to the third drink, we are both saying we'd like to proceed. We've just said to each other that this is a done deal.

"You got it, doll."

He flags the waitress and she brings us another round. I take this one more quickly than the last– I'm a nervous drinker.

Kyle puts his hand on my leg; the warmth of his palm is nice.

"What do you do for fun?" he asks, idly running his fingers along the inseam of my jeans.

"I don't really have time for fun."

"That's no way to live."

"Well, what do you do for fun?" It's getting hard to concentrate, his fingers are getting progressively higher on my leg, inching toward my pussy.

"I'm having fun now."

I spread my legs apart, giving him more room to move. His eyes widen and I watch his pupils dilate.

He reaches over, grabs me by my chin and pushes his mouth against mine, planting tiny kisses around my lips, slowly, tracing them with his tongue before moving forward. He pushes inside my mouth, hungrily searching for my return, thrusting deeply, as any horny woman wants it.

Deep and frantic.

His soft mouth tells me everything I need to know about how he will fuck me. And I can't fucking wait. We share the air in our lungs back and forth, unable to pull away for even a second to catch our own.

His hands are all over me, I can feel him up my shirt again, and I press against his hand, craving more of him. I want him to ravage me.

"Do you want to know what I'm going to do to you?"

"Yes." I hardly form the word in my mouth; it's really more of a hiss. I'm getting greedy for him.

He gets up close to my ear again, "I'm going to peel these pants off of you. Then, starting with your feet, I'm going to kiss up your legs until I come to your pussy. I'm going to lick you from asshole to clit." He pulls my ear into his mouth; his hand massages me through my pants, right on the spot in question. "I'm going to smell the sweet scent of you and bury myself inside."

"Ok," I breathe. My head is dizzy, and I'm lost in all of his dirty talk, as if I needed more incentive to lose it right here.

"You make me so hard." Another suck on my ear lobe. "I can't remember a time I was this hard."

"I bet you say that to all the girls." I joke.

"Absolutely not," he says seriously, "you are fucking amazing."

He takes his hand off me and fumbles with the button of his jeans. I look around the dining area for onlookers, moving my attention to his hands when I confirm it's all clear.

He unzips and pulls his cock out from his pants. It's massive, thick and definitely as hard as he'd been explaining, purple, in fact, from all the blood forced south. He doesn't touch it after removing it, just releases it and asks me, "You know what you're going to do with this?"

"What?" I don't want to give him the wrong answer, so I wait for him to say.

"You're going to wrap your hand around it... tightly. Then you're going to jerk me off until I come."

I've never been one for public displays, and this surpasses what I think my limits are, but I want to. So, I do. I take him into my hand, squeezing as tight as I can, realizing my fingers won't meet. My mind goes wild with the thought of him buried inside of me.

He pulls me against him, wrapping his big arm around me. I rest my head on his chest and watch as the tip of his dick leaks pre- come.

"That's right, nice and tight," he says into my ear as it rests against his mouth. I hear him breathing slowly in and out, hissing every now and then when it becomes too much.

He moves his arm from my shoulder and slips his hand under my shirt, my pace quickens. "I'm going fuck these too, squeeze them together and fuck right in the middle of them."

"Oh, god." He has me so worked up my hand is trembling, my body alive with anticipation.

"Salem...I'm almost ready, don't change anything... just keep fucking it."

I watch until ribbons of his come shoot out, narrowly missing my face. It covers the back of my hand as I continue to milk it.

He groans low in his throat until it's done. I reach for a napkin "Lick my come off your hand, clean it up with your mouth."

I look at him to be sure I heard him right. I want to have heard that right. So, when I don't see a joke his eyes, I do it. I take each finger into my mouth and suck until they're clean, then do the same to back of my hand.

"Is your pussy wet?"

"Yes." More wet than I care to say, my panties are soaked.

"Show me."

My heart pounds, his words excite me. I put my hand down the front of my pants, dip my fingers into my very-wet hole and pull it out before I'm ready, knowing that if I keep it down there, I'd need to finish myself off.

I show him my first two fingers, glistening in the overhead light.

He takes my hand, brings in to his face, inhaling the scent of my wet fingers, and then sucks them into his mouth, twirling his tongue around each one individually and then in between. "You taste so fucking good, Salem. I'm going to enjoy this."

He pulls his still semi- hard cock back into his pants and I excuse myself to the bathroom, the alcohol has caught up with me.

I want him to know I'm ready, that I can't wait another second for him. "I'll take another one of those," I say, and wink at him.

KYLE

She heads to the bathroom after I let her out of the booth. I see the waitress and order both of us one more drink then pay the tab. The drinks come and I take a long swig of mine, dig in my pocket for the little baggie, take two of the pills from it, and place them into her drink. They dissolve before she returns.

I see her coming and stand to let her back in. She sees her drink and takes it quickly, all of it, until it's gone.

"Yum," she says, licking her lips.

I can't wait to get her home, tonight has been one of the best I've had. I can hardly wait for the rest.

We talk a few minutes, just until she starts to slur her words.

"I feel dizzy."

"I should get you home before you pass out right here." I could manage, I'd simply throw her over my shoulder and carry her out, but I don't think the wait staff would take to kindly to me doing that. So, I help her to her feet, wrapping an arm around her for balance, and lead her out to the street.

I hail a cab, too many drinks for driving now, good thing it's early enough that they're still out looking for fares. One stops right away, and I'm able to finagle her limp body into the backseat.

"Whoa, one too many for the lady, huh?"

"Yep." I don't feel like conversing right now, so I keep my answer short, assuming he will take the hint and not delve deeper into my situation. I have a lot to think about, number one on the list is all the fun things I'm about to do to this woman.

We pull up to her house a few minutes later with nothing else from the cabbie, and I help myself to her purse for the keys. This time I did take the easier route and threw her over my shoulder— fireman style.

Once in the house, I take a look around, familiarizing myself with the surroundings. She is neat and it looks like everything has a place. I scope out the rest of the house after setting her down on the bed, also, I need to take a leak. I follow the long hallway; leading to what I can only assume is the bathroom. Every house is different, but for the most part, it's easy to tell what the layout is.

I finish in the restroom and make my way back to her; she hasn't moved an inch. I feel very excited to move forward with her, and I only have a few hours to get this done before she wakes up. I set my phone up on her dresser and position it so the bed is in frame. Then I double- check. I can't miss a second of this.

I tug her skin- tight pants down her legs, removing her shoes as I go. Her legs are great, silky smooth and just a hint of a tan. I slide her black thong down next, exposing her hairless pussy. I'm met with puffy lips and bubble gum labia— my favorite. I spread her legs and get a closer look at what she has to offer down there. She is still wet, absolutely saturated. I slide my finger into her seam and collect the juice, tasting her again.

Fuck. It goes right to my dick, I thought I was hard before, but it's nothing compared to now.

I step to the side showing the camera how wet she is.

I lift up her shirt and maneuver it over her head, careful not to rip it. It would be a shame to ruin it; it looks so good on her. Her tits are as spectacular as I knew they'd be. Round and high, soft pink nipples that seem to always be hard. Fake, if I had to guess. They were done well, in my opinion. I pinch each one between my fingers further hardening them.

I run my hands down her trim waist, passed her flared hips, and between her thighs— she is so soft.

I know it may seem strange, that I had a very willing woman in the palm of my hand, and drugged her. I have a compulsion; something inside of me loves the feel of an unconscious body underneath me. The things I can get away with when the other person is unaware of what I'm doing. The thrill of knowing she will have no idea what I'd done to her, waking up in the morning with a foggy memory of what happened between us is all I want her privy to.

I don't consider myself strange for wanting this. We all have our vices; the things we want deep down inside, most of us not brave enough to bring it to fruition. I embrace mine– I thrive on it.

I go in search for things around her bedroom, things I want to use to play with her. I see a few interesting items right away, and toss them next to her on the bed. I come back after collecting from the rest of the house.

I move her to the head of the bed, her back propped against the headboard and tie her wrists to the posts. It's not necessary to do this, the girl is unconscious, but I don't like to fumble around with limbs while I'm doing what I do.

I walk around the bed, dragging one of her legs as I go, and affix it to her wrist, then the next, effectively spreading her. Her head lulls to the side, she is beautiful.

She'll be sore in the morning, I'm sure, but she won't know a reason for it. Luckily, she is flexible; I have a clear view of everything.

I take my clothes off and slide up the bed where my face meets her crotch, taking a deep breath; I get a heady rush from it. I taste her with my tongue, slowly and almost hesitant at first, then progressively more rhythmic.

She may be unconscious, but her body still responds, her clit swells as I work my fingers inside her hole. I feel her getting wetter. I suck hard on her little nub and then flick my tongue. I feel the liquid flow and her body quiver. I lap up every bit– she tastes even sweeter now.

seven

Salem

I woke up in the morning with a splitting headache, a foggy memory, and a soreness across my whole body. But nothing compared to the tender bruised feeling I had between my legs. I could hardly walk.

I took a pain reliever and went into work, I was a few hours late, but they do fine without me, really.

I went home and took a bath and went to sleep, I did that for four days. None of my memories came back, the soreness faded, as did the bruises– good as new.

***

I got home today, reached my hand into my mailbox and came out with a memory stick. I walked right through the door and plugged it into my laptop.

I click on the folder and it plays. My bedroom is the setting– my bed, in particular. I watch as Kyle, my last date, ties me to my bed. My heart is pounding so hard I feel the rush of blood in my ears. I swallow hard, my mouth has gone dry.

I watch him restrain me, in a position I might not be able to recreate when I'm not limber and drugged. My hands and feet are bound together and then over my head to the headboard, it looks like it hurts, and accounts for the pain I had in my legs the few days following.

My eyes are glued to the screen, I can't look away. I watch as he buries his face and eats me; I don't see myself move as he manipulates me. Then I see a tremor, it's subtle, but I see a small twitch, followed by a moan, it has to be coming from me, his mouth is occupied. I can't believe that he brought me to orgasm while I was unconscious. I didn't even know that was possible.

I watch him fuck me, quite brutally, in fact. My hands shake as I watch him ruthlessly pounding inside of me. My head is knocking against the headboard– that may explain my headache I chalked up to a hangover the next morning.

The sounds are a mixture of grunts, the relentless banging coming from my head meeting the headboard and the headboard hitting the wall. I can't imagine what that would feel like if I were conscious, it looks as though he's trying to fuck through me, his ass cheeks clench together hard with each hard push he thrusts into me.

The picture over my bed starts shaking as he moves faster. I look up to it now, see that it is secure, and probably hadn't fallen off the nail. My god, I don't know how it didn't.

He finishes finally, collapsing on top of my body. I'm relieved that it's over, I can't imagine what my body would have felt like if his was able to hold out much longer.

I've only ever been with men who were able to make it last fifteen minutes tops, even less at the rate he was going. I look at the streaming bar at the bottom and realize that it lasted well over half an hour. I also realize he wasn't done with me. The progress bar sits well under the half way mark.

How long was he here?

The scene cuts to another frame. He must have done some editing before giving this to me. I collect myself and prepare to watch the rest. I have to know what happened, what he did while I was out.

He has the camera in his hand now, and there is a close up shot of my pussy. It's wet, still responding, even if my brain was not alert to tell it to be.

He is fingering me at first, but he replaces them with a cucumber. My jaw drops as I watch him insert the entire thing inside of me. I hear him say something, but can't focus enough to decipher the words. It's pretty nonsensical, a bunch of gibberish one might hear from someone while fucking them.

He draws the veggie out of me, only to push it back inside, over and over while rubbing the little nub above it.

I can't imagine why he is trying to make my body come. I've not had this much attention paid to my orgasms when I'm alert. But there it is again, that shudder and the telltale cream that covers the cucumber when he pulls it out of me finally.

I'm a little embarrassed by that, I can't help it. My face flushes as I watch him slide his finger through my come, then turn the camera to himself– selfie style, and suck it off his finger. "You're delicious," he groans, closing his eyes and savoring it.

A new wave of embarrassment hits me as I watch him lick me, his long tongue slipping between my folds and lapping it all up.

"I wonder if you've ever tried any ass play? We didn't really get much conversation in." He's talking to me through the camera, to the real me, the one watching this.

To be honest I've never had anything in there, I can't imagine it would be easy for him to get anything inside of me back there.

The editing he's done brings me back in a different position. My knees are folded under me and my ass is high in the air. My cheek rests against the bed, my eyes are slightly open, but I can tell they see nothing.

Kyle brings the camera close as he pushes his fingers inside my ass. They look wet, and I assume he's smeared a lubricant of some sort on– which I can't help but be thankful for. He continues adding fingers, loosening the tight hole, and when he deems it's wide enough, he replaces them with his cock.

I remember how my fingers were barely able to touch when I jerked him off in the restaurant, and somehow it looks even bigger on screen. The shaft is so much thicker than you would find on even the shelves of a sex- shop.

Somehow, my ass lets him in, he is not gentle when entering, and he just shoves himself against the opening until he's buried inside.

"You are so fucking tight; I bet I'm the first in here."

He wraps his hand around my hip tightly— holding me in place, so when he starts to move, I don't topple over. The other hand is doing an expert job of holding the camera at an angle that lets me witness every gory detail of what he's doing to me.

Slowly, he moves, in and then back out, pushing his entire cock inside. I watch as my hole becomes more welcoming to him.

He stretches out his arm, grabs hold of my hair, twists my face up toward the camera, and zooms in on a trickle of drool that seeped past my lips. Then he pulls my head off the bed using my hair after tightly wrapping his hand around it, then brings the camera back to where we are joined and moves at a quicker pace.

My head is at an awkward angle and doesn't look comfortable. He obviously doesn't care about my comfort though, I can tell as he starts to move quicker, thrusting harder.

I have never seen a man so ready again after just having come— twice. I don't know how much recovery time he gave himself in between. For all I know it was hours and he made a fucking sandwich while waiting for the next round. He has the stamina of a racehorse; I can see the sweat glistening on his belly and still he pounds.

I am absolutely shocked as he pulls out of me, releasing my head unceremoniously, dropping it to the bed. He takes his cock in his hand and directs it to the gaping hole that is my ass and spirts inside of it. The bit that misses, he drags his finger through and deposits it inside. "Oops, missed a spot," he says, while doing it.

He turns the camera to his face, the hair on his forehead is wet from sweat, he wipes across it, sweeping the hair away from his face and wicking the droplets away.

He is short of breath as he speaks to me, his chest heaving from exertion. "I had a really great time with you tonight. I've never been happier to go out on a work night, may take some recovering on your part, I hope it doesn't take too long. You brought something out of me tonight; I hadn't been able to appreciate before. I am grateful to you for having that last drink, giving me the opportunity to enjoy you as only my sick cock likes. We all have our quirks and I thank you for letting me use you for mine."

The screen goes black, he must have either cut the camera then or edited the part where he dressed me and tucked me into my bed.

How thoughtful.

eight

My heart begins to beat normal again; it's quite a weird experience watching yourself go through things you have no recollection of.

That was seriously the hottest thing I've ever seen, I think about logging on to message Kyle right now, for a repeat performance, but that is frowned upon, this is supposed to be for one- time experiences. But even still, I hit the icon and open up the Date Rape™ app, looking for him.

They really do have an app for everything.

The End

THE EMBALMER

SADIE IS TEMPTED BY A BODY IN THE FUNERAL
HOME. SHE CAN'T HELP HERSELF; HER CURIOSITY
IS TOO STRONG. THE DEPRAVED AND OBSCENE
THOUGHTS WON'T DISAPPEAR, AND WITH
NOTHING HOLDING HER BACK, SHE SUCCUMBS
TO HER SICK DESIRES.

ONE

The thin white sheet is tenting. I can't keep my eyes off of it.

There is a common misconception that when men die, they get an erection, and unless you are face down with the blood pooling in that direction, it's simply untrue.

That guy, however, is sporting a huge erection. Cause of death, heart attack. He's not the body I'm working on right now, he is next in line, though.

James has been working on the same old man for over an hour, they're always a challenge, their faces sag and it's hard to make them look life- like in order for their families to recognize them. He's an expert though, and I have every confidence that he will do an excellent job. His back is to me, and I'm glad, I definitely can't get caught eyeballing the dead dude's junk.

I can't seem to get over how big it is, I keep catching myself losing track of what I'm doing and fantasizing about what might be under there.

I've honestly never given any other body more than a cursory look, nothing but business for the greying and flaccid ones. But this man, whose sheet is tucked under the chiseled chin of a god, has me curious. The sheet can't hide how sculpted his body is, I can tell he is in perfect shape, I can't imagine the reason for the heart attack unless it was genetic. Sad, really, seems like such a waste.

I catch myself breathing heavy, and when James asks me if I'm ok, I drag my tongue across my dry lips and swallow hard, trying to recoup the semblance of normalcy. Then tell him I'm fine, that I have a headache and I need a moment.

I take a cigarette from my pack and head up the stairs to the main floor of the house and as far away from the converted basement as I can get right now. I light it before I'm outside and I pull the drag deep into my lungs before blowing it out, along with the thoughts that really shouldn't be there anyway.

What the fuck is wrong with you?

I cannot get over how affected I am by this whole thing. I've never been so interested in something like this before, sure there have been times where curiosity had gotten the better of me and maybe I wondered. But this, this is not wondering, this is fantasizing– this is lust.

I'm soaked between my legs, the heat is practically radiating throughout my core, even while standing outside on a brisk day without my coat, which I left in my hasty getaway, I'm hot.

I take another long pull and slowly let the smoke out, expelling even more air than needed, in hopes that I can get that sheet and all the implications hiding under it out from under my skin.

I flick the butt near the ashtray, not giving it too much of an effort, and then head back down the stairs.

James is grabbing the keys to the transport van and I ask him 'what's up?'

"Twenty something female, gunshot wound."

I look at the taboo man lying on the table, and before I can stop myself, I say, "I can get her, you could take care of this one."

He gives me a strange look. I never volunteer for transport. He brushes my offer to the side and grabs his jacket.

"I'll be back as soon as I can."

"Thanks," I say back, hoping I haven't confused him too much.

I wait until the door closes before returning to the forty- two- year- old suicide on my table, I just have to finish her neck, she hung herself and did quite a bit of damage in the process.

I'm annoyed that I'm not done already, I should have been able to knock this one out quickly and moved on to the next, except that's what I'm procrastinating. I can't imagine putting my hands on him in any capacity and not touching him inappropriately. Wrapping my fingers around that big cock I see, barely hiding under there.

I can't keep my feet from walking forward, my head keeps telling them to stop, but they hear the half-heartedness behind the pleas. I need to see what's under there.

Just a peak to quench the curiosity. Then I can get the fuck back to work.

I take that peek, but I don't cover him back up like I thought I would, instead I'm stuck staring. He must have had some sort of augmentation done on it. That would explain the rigidity and the slight scar I see around the circumference about midway up his thick shaft.

I can't stop my shaking hand from reaching out. My mind is foggy with confusion and lust. I know I want this, but I don't *want* to want this. I don't want to feel the need, the desire to do this, to touch him. I want to remain the normal girl, with normal thoughts. I want to think this is repulsive, but I can't.

The smoothness of his cock sends a thrill across my body. I've never touched a corpse with anything other than professional intentions. Never given it a single thought.

This man, for some reason, has me twisted inside, conflicted, and fucking *horny*.

The excitement inside of me is overflowing; I can't stop myself from stroking him. He can't feel it, so I know it's only for my own sake. I must want to feel him like this, sliding inside my fisted hand. Slowly, I glide my hand from base to tip, squeezing hard at the tip, then back down.

I can feel the rhythm inside my core, images of him inside of me, accepting his full length deeply. Then the thoughts of him lying here while I do it spring into my mind. I like that he's here on the gurney, that he can't say anything, that he would be used for my pleasure alone. I hold myself back but let my imagination run away, let it go toward what it's craving.

It takes me to the very depths of the disgusting thoughts that I'm only now realizing I have inside me. I have a very healthy and active sex life, but I can say with a hundred percent certainty, that I've not been this wet for any other man, or reason, in my life. I let go of his shaft only long enough to grab his chart, I don't know what I'm looking for until I find it. His STD results. They'd done a swab of it and the results are negative.

I can't wrap my head around why I even care. What does that mean? Is this feeling right now so strong that I know I'm going to do something about it? Does it mean I want to?

Before I can answer any of those questions, the double doors swing open and James pulls the gurney in through the door. Luckily, his back is to me and I have time to right the sheet. I can't believe how distracted I let myself become, how overwhelming this pull is for me that I'd almost lost everything for it. My god, that would have been awful.

"Hey, James," is all I can say, and it probably shouldn't have been said in the first place, I never welcome him back.

He must realize it too, because he looks at me with his brows raised. "You need something, Sadie?"

"Nope... just this damn headache again."

"I think it must be the chemicals today."

I notice, then, that his face is flush and looks a little green. "What's going on with you?"

"I think I've got a cold coming on, can't get over this nausea thing." I see it then, just how bad he looks, and it makes me feel horrible for him.

"We could just put her in the fridge and you could take off. I'll get these two sorted out," I offer.

His face looks like he'll take me up on it, but he says he'll stay.

"Really, don't worry about it. I need to finish with the suicide anyway. I'll just tuck these ones away; we'll get to them tomorrow. You look like shit. I can take an aspirin for mine. You need bedrest, plus, you're probably contagious, and I don't want to catch that shit." It comes out a little harder than I intend, but seriously... gross.

"Yea, that might be for the best." He drags her body to the fridge and slides it inside.

"I'll get these two." I say a little too quickly, hopefully his ailment is keeping him a little slower mentally than normal, and not as keen to notice how weird I'm acting.

He doesn't seem to notice my oddities and I'm grateful for it.

I watch, without moving an inch, out of fear alone, as he gathers his things and heads to the door.

Relief floods when I realize I'm alone. I can hardly think straight since almost being caught in the act of defiling the corpse.

I do the only thing I can do right now, while holding tightly to my rational self. I put this fucker in the fridge, shoving the door hard to latch it. Then I finish with the woman who should have been done already and joining him, but still, she needs my attention. Her funeral is tomorrow, and I have to get her looking her best for it.

I think of anything I can to keep my mind free of him and it works. I'm able to nearly forget about him in the cooler. And by the time the woman looks as near perfect as she's going to get, he is a distant memory.

Almost.

I do have to jog up the stairs to fight a bit of curiosity creeping back in. But, once I'm upstairs, I am able to eat and watch some television before tucking in to bed for the night.

TWO

I'm having trouble sleeping, obviously my subconscious is not able to calm down from all the excitement. As soon as my eyes are open, my thoughts are on that man downstairs. Maybe it's living in such close proximity to him. Maybe it's my morbid fascination with him, for some reason I cannot understand, he has me trapped inside a loop of curiosity.

As I lay in bed, I try very hard to focus on the realization of what would happen if I gave in to my thoughts, if I stoked them with a bit more reality. If I followed, what my legs want me to do right now, and walked down the stairs to him, peacefully lying there on the slab of frigid metal. What would it take from me if I did that? What would be the consequences to my soul?

I can hardly think. The rambling and scrambled thoughts have been obscured by the picture my head has created of him down there, completely naked beneath the thin sheet, his thick muscles hardened by physical activity and a gorgeous face to boot.

Fuck.

I can't stay here; I can't just pretend like I am able to accomplish that. I know I don't morally find anything wrong with what I have in my mind. It is a crime, but a victimless one. Honestly, if I think about it, I know that I don't abide by all of societies laws, I don't let a red light stop me if no one is around, I don't let the grapes eaten in the grocery store bog me down with guilt.

I shouldn't let this weigh on me, shouldn't let what society thinks is appropriate define what I think is nothing more than getting off. No matter what, I'm the only one who has to live with this, and I am willing. For fucks sake, the guy is dead. What does he care?

I let my feet take me down the winding staircase and around the corner to flip the light switch, the fluorescent bulbs flicker until they charge and brighten the room.

My slippers drag on the floor, making the only noise in the silent room. It is always so quiet down here after hours. Not that it has the hustle and bustle during operating hours, but it's eerie in here at night.

I go to the drawer that holds my heart attack guy with the boner and pull on the door, then slide the drawer out. I catch myself looking around the room, subconsciously aware that what I'm about to do is wrong, but still wanting to do it. Almost needing to do it, the compulsion is driving me mad.

I move the sheet slowly down his body, uncovering his hairy chest. He has the light shade of grey that people have once they're dead, it doesn't even phase me. I don't pause, I continue moving down his body. Standing next to him, I lean over the bottom drawer and take his cock in my hand again. This time I intend to do something other than just groping. There is no stopping me now.

I lift up my long shirt over my head and straddle the man, resting my ass on his thighs. The cool feel of his body sends a shiver up my spine. The rush of cold hits me fast, he's hard underneath me.

I put my hands on him and feel the tightness of his chest. I close my eyes and feel him, touch everywhere. Run my fingers across his body and down to the meaty cock that interrupted my sleep, then I raise up to hover over it, rubbing it against my clit. I hiss. The feel of it against my hotness is a sensation I will never forget. I thought it might cool me down, but it does not, the drastic temperature change exhilarates me.

I let it enter me slowly, gingerly lowering myself down on it. It does the same thing to my insides— cools them, but only in temperature, nothing can take this from the top of my hot and naughty list.

Moving with purpose, I let myself experience every inch of this man's big cock. I feel the fullness of him and am compelled to move faster, running my hand down my chest, across my trembling stomach, until I find the little nub that's begging to be touched, then rub circles around it.

My breathing, the sound I can't hold in when being fucked, and the tiny moans that escape me interrupt the quiet room. I keep one hand on him for balance as I quicken the pace. I get lost with him inside of me, the feel of my orgasm creeps in and I rub harder— fuck harder— deeper than I've ever been reached.

I come hard and loud, then fuck myself frantically on top of him. So frantic, in fact, that I don't hear the noise. The noise that I should have heard, that would not have happened if I wasn't preoccupied with this man. If I could have just kept my wits about me, I would have remembered to lock the lower entrance doors to the room.

But, instead, they swing wide open. The heavy door hits the wall and it only slightly alarms me. I don't stop, I can't, not until the voice comes. The voice that doesn't belong to James, but instead a stranger.

"Holy fuck!" says the voice, which I match to the man as soon as my eyes open. He has a phone in his hand, and it's pointed right at me.

I'm at a loss for what to do. I stumble off the slab, to the floor, on my hands and knees.

I'd be embarrassed by that if I weren't mortified from being caught fucking a dead body.

My face is red, the heat of shame crept up my neck, I'm flushed. I can't get to my feet; I can't do anything but bury my face on the cold cement floor.

I hardly realize that I should be concerned about the three men standing in front of me. It dawns on me that I shouldn't be thinking of my embarrassment, instead, I should be pissed, or at the very least, I should be scared.

They are huge men. Three. Huge. Men.

I get to my feet with very little grace, but it's done now, and I square my shoulders and meet their faces. Each one of them.

The first is tallest and thinnest, but that doesn't mean he is not intimidating.

He is.

The second is slightly shorter, thick, in the way that you know he has muscles, but they're hiding underneath a layer of fat. He's glaring at me.

I move quickly to the last, he's tall and muscular, covered in tattoos up to his neck. Bright and colorful. His hair is short, making it easier to see them all. He has a smile on his face– more of a smirk, really, watching me through the lens of his phone.

"Nice to meet you," he says, finally meeting my eyes.

The accent is thick, I can't place it. I'm not good at pinpointing regions, if it weren't so apparent, I might not have even noticed it.

"Shut up, Rhys," the glaring fat man says.

"Just being polite," he says back at him without looking away from me.

The blush comes back, this time it's from the thoughts that just came into my head of him whispering into my ear, telling me such dirty things with that voice. It's low and gravely, and coupled with the accent, sends me over the top.

I swallow hard and avert my eyes. I don't miss the huge grin that crosses his face before I can get away. My mouth dries until it feels like a desert, making me anxious. I have to be able to speak to these men. And hopefully that's all they'll be doing to me tonight.

"You get a lady in here tonight?" the thin one asks.

"Uhhh." I can't remember anything at this point, I can't recall something to help him.

"She'd be blonde, big tits– she got shot." The fat man cuts off his friend, obviously taking the lead.

I gather my thoughts and realize; they're looking for the lady James brought in earlier. I didn't get a good look at her but I know she is blonde. I try and rack my brain for the number of the cubby we put her in.

They look impatient. I get nervous. I don't do well under pressure. That's why I work with dead people. It has always promised little to no social interactions. But, I guess, if you start fucking them, bad things happen. I just never imagined it would be thugs showing up in the middle of the night looking for a corpse.

I point to the door they should open to find her. Rhys walks over and pulls on it. Luckily, I was right; there she is, covered with a sheet, completely untouched by us. He pulls the sheet off her and lets it fall to the floor.

"Give me the shit you found in her," the fat leader says.

I forgo the on-the-tip-of-my-tongue sarcastic remark and keep my composure.

"We haven't done anything to her, yet," I say.

"Really? Why is she all cut up then?" Rhys says in his sexy accented way.

I can't help it; it flusters me and makes me so fucking hot. He has one of those rolling r's.

"Um," I take a deep breath. "She had an autopsy done; we didn't embalm her yet." I hope it sounds as strong as I planned, I'm practically swooning. I have always had a thing for accents. The way I imagine his tongue would feel on me, using it to give me exactly what I want. Buried between my legs– eating me– fucking me with the very thing that is making me wet right now.

"So, it should still be in here, the guy at the hospital said they hadn't found anything," Rhys says to me.

"I don't know what you're looking for. I haven't seen her before."

"She had drugs in her tits when she died. We need to get them back." He looks at me expectantly.

"I don't want any part of this," I say.

"Listen, bitch, you are a part of this. And if you want to walk away right now, I'm sure I could show a few of the right fucking people that you were caught fucking Mr. Big Cock over there when we walked in," the fat boss says.

He's angry and I don't try and tell him he would implicate himself in some pretty bad things if he were to do that.

"Calm the fuck down, Leo," Rhys tells him, putting his phone in his back pocket. As if I needed one more reason for him to be attractive. Coming to a lady's rescue, even when you are a strong female, is always nice. It does get him a glare from the leader, Leo.

Knowing their names worries me; I hope they don't think they need to kill me.

Leo takes over the conversation, but does so with a little less hatred spewing remarks. "I need you to get our shit out of her titties."

I'm confused as to how it may have been missed during autopsy. I mean, things are overlooked, but implants are usually found pretty easily, without even looking for them.

I walk over to see if it was in this case. I feel around her chest and can easily confirm she's got her implants still inside. Reaching for a scalpel I cut across the stitches put there by a lazy M.E.— or assistant, I'd say, by the lack of precision.

I fold back the skin and see that the implants are intact and inside. I remove the first, after putting a glove on, and hand it over to the thin man, whose hand is reaching for it.

I don't have too much time with it, but I can confirm the implant is full of drugs, a black substance in tiny bags within the implant sack– whatever that might be, I have no idea.

"And the other," Leo says, impatiently.

I quickly go after the other one, handing it over swiftly. The thin guy holds one in each hand, not really knowing what to do with them. It might look funny, if I weren't so fucked right now.

"Ok," I say, more to fill the silence.

"Let's go, Leo," Rhys says, turning his back to me, effectively blocking me from seeing the intense conversation they're having with each other using only their eyes.

"Fine, but if she gets even a *little* messy, she's fuckin' done. And I know you know what I mean by *done*," Leo says to Rhys, before turning to the thin guy and saying, "Let's go."

They leave me alone with Rhys to explain how shit is going to go, assuming I'm willing to comply. Although, if I'm not, I am certain he is supposed to kill me. I can see it in his eyes. There's a hint of pleading in them. I can't hold his gaze; I look down at his colorful arms instead. Then down to his thick fingers, then over a few inches to his crotch.

Damn it.

This man has seriously affected me; something about him, I couldn't name it if I tried, has gotten to me and wrapped itself around my insides.

"Listen, beautiful lady, I need you to behave."

"Ok," I say, but I don't know if he is referring to me looking at his crotch or if he means the task at hand. The thing they talked about without words.

"Thanks for such a nice compliment, by the way." He brings his eyes to the front of his pants and I know he did catch me.

I wish I didn't blush every fucking time I heard him speak. I wish he didn't have this thing that captivated me. I'm completely lost in whatever this attraction I have to him.

The way he speaks, the simple words, whatever they are, completely hypnotize me. The cadence of his accent, and the ease in which he forms his words, is wrapping around my head and swirling inside my tummy.

Standing here fully naked, and literally caught with a dead guy inside of me, doesn't stop my nipples from exposing my state of complete arousal. I can feel my lust trickling down the inside of my clenched thighs. Somehow it is not as awkward as it clearly should be. He has this ease about him, some sort of swagger that screams to me and makes all my inhibitions melt away.

"I'm sure you know, that Leo will follow through with what he said. He will leak the video."

I can only shake my head; my voice wouldn't work even if I tried.

"You heard Leo, he's ok with you, so long as you can help us out with a few things. The people we have dealings with that may end up going south," he looks at me poignantly. "We need you to help with those. You can do that, right?"

I don't know what the fuck I can do for them. I have James here most days and I can't necessarily have a stream of people coming and going as they please without raising suspicion. But I tell him yes. I know I don't want to fuck with these men, I don't want to end up dead, and they look exactly the type to do something like that if I can't be useful.

"Ok, so for now, you just hold tight and wait, I can't say when we may need you."

"How are you going to let me know you need my help? I have a partner that will start asking questions and possibly get suspicious if he sees people like you hanging around."

"People like me?" he has a flirty smirk on his face. "What are people like *me*?"

"I don't know, thugs?" I regret it the second it's out of my mouth, I really shouldn't be tempting fate, I should be being on my best behavior, considering who I'm in front of.

"Little lady, I suggest you watch your mouth when we are not alone, I know Leo and Thomas wouldn't like hearing that."

I can hear the seriousness in his voice, which is even hotter when he's laying down the law and being stern. "Ok," I say. I can hardly contain the shiver I feel cover my body.

I can see he is aware of the effect he has on me, his eyes follow the length of my body, and the scrutiny arouses me. "Anyway," he shakes his head and refocuses on my eyes. "We can be discreet, so long as you can be helpful. I'll make sure the others know that we'd have to wait for after hours to do business."

"Thank you." I don't know why it sounds like he's conceding, I wonder what it would be like for me here if he weren't being so reasonable— if I could even use that word in this context.

"I'll take a key for the doors here."

"Uh... I think you can just ring the bell." I don't want them down here fishing around in things while I'm upstairs sleeping, or if James shows up earlier than me, I can't have him find things.

"That won't do. Key. Now."

Well, since he's using his stern voice again, I really can't deny him. I take the spare from the ring by the door and put it inside his waiting hand. "You need to put whoever it is in the drawer right here." I point to the one that we never use, center row, last box. It has a sticky roller that makes it a pain in the ass to pull out.

"Got it." He's all business now, the spark of flirtation is gone. It makes me want to cover up more than ever. I finally *feel* naked.

"See you later, love," he says, then turns to go.

I wait until the heavy door closes completely before I move. The first thing I do is lock it.

THREE

The next few days I have some of the most vivid dreams of Rhys. I wake covered in cold sweats of arousal. Obsession— if I'm actually honest with myself. His voice pulls me awake, even though he's not here, I hear him perfectly inside my brain.

The days pass, and I find nothing in the drawer, I'm jittery and jumpy at every sound. James takes notice right away. I didn't have an answer for the reason, so our relationship is strained. I'm sure he is thinking it's something he has done. But how can I explain the real reason for the distance and weird behavior? I can't.

I'm almost able to pretend that the night never happened, when I hear the lock click. I'm alone, and cleaning everything for the next day, when the doors swing open. The three men file inside, Thomas, the tall, thin one, carrying a body.

Fuck.

"Nice to see you in something other than your birthday suit," Leo says.

"Not really," Rhys says under his breath. That gets him a look of disapproval from Leo.

He shrugs it off. "What? She's hot."

"Anyway... we got something for you." He nods to Thomas, who then brings the body forward. I point to the table and he sets the man down. Both Thomas and the body are covered in blood.

"What am I supposed to do with him? You got something inside of him too?"

"No, we need you to get rid of him," Rhys says.

I look up at him, a better place to focus my attention anyway. "Why?" I regret the question right away, I shouldn't ask these things that I know could be detrimental to my health, but I've never been in a situation where I had to watch myself so closely. "I'm sorry. I don't need to know that," I say to no one in particular.

Leo moves forward, putting himself close enough that I could touch him. "Don't push me, bitch. You will not like what I do to people taking an interest in what I do."

I press my lips together and nod at him, trying my hardest not to cower. I hate being called a bitch simply for my gender, but I let it go. I mean, what else am I supposed to do?

"So, you want me to make the body disappear. Is that it?"

"Yes."

"In the chamber? You want me to cremate him?" I hope that's what he's asking, I can't imagine what else he wants me to do. Burying him is out of the question, but I could easily run the incinerator if he wanted me to.

"You got it. No trace, fast and easy."

"Alright." Relief takes the weight from my shoulders and I relax. If this is all they want from me, I could be all right. I do it all day anyway.

They stand around, instead of leaving as I thought they would.

Rhys walks over and helps me lift the man from the table. "Leo has some trust issues," he whispers into my ear. I cannot imagine a better way to get through this than him whispering directions to me.

In a way, I'm kind of glad this is all happening. As fucked up as it seems, and all things considered, it hasn't been as bad as it could be. Disposing of a few bodies here and there isn't awful. I do it on a daily basis for work, and as we've recently learned, my morals are not that of an upstanding citizen.

After closing the door on the oven, Rhys comes to stand right behind me; he puts his hands on my shoulders then leans in close to whisper in my ear, "it will get easier." The t's and s fall softly from his lips onto the hair of my neck, sending electricity through my skin before the r rolls its way into my ear, goosebumps erupt along my spine.

I don't know if he's picking up on some other sort of dilemma I'm having and assigning the agitation to this ordeal, but I do have to say, it's nice that he notices these things.

He squeezes my shoulders a couple times, digging deep into the muscles, and if we were alone, I'd turn right now and put my mouth on his. Instead, I struggle to restrain the moan that is threatening to escape, and then I take a step away before it's impossible.

He doesn't move away, so I come face to face with him when I turn, his eyes burn right into mine. I can feel his thoughts; feel everything they're saying to me. He's so reassuring in them, without words, his beautiful blue eyes tell me he will keep me safe, and I trust that he will.

The only thing that can take my eyes from his is what he does next. I catch a glimpse of his pink tongue, the same tongue that has become my obsession, licking his full bottom lip, leaving behind wetness that I can't help but want to taste.

My own comes out on a subconscious adventure and I bite my lip to keep from saying anything about it, balling my hands into fists at my side to keep from touching him. The pain in my lip hits me seconds later, and I let it go before I draw blood.

The whole thing only takes a minute, at the most, but it feels like so much has happened. So many tiny and intricate things transpired in that time that I feel overwhelmed. The feelings that I can't accept, because it makes me crazy to think that love at first sight might exist. And that I'm staring at it in the face. It scares me to no end. But I can't help myself, I know that this is real, I know that what I feel is something otherworldly. Something that happens when two people have the same need, that someone could pick up on that and meet it. I can't help but feel this man is my need, and only he will do to fill it.

He finally steps back; I see the miniscule tick of regret on his face. I know he was where I was mentally, thinking all the same things. He also knows that now is not the time, so he takes himself out of it.

"Alright, we done here?" he asks Leo.

"Yep, looks like the lady is useful after all, good call, Rhys." Then he turns to me. "Be seeing you, little lady."

The two men leave ahead of Rhys, who I think will say something to me in confidence, but he doesn't. He just looks into my hungry eyes and does his rendition of the sexiest smile I've ever seen. It takes the breath from my lungs, stirs up the little sleeping butterflies in my stomach and fucks my mind into a complete mess.

Then he leaves, and I'm feeling the loss instantly, the room is empty, and feels cold without him in it. I take a deep breath before I pass out and crumble to the floor. My legs won't work to move, so I stay planted, staring at the door. Eventually, I find the strength to tame the tremors so I can leave.

Knowing I'll just lie in bed, shuffling through the thoughts, the what- ifs, and possibilities of him. His words, however few, replaying in my head, hearing all the meaning behind the limited words we can say in those brief moments. I am able to survive this whole ordeal only because of those times I get to spend near him.

FOUR

I do just as I assume, and lie awake, alone and yet somehow not. He's right here with me even if it is only in thought. Sleep is hard to chase down, and when I finally fall, it is at the very tip, restless and fidgety. I wake with the sun, much earlier than I like, but what I have become accustomed to since meeting Rhys.

I lie in my bed; full minutes pass, as I try to rid my thoughts of him. I can't help but bring my hand between my legs, swollen and aching. I rub that pesky little nub until I come, and still, I find no relief. Frustrated and unsatisfied, I leave the bed in a pissed off mood.

I get ready to start the day, I'd be early going downstairs to work, but I have nothing else to put my focus into, so I get ready and rush downstairs to drown in routine.

It's dark until I turn the light on, I pull open the cadaver drawer and get to work immediately on the man I left here last night. His funeral is this evening and I shouldn't have put him off this long, but I can hardly focus on what needs to be done.

He only needs a few touch ups, he's relatively young and there was no trauma to his exterior. I get lost in the particulars of my job, humming to the music that fills the air.

I hear the door open and look up a moment later, expecting to see James, but am confronted by the three men I have grown to both love and hate.

"You do know that it's business hours," I say to the group, a little harsher than is smart.

"Got a job, can't wait around all day for you to be available," Leo, ever the friendly guy, says.

"Then, by all fucking means, what can I do to serve you?" I put my hand on my hip to emphasize my irritation. It's still early, and I'm not really expecting James, but the deal was agreed upon and I can't let them get away without, at the very least, letting them know I'm annoyed.

It's the fucking principle.

"Got one of our own, he needs to be looked after," Rhys chimes in, and simply hearing that accented voice calms everything inside of me.

"K, bring him in." I roll my eyes, more at myself, than anyone else. This man truly could ask me for anything at this point and I'd drop everything for him to make him happy.

Leo and Thomas leave together, I assume to do what I said, and Rhys comes toward me. The butterflies are back, the freefalling starts, and I try and hold myself upright.

"Thank you, he means a lot to us, wouldn't want anyone else to handle this," he says, reaching out and tucking a stray hair behind my ear. The brief touch warms my skin and flushes my face. I suck my lip into my mouth, this time I don't bite down, this time I'm only trying to stop myself from saying something stupid.

My eyes tick across his face, from the top of his forehead down, so I can remember every detail, memorize it for later, when I can close them and recall every tiny nuance of him. The tiny scar across his eyebrow, the light freckles that dot the bridge of his nose, which has a slight bump on the bridge, I can't tell if it's from a break or just how it's always been. I don't miss a single thing, though.

I feel compelled to ask him, but I don't, instead, I let my eyes wander lower. The neck of his wife- beater is low enough to see the spatter of hair that would be hidden in another type of shirt. There are tons of women that love a smooth and hairless chest; I however, have never been one.

I catch all the intricate detail of his artwork and find a small coin shaped scar under one of them, slightly raised.

"What's that from?" I ask, meeting his eyes that were busy watching me during my inspection.

"Had a bad step dad who used me like an ashtray for his cigars. It's not the only one down there."

He doesn't sound like it traumatized him, it does, however, sound like it still pisses him off.

"Oh." It's the only thing I can get out before the doors slam open. I startle and scramble away like I'd been caught doing something awful.

I look over to him when I hear the chuckle that tells me I'm being ridiculous. I can't help but smile back at him.

"Put him in the cooler," I tell the men, who look at me for direction.

I see Leo may have a problem with the instruction and I tell him, "I can't do anything with him right now, James will be here soon and I can't explain to him why the incinerator is on when we have no scheduled cremations today."

"Fine," Leo concedes, "but I want it done tonight, if I find out you fucked off and didn't, you'll fucking regret it."

"I got it. Not my first time." I hold his stare until he breaks it on his end. Following my lead to the cooler, I open the door and slide out the metal table for them. They get him situated and I can't help but notice the resemblance to Rhys. They both have dark hair and a softer looking face, some might call it a baby face, but for the dotting of hair that looks as though they've missed a few days of shaving.

I look over to Rhys, checking to see if there is a familial resemblance, or if it is just a coincidence. The look on his face is not that of someone who has lost anyone other than a friend. So, I feel better for him— guessing I'm right in my assumption.

I shut the door, and just in time. I hear the roar of James's truck. It's a too- big thing that makes all sorts of unnecessary noise. I'm grateful for it now, and rush them up the stairs, telling them, that unless they want to get caught in here and ruin a good thing, they'll follow me. I hear nothing but footsteps from them as they rush up behind me.

I unlock the door and close it behind us all, just as I hear James downstairs slamming the door shut.

I walk them straight to the front door, holding it open expectantly. The men take their leave and I have a rush of relief as they don't argue or take liberties with my house. It's one thing for them to be in the basement, a completely different thing when invited into my home, where they may now feel is open to them.

I watch Rhys walk away, he doesn't turn and I don't really expect him to. The sure way he carries himself is fucking beautiful, he has a swagger that can only come from confidence. His low hung jeans hanging on by the roundedness of his ass, it is truly hypnotic. I take a shaky breath and head downstairs when I no longer have my eye candy to look at.

"You get here early?" James asks.

"Yea, couldn't sleep, I am about finished with number eight though, so he'll be ready for tonight." I head in that direction now, keeping my head down and eyes averted, jumping right back in where I left off. A few finishing touches, and I'm done in no time.

We have gotten back into our work- flow again, letting the awkwardness go, working together nicely. The day passes quickly and James heads out when he is done with his last job, leaving me to finish with mine, and what I almost forgot— the body in the cooler. I can't believe I hadn't given it another thought. I really must be made for this type of thing. Hiding bodies for thugs must be a calling.

I put my finished work into the cooler and make my way over to the Rhys look- alike. I pull the drawer out and look again at his face. He doesn't have many similarities once I'm in full blown comparison- mode— just enough to intrigue me.

He's wearing the same wife- beater tank- top and I find he has the same exact tattoo as Rhys. An eagle with wide spread wings, right across his chest. It must be some sort of insignia for their club, or whatever you call it.

I picture the quarter sized burn scar under the left wing, and can't help but think that he would make a fine substitution for what I need from Rhys. The thought seems to have hit the nail on the head; I feel that strong tingle between my legs that has only ever come from Rhys.

I trace the tattoo, running my finger across the full outline of it. I get lost in a sort of trance while my fingers work across his flesh, cool from the refrigerator.

The heat swells inside of me, hitting me deep inside my core. I can picture Rhys here right now; I can see all the things I want to see— need to see. I pull the scalpel from my pocket, cutting the fabric from his chest, opening it wide to display the rest of his tattoos. Although, very different from what Rhys has adorned, it still does the trick. The only thing missing is the hint of a scar under the wing.

I go to my purse, pulling a cigarette from the pack, and light it. I take a long satisfying pull from it and touch it to his chest, branding him with the mark of Rhys. I run my finger over it, and feel what it would be like to touch Rhys.

All I need now is something to enhance him. I go to the cupboard and find my hardening filler, mix the proper ratio and inject it into the underside of his cock, stretching it and massaging it to distribute the filler evenly throughout his shaft. The stroking motion of this cock adds to my excitement.

My mouth begins to water as I imagine my hand wrapped around Rhys. I have trouble getting the filler into the head of his cock and suddenly I find myself wrapping my lips around it and sucking hard in an effort to draw some up into the tip. It's so exhilarating I nearly get lost in it till I feel the compound start to harden against my tongue. This should effectively give him a hard and usable cock; it's fast acting and it should be done in under a minute. I watch as the solution swells, he is hung and thick, once it's full and standing at attention.

I give the taut cock a little squeeze to test its ability to handle what I have planned for it. It's firm and should be ready for me. I go first to the door and make sure to lock it, not wanting a repeat of what happened last time.

I peel my clothes off, leaving them scattered on the floor as I go. I can hardly wait to get him inside of me. I take it slow, lowering myself down on top of him inch by inch– and there are many inches.

I'm trying my hardest to take my time with him. To feel everything, I crave. His cock is warm, heated by the activation of the mixture, and feels so good as it slides deep inside of me.

I hone in on the similarities of Rhys, picking out each inch that reminds me of him. And in no time, it is Rhys I find under me. It's him I'm fucking, and it is the most dizzying feeling, capturing him like this in my mind. Once I get to that place, I lose control and have no choice but to submit. My pace goes from slow to frenzied within seconds.

Soon after, I come hard, shivering goosebumps across my flesh. I collapse on top of him, a sheen of sweat covers my tired body, and the contrast of my heat and his cool only amplifies the experience. It's a completely orgasmic feeling. A girl could really get used to this.

I climb off him and go get the furnace ready for him. I can't necessarily keep him, even if I'd very much like to. I send him into it with a little regret. Then I get dressed and do some of the cleaning that needs to be done for the evening.

FIVE

I sleep better than I have in weeks. Quenching a little of my obsessive need for Rhys, through the use of his friend, really did a number on my moral. The day flies by, and just as I'm heading upstairs for the night, Rhys walks in alone; I'm startled that I didn't hear him before I saw him.

"Hey, pretty lady," he says, turning my panties wet.

I don't have any idea why he would be here tonight, and without a body for me to handle. My thoughts run wild of what it could be; maybe he's here off the clock and hoping I'll be available for him.

Oh my god, if only.

I want it to be true so badly that I can taste it. Right on the tip of my tongue, the way I want to taste him. I lick my lips, as the flavor of him actually turns tangible. I salivate at the thought of him rolling his tongue around mine and fucking deep into my mouth, showing just how badly he needs to taste me, as well.

I step closer to him, his body calling to me, the magnetic pull I feel when around him is greater than gravity. The pull of him calling me nearer still, until I am mere inches from him, he doesn't step back and I take that as an invitation to climb up on the tips of my toes and reach for his mouth.

I don't feel it right away and have to open my eyes to find it. What I see though, crushes me; his face is twisted in repulsion. He puts his hands up and pushes me back by my shoulders, bringing us arms- length apart.

He holds my eyes with his, his face only slightly loosening and becoming more natural. "Listen, you're stunning, and we can still be tender to each other, but under no circumstances am I going to get anywhere near that hole of yours, I may be a lot of things, things that you think you like, and things that you have no idea about, but I'm not a man who follows after a dead guy. I will be making no concessions. It will be over my dead body that something like that will ever happen."

The words are harsh; they hit me in the pit of my soul. I can't hear anything else, the rush of blood is pumping hard, and taking away that sense. My vision blurs in rage. I never imagined this was a possibility, all the times I've thought about this, run it through my head, I never once thought the outcome could be anything other than us together, fucking like rabbits, ravaging each other. I can't wrap my head around this version. This fucked up version where he is not just as excited and eager for me. I feel duped, stupid, or both.

I am spitting mad, gritting my teeth hard enough to cause an ache. I don't realize the extent of what I'm capable of until I feel it. The scalpel tucked into my coat pocket, the cool metal feel of it in my fist.

I'm on him before he can react and stop me. My blade slicing right into his jugular, the arterial spray blinding me as it comes gushing out. I spit what gets in my mouth, but I still taste it, the tangy fluid dripping down my face, covering me in its warm wetness. He stumbles back clenching at his throat in an attempt to somehow save his blood from leaving his body. I push him down onto his back and sit on his chest, my knees pinning his arms beneath them.

I get close to his face, looking right in his knowing eyes and whisper, "as you wish."

I watch him die, no strength to even fight for his life. It flowed from him quicker than his blood left. I see in his eyes the horror that I am. He knows what I've done to him, he may even have some regret for being so mean, but it's too late now, nothing can bring him back from this.

And now, he's all mine.

SIX

I get control of my heart rate as I stand and look at what I've done, what my impulsive reaction caused. I am both horrified and turned on. I'm so fucked up, he had me so twisted, so obsessed, that I couldn't handle those words, I couldn't fathom the possibility that he didn't want me just as much. How could my feelings be so strong for him and his not be the same for me? I suppose I could have been projecting my feelings for him onto him, manifesting it into reality. The thought hurts to my very core.

The loss is in the back of my mind, as the reality of having him available to me now, takes a leap to the forefront. I feel that tingle he gives me, deep between my legs. The butterflies in my tummy start dancing around, making me light- headed and excited.

I lower the table to floor height and heave his body on to it, undress and wash him. I need him looking as close to alive as I can get. I get lost in the process, his cock mostly, I touch it, feel the softness of it. Unless it was him putting his hands on me, I've never touched him, and now I have free reign to do with him all the things I have literally been dreaming of for all this time.

I push my finger into his mouth to feel his tongue, the piece of him I want with a desperation unparalleled by anything else in this world.

I need it.

I put my mouth to his, dipping my tongue into it, tasting him for the first time. His lips are soft, softer than I'd imagined they'd be. I suck his lip into my mouth and pull hard on it, biting a little to feel it between my teeth. I'm so hungry for him.

I slide my hands around his body, tracing all the detailed artwork and the muscle's divots along the way. He's still warm and soft, it's almost possible to imagine he's still alive. I lift his arm and put his hand on my chest, manipulating him to squeeze my tit. The feel of him touching me is overwhelming; it sends a rush between my legs. I make him squeeze harder.

The urge to have these fingers inside of me takes over, I pull my soaked panties off then bring his hand to my pussy, turn it upward, and push them inside of me. I want him to touch me everywhere; I want to feel him all over me. It doesn't even matter that he is not doing it on his own, it's still his hands touching me, even though I'm the one in control of them.

His thick fingers spread me wide and fill me up; I grind my hips and push him deeper, putting my own inside to guide his fingers to the spot that makes me so wet. My legs get weak, and I know I won't be able to stand for much longer. Regretfully, I pull his hand away from me.

I move to the tray with all my implements on it and take the suture kit over to him. I need that tongue, but without his muscles, it won't do me any good. I pull it out of his mouth and cut the underside to elongate it and make it usable. Then use a thread and needle to sew it to his lips, making it look like he's sticking it out. I taste it again, twirling mine around his. I can almost imagine all the words he's ever said to me in his beautiful accent, using this tongue to do so.

I take the rest of my clothes off and climb on him, pressing my body against the full length of his. I put a dab of lubricant on his tongue to wet it, then turn around and push my pussy right against it, grinding myself against him. I want his cock in my mouth and in this position; I simply lean over and suck it. I wish I could taste him, have him fill my mouth with come and really savor it, have him feed me.

I'm disappointed that it will never happen, but it doesn't stop me from sucking it into my mouth until my lips kiss his skin. He tastes so good. Feels so good inside of my mouth.

I make circles around the head with my tongue and imagine that he'd love that, that he would be so fucking hard for me, that I'd never be able to fit him inside my mouth from being so turned on by me.

I work my pussy up and down his mouth, sliding quicker as I feel that little tickle that tells me I'm ready. I can't stop myself, although I want to. I want it to last forever, but I can't pull away for even a second, it's been too long, and the tension has built up so much inside that little nub, that I need it gone.

A moan wells up from deep inside my throat and escapes around Rhys's cock, muffled only slightly by it, as I orgasm against his mouth. I keep myself pressed hard against him until the tremors stop.

My breathing slows and I can finally think straight, the constant state of arousal the last month was too much for my body, and the only thing that could satiate it, and help me be able to get back to the monotony of my life, was to have him. I just didn't know it would be instantaneous. I can feel all the tension fall away and the knots loosen around my body.

I lay my head against his thigh, pressing my mouth to it to put a few kisses around. I'm so grateful for the release, more than any other time in my life.

SEVEN

I don't even realize that I had fallen asleep until I'm waking to the sound of the door crashing open. I can't remember why it should be frightening, why my heart pounds in my chest like a drum. Then it hits me— the flash of blood, the things that followed... me lying naked on a very dead Rhys.

Oh fuck.

I barely get my head turned in the direction of the door, when the loudest bang I've ever heard rings out in the tiny room. I never see what it was, but I feel right away that it hits me. And I know I'm dying, the bullet has gone through my neck, hard.

"That sick fucking bitch," I hear Leo say. The words are hard to hold on to. They leave my head a second later.

"She fucking killed him!" Thomas says.

There is a lot of blood pouring from me, so much I can't believe I'm still alive, my vision is hazy and I can't see anything individually, it's all just a blurry mess of colors. I can't breathe, I can't swallow to clear my throat. I can't hear them anymore. All I can do is lie here and wait, but I can't find a single regret here, as everything flashes by, I don't wish it had gone differently. I get to take my final breath while connected to Rhys. The last thing I do on this earth is turn my head and press it into the warmth of his skin. And there's never been a better, more complete feeling.

The End

Thank you for reading.

Liked this one?

Check out Volume Two